Worth The Weight

Lizzie looked up at him and smiled. "You weren't waiting for me, Finn. I'm willing to bet you haven't thought about me once in all that time, so don't give me that."

"You'd lose that bet. I thought about you plenty for the first few years. Then, well, you know, life kind of happens and your priorities shift."

She laughed. "You mean taking me to bed wasn't a lifelong priority for you? I'm hurt."

His smile went right to her gut. Maybe a little lower. He stuck a workboot-clad foot between her sandals and nudged her feet apart, creating a nest for himself between her legs, which he flew into like a homing pigeon. "Oh, it was a priority all right, it just slipped a few notches on the list."

"Yeah, like a thousand notches." She put a slight pressure on his neck, coaxing him even closer. The heat of his body in front of her a stark contrast to the cool metal of her car along her backside.

"Well, E-liz-a-beth, you're right back at the top of the list now."

WORTH THE WEIGHT

The Worth Series, Book One:
The Nice One

MARA JACOBS

Published by Mara Jacobs
©Copyright 2012 Mara Jacobs
Cover design by Kim Killion

ISBN: 978-0-9852586-5-8

For more information on the author and her works, please
see www.marajacobs.com

For Amy

Prologue

—◊◊◊—

Make no little plans; they have no magic to stir men's blood.
Make big plans, aim high in hope and work.
~ Daniel H. Burnham

LIZZIE HAMPTON HAD A PLAN. Now she just needed the nerve to carry it out. As she drove into the Copper Country, the three-county western tip of Michigan's Upper Peninsula, she started to have second thoughts. Determined to follow through, she repeated to herself, like that little engine, "I think I can. I think I can."

The sun shone brightly, which was not always the case in the Copper Country, even in mid-June. She took the blinding light as a good sign, a sort of welcoming committee. She drove through downtown Houghton, the small city that neighbored her equally small hometown of Hancock.

Some would call it quaint. Some would call it run-down. Lizzie called it home.

She crossed the Portage Lake Lift Bridge to Hancock. The swelling of her heart surprised her, as it did every time she came back. She truly loved it.

She unclipped her long black hair, shook it out, then rubbed her neck and rolled her stiff shoulders. The 10-hour drive from Detroit felt like 20. She slipped her oldest Springsteen CD into the player. Her love affair with Bruce had begun at the tender age of 13, and he was still bringing her home 22 years later.

Just over the bridge separating Houghton and Hancock, she pulled into Bob's Mobil, famed in the area because of its marquee. Just below the ever-increasing gas prices read a daily changing Bible verse.

What made this sign so special was that no one had ever seen Bob, or anyone on his staff, change the marquee. And people had tried…hard. There had been stakeouts commanded by drunken Michigan Tech students. Local law enforcement—who really had nothing else to do in the peaceful area at 4am—would keep an eye out. Even Lizzie herself, aided by her two best friends and a bottle of Boone's Farm Tickled Pink, had given it a shot years ago.

No one had ever seen the "changing of the verse", and it was jokingly discussed that maybe it wasn't Bob who did the rotating, but a higher power.

Today's verse was *"Blessed are the meek, for they shall inherit the earth."*

She sighed over that. Guess she wasn't in line for the earth, because she sure as hell had no intention of being meek on this visit.

She gassed at the pump, then walked into the station to pay. Inside, she went to the coolers and pulled out a Diet Pepsi. She stood for a long time in front of the candy aisle, the glorious bright colors of red, orange, and yellow wrappers invited her into their world of secret treasures.

Old habits, dark feelings, and strong yearnings waged war within her. God, would it always be this hard? Would she always have to rely on sheer willpower? Would the cravings ever go away?

Turning quickly away from the aisle, lest the lonesome call of the Kit Kat make her succumb, she made her way to the checkout.

"Hi Bob," she said as she grabbed a *USA Today*, both Detroit papers, and the local paper, *The Copper Ingot*, scanning its front page for her best friend Katie's byline. She put them all on the counter.

"Lizzie." Bob acknowledged her presence and rang up her gas, pop and papers. Bob never said more than a grudging first name to his customers, but, amazingly enough, he remembered everyone, whether they stopped by every day or once every four or five years as Lizzie did. Throw in her startling change in appearance since she'd last been in Bob's, and his recognizing her was even more impressive.

During her ten years of obesity, she'd only come home three times. The imagined embarrassment at seeing high school friends had kept her from venturing too far from her parents' place during those visits. Just to Alison and Katie's places, occasionally to the Commodore for pizza, and to Bob's for pop and the papers.

She hadn't walked away from the candy aisle unscathed during those years.

As she gathered her purchases, she looked around for somewhere to get rid of her fifty-eight cents in change. As she knew there would be, a canister sat next to the register. A picture of an angelic and tragic looking girl of around nine or ten, sitting in a wheelchair, adorned the converted tennis ball can. The only inscription read "Help Hannah" in crude, hand-written letters above the photo. Lizzie dropped the coins into the canister. She turned to close her purse, then opened her wallet and gathered out her single bills and stuffed them in as well.

"See ya, Bob," she said, getting only a grunt in reply.

She got in her SUV and grabbed her notebook from the passenger seat. She'd written "The Plan" across the front in red marker. All her tablets were labeled in front. It made it easier to find the one she was looking for amongst the two or three she'd have in her large purse at any given time. She easily flipped to the page she sought. The page had a Diet Pepsi stain and was slightly curled up at the bottom edges. She'd flipped to this page often in the three months since she'd first begun her planning.

The familiar tingling that putting a plan to paper gave her returned. She looked through the bullet points and felt a rush of accomplishment at the check marks that accompanied all but one of the items.

Secure loose ends at work. This item was first, of course, and had taken the most time. There were several sub-heads beneath it, all completed. Still, she'd check in with a call at least once a day while she was gone, plus she was always available through text, email, IM, Skype, you name it.

Make arrangements with Robin. Her cleaning lady was up to speed on looking after her condo while she was gone. Nothing to worry about there.

Have mail transferred to Mom & Dad's. A quick form dropped at the Post Office on her way out of the city had taken care of that.

Buy new wardrobe. That had been tough and had given her hours of anxiety at the department store. She'd bought lots of work clothes in her new size, but had been content to spend her leisure time at home in her old sweats and shorts. No longer. The number of suitcases in the back of her Navigator attested to that task being checked-off.

Bruce moaned *Born To Run* as she pulled out of Bob's parking lot and turned up the hill toward her parent's house. Her eyes scanned the last item on the list.

The only item left unchecked.

The reason she was here.

Find, fuck, and forget Finn Robbins.

One

~m~

√ Call K & A about movie times

"GOD, I LOVE THE SMELL of theater popcorn, there's nothing else like it."

Finn Robbins heard the female voice from behind him. He couldn't say the same. The smell of fresh popcorn made him sick. It seemed the aroma stayed with him wherever he was, the buttery stuff burning into his nose with every breath. It was enough to make him puke.

It'd been okay when he'd worked here years ago, but this time around it was too much. Everything was too much.

Something about the voice made him turn. Three women stood at the concession stand counter, one of the new high school kids waiting on them. Finn had his head buried, connecting a new Coke tank. The old tank had just died, spraying Coke all over his white shirt. Just another sign that the universe was having a good laugh at him.

He checked out the women. Mostly all he saw were packs of kids and couples at the theater. It was refreshing to see a group of thirty-something women together. The two he could see were striking, but in very different ways. Completely opposite in looks. The first was tall and Nordic looking, and strikingly beautiful. A Viking princess. The other was all soft curves, darker skin and hair, but still blonde. A dark Finlander and a light Finlander, the two mainstays of the Copper Country.

There was something a little familiar about them. Maybe they came to the theaters often? He dismissed that. He'd have definitely remembered the Viking.

The woman behind the two got her order and turned, allowing Finn to see only a flash of long black hair ending just above a wonderfully lush butt. He tried craning his neck, but from where he stood he couldn't get a clear view of her.

Those damn high school kids were too fast. They had the women's orders done before Finn had a chance to get out from behind the counter and get a proper look. He wanted to figure out where he knew the two from, and definitely wanted to see the third.

There was something about that voice. Maybe he could catch a glimpse of them after the movie as they left the theater.

—ᴍ—

Lizzie couldn't concentrate on the movie, which was unusual. She, Katie and Alison had been seeing movies at the Mine Shaft together since sixth grade when they were finally allowed to go without parental supervision.

One parent would drop the three girls off in downtown Houghton. They would see the movie, then cross the street to the Big Boy for a hot fudge ice cream cake. One of the other girls' parents would pick them up in front of the Big Boy exactly one and a half hours after the movie was scheduled to get out. In that time, the girls would dissect the movie while plying themselves with the decadent dessert.

Over time, the girls' critiques of the movies went from "isn't he dreamy" to "the use of the wide-angle lens by the director was really effective." Although "isn't he dreamy" never really went out of style. They had progressed from their parents' pick-up and delivery service, to being old enough to walk on their own, to driving their parents' cars, to driving their own.

Now they were back to walking across the bridge from Hancock to Houghton, but this time for the exercise. The Big Boy had long closed down, but Lizzie fully expected the Pavlovian response of craving hot fudge the moment the credits rolled.

Except tonight, she wasn't immersed in the movie. "He didn't even know me. Not a flicker of recognition," she said out loud, as much to herself as her friends.

"SSSHHHHH," came a voice from behind them.

"My plan centers around him, and he has absolutely no idea who I am." She could hear the dismay in her voice. She put her head in her hands, slowly shaking it. Then she grabbed hold of herself, snapped her head up and concluded, "It may take a little longer than I thought, that's all."

"SSSHHH," repeated the voice.

"Get a grip, Lizard, we're being shushed," Alison whispered. "I don't think he even saw you, you were so quick getting your popcorn. We'll figure it out at the Big Boy. I mean, wherever we go after here."

Apparently Alison was still programmed, too. The thought cheered Lizzie.

—⁓—

Finn looked up from the desk when he heard people leaving the theater. He was in the office going over how to fill out a time sheet with one of the new workers. As he heard the small crowd leaving, he quickly tried to wrap up his tutorial and get out to the lobby.

The three women had just passed the office. Another view from the back. It was a hell of a view, but not the one he wanted. Damn, he wouldn't get a chance to solve the mystery of from where he knew the women. The Viking was telling a story and as she finished, the other two laughed. He froze at the sound of the dark-haired woman's laugh.

He knew that laugh. Nothing dainty or feminine about it. Loud and boisterous, it came from the gut, full of heart.

He dashed out the doors trying to catch the women. "Elizabeth? Liz?" he yelled after them.

A few steps down the sidewalk, Lizzie turned to face Finn. Excitement buzzed through her. Triumph…he did remember her. Her excitement was quickly replaced by nerves.

Now what? Should she play games? Pretend she didn't know him? No, she decided, it had to be honest or she wouldn't be able to live with herself. Her plan was cold-blooded enough without bringing deceit into it as well.

"Hi, Finn. I thought that was you, but I wasn't sure you'd remember me."

It felt surreal. Face to face with Finn Robbins after eighteen years. She moved closer to him and tried to take him in. His face, which in his youth had seemed chiseled, was now angular and hard, his blue eyes still deep and vivid. He stood right around six feet. Lizzie had always loved his height; it fit so perfectly with her own five nine. His then-lanky build was now muscular. His hair, still close cropped and sandy brown, was sprinkled with sun streaks and just a touch of gray.

Even though it was only early June, and summer hadn't even begun in the Copper Country, his neck and forearms were tanned a golden brown. He wore old jeans that looked like a pair any teen would wear, but Lizzie guessed the holes and stains weren't placed there for fashion. Some brown substance splattered the front of his white shirt.

She couldn't believe it. Eighteen years later and she was still drawn to him. Still wanted to touch him, wanted to place her hands on his chest, wrap her arms around his neck and press her body into his.

She held out her hand instead.

"I didn't see you when you first came in. It was hearing your laugh that tipped me off." He shook her hand, but didn't release it, just held it awkwardly, as if he couldn't believe she was real. She felt the same way, and she'd known she was going to see him. He must really be surprised. Pleasantly, she hoped.

"God, Liz. I…I can't believe it's you," the shock was evident in his voice. "You're so…so…old." His hand left hers as he covered his eyes, shaking his head. "I mean. I didn't mean."

He placed his hands on his hips and let out a deep sigh. "What I mean is, it's been a long time, Liz. I guess I still think of you as eighteen. But, here you are." As if trying to put himself out of his misery, he finished, "It's incredible to see you, Liz. You look beautiful."

He should have seen her three years ago. But that was then, and this is now. And right now Finn Robbins was telling her she looked beautiful.

Take it and run.

"God, it's such a shock to see you. Did you move back to town?"

"No. I live in Detroit now, have for quite some time. I'm just home visiting. Finn, do you remember my friends Alison Jukuri and Katie Maki, though Katie is Lipton now."

Finn nodded to Katie and Alison and they nodded in response.

"And are you still Hampton, Liz?"

It took her a second to figure out what Finn was asking. "Oh, yes, still Hampton. I'm not married. And you?" She held her breath. She had known of one divorce, but that didn't mean he hadn't remarried somewhere along the line. Finn had never traveled in the same circles as she and her friends, so they wouldn't necessarily have known if he had.

And Google came up woefully short on Finn Robbins searches over the years.

"Married and divorced, about, let's see, seven years ago, I guess."

So it had only been the once, she happily thought, and that had ended seven years ago. She mustered up her courage. She could do this. If she couldn't ask out Finn Robbins, how on earth would she hold her own with someone like Davis Cummings? And that's what this plan all boiled down to.

"Listen, Finn, we have to get going…but I'd love to get together sometime and catch up on what's been happening with you. I'll be in town for a couple of months, at most." She added the last part so he wouldn't feel like she was trying to start anything permanent with him. She also brought her hand to his and squeezed, just so he wouldn't think her interest was only platonic.

—⁓—

"That'd be great, but I'm pretty swamped right now with berry season…." Finn didn't want to let her go. The shock of seeing her after all these years was wearing off and he now looked at her through new, older eyes.

She was breathtaking, but he'd always thought so. He wanted her, and if her body was sending the signals he thought it was, she wanted him too. He did some quick juggling of events in his head. He had a night off from the theater on Wednesday, but he'd have to do something about Annie. He'd figure that one out later, he wasn't going to let Liz go without a firm date.

"How about dinner Wednesday?" he asked.

She stepped closer to him, her bountiful breasts nearly grazing his chest. She gave his hand another squeeze. Damn, he'd sure like to squeeze more than just her hand.

"That sounds great. Meet at the Commodore at eight?"

"I'll see you then, Elizabeth." He dragged out her name into four long syllables, just like he used to, years ago. Only then, it would be a soft whisper, breathed close to her ear, prompting an answering sigh. He was the only person who ever called her Elizabeth. He mostly called her Liz, but he never called her Lizzie as everyone else did. He didn't want to be just like everybody else to her.

She'd been like nobody else to him.

He felt her shudder. He'd always had that effect on her. Back then, she'd been too innocent to know how to hide it. It was refreshing to see that she still couldn't mask her attraction.

She smiled, placed a soft kiss on each of his cheeks, and then pulled away from him and returned to her friends. The women walked down the sidewalk toward the bridge. Leaving Finn staring after them. And counting the hours until Wednesday night.

—⁓—

"I did it! I did it!" Lizzie muttered to herself while the women walked home. The early summer was warmer than usual, a soft breeze drifting off the canal. It was warm enough for shorts and tee-shirts, yet not muggy. It never got too humid in the Copper Country, the breezes off nearby Lake Superior saw to that. "If I'd known how easy it was to ask a man out, I'd have done it before."

"That's the first time you asked a man out?" Katie said incredulously.

"Oh, big talk, how many men have you asked out? You had boyfriends who came after you all through high school. Ron asked you out freshman year in college, and you married him after graduation. So, don't be playing all Miss Sex and the City with me," she good-naturedly shot back at Katie.

"What was with the cheek kissing? Very European," Alison piped in.

"Milan, Paris, the Copper Country…we do it in all the chicest places," Lizzie answered. "Honestly, I don't know where that came from, I just…" She let the thought slide away.

"You just what?"

"I just…I needed to…I wanted to smell him, okay?" It came out sounding defensive, and she quickly continued, feeling the need to justify herself. "He always had this unique scent about him. I wouldn't even call it a good scent. Not clean and fresh, but…I don't know, he smelled of work, Brut, a little of horses, and what I assumed sex smelled like."

"Oh, brother," Alison said. "Brut? Are you kidding me? My dad used to wear Brut, and that was thirty years ago."

Katie nodded her head, seeming to understand the intangible quality Lizzie was trying to describe.

"How about that 'Liz you look so…so…old,' God that was priceless," Alison hooted.

Lizzie cringed. "Too much to hope for that you guys didn't hear that, eh?"

Katie laughed. "Oh, we heard it all right. But don't worry, we won't bring it up if you don't. Because if you look old, I guess that means…"

"Speak for yourself," Alison said. All three laughed.

They walked on in silence, until Katie asked, "Lizzie, are you sure about this plan of yours? Are you sure it's something you want to do? It's so unlike you."

Lizzie nodded her head. "Yes. I'm sure." At her friends' skeptical looks, she continued, "Look, I'll be up front with him. I'm in town for a couple of months, I'd love to spend some time with him…" She paused wiggling her eyebrows. "…*Intimate* time with him. Then I'm gone. No strings, just a summer fling. Either he's in or he's out."

"Or in and out, in and out," Alison said, her voice a mocking sexual tone.

"If I'm lucky," Lizzie said.

"But why Finn? You guys didn't even date that long. I didn't even remember his name when you called us last month with this plan of yours," Katie said.

"You're right, we didn't date that long, it wasn't all that serious, but…" She stopped for a moment, gathering her thoughts. "You know how they say you don't regret the things you did in life, you regret the things you didn't do? Well, I regret not sleeping with Finn back then."

"Why didn't you? I mean, I know you were still a virgin, and you hadn't planned on 'doing it' until college," Katie said, making air quotes.

"The life plan of Lizzie Hampton, I remember it well," Alison teased.

A sad smile curled on Lizzie's lips. "Funny how that life plan worked out. But, much as I was attracted to Finn, I was determined to stick to my plan back then. The irony is that he dumped me because I wouldn't sleep with him, and I desperately wanted to."

"The jerk," Alison said.

"No, not really," Lizzie went on. "I'm sure it was the real reason he dumped me, but the excuses he gave at the time were actually true."

"Like?" Katie asked.

"Like I was going off to State in the fall. Like we came from totally different backgrounds. Like he didn't want to get too serious because he wanted to leave town as soon as he could. " She spoke of it clinically, like it had happened to someone else. In a way it had. That girl was a different person. "He was absolutely right, though he probably didn't realize it at the time."

"So he's just a ghost to exorcise, eh?" Alison asked.

Lizzie shrugged. "That too."

"And you're not going to say anything to him about this Davis guy you told us about?" Katie asked.

Lizzie shook her head. "No need. Davis isn't anything more than a man I've met and I'd like to get to know better. Yet. Finn has nothing to do with my life in Detroit. My real life."

The women said nothing for a few moments. Lizzie could feel their concern. She knew they didn't understand what she'd come home to do. She tried to explain in the most basic terms. "Listen, it's been a long time since I've had sex. I have no idea what will happen the first time out with my body. I could break into hives. I could break into giggles. I could be so insecure about stretch marks and jiggly thighs that I totally freak out."

They nodded and waited. She took a deep breath and continued. "I don't want those things happening with a man who I really want a future with. And I don't just want to sleep with any random guy I meet to get over this hurdle. That would freak me out in a different way. I know I'm attracted to Finn. I know I desperately wanted to sleep with him years ago, and he with me. He's safe, non-threatening."

Alison started to jump in, but Lizzie raised her hand to stop her. "I know. He did hurt me years ago—but that was kid stuff. Sure, I cried for a few weeks, but I got over it. Teen angst, that's all it was." She saw Katie and Alison shoot each other doubtful looks, but she ignored them. "It's not like that this time. No expectations, for either of us. Hearts are not involved." She paused. "Just bodies."

"Are you so sure that Finn can't be the man for your future? You could be killing two birds," Katie asked.

Lizzie threw her friend a sad smile. "Come on, Kat. Can you really see me with a man with no more ambition than to still be working part time in the same theater for seventeen years?" Alison and Katie both slowly shook their heads. "Thanks again for doing the legwork, Kat, and finding out where I could find Finn before I got up here. That cut a lot of time off my timeline."

"You have a timeline to fuck Finn Robbins?" Alison teased.

Lizzie shrugged her shoulders. "Of course. Every important plan needs a timeline, how else would you know if you're on target?"

Katie ignored Alison. "You're welcome, though it wasn't easy. I had to ask around at the paper and finally the ad rep that handles the theaters knew Finn from picking up ad copy. That guy really flies under the radar."

He always did, Lizzie thought to herself. Wanting to change the subject, she said, "Wednesday. Let's see, today is Monday, so do you know what you'll both be doing Wednesday afternoon?"

"Of course, helping you pick out what to wear," Alison said laughing.

"I can't wait to see all the new clothes you must've bought now that you're thin again," Katie said. She shared Lizzie's love of clothes.

"Thanks, Kat, but I'd hardly say thin," she said as they neared the end of Houghton's main drag, soon to cross the bridge to Hancock.

Katie and Alison gave each other a look and Katie laid her hand on Lizzie's arm causing her to stop. She looked at her two closest friends in the world. "Okay. You may never be skinny, you have too many curves for that—wonderful curves...but Lizard, you must realize you have a great figure again."

Stunned, she looked first at Katie, then Alison. Katie was telling her she had a good body. Katie was drop-dead gorgeous. Katie was the pretty one, while Alison was the smart one. Lizzie, of course, was the nice one. Or so they'd been dubbed in elementary school.

She *had* been the nice one. Now, she wasn't so sure. Now it was time to grab life for herself, and if she had to sacrifice some of the niceties to do it, so be it.

But these two had always loved her—no matter what. Fat. Thin. Nice. Even a woman embarking on a summertime fling with an old flame.

"It's so nice to be home with you guys, again," Lizzie hugged them both.

"Oooh yah, it's good to be back in da Yoop, eh?" Katie crowed out in an exaggerated Yooper accent as they crossed the bridge to Hancock.

TWO

—ᵐ—

√ Revise timeline?? Do I dare?
√ Call Sybil about contracts

ELIZABETH HAMPTON. LIZ. He couldn't believe it. Just when he'd been feeling like such a failure, Liz waltzes into his life. This was just what he needed to get out of his funk.

There had always been something so innocent, so special about her. Something that made him feel just a little…better… when he was with her. Although he'd been hung up on the idea of being her first, he hadn't been sure he wanted the responsibility that went with such an honor. Plus, she'd just graduated from high school when they met. She'd be heading to State in the fall. The thought of the only good thing in his life leaving him behind had terrified Finn.

So he'd ended it.

He'd done it coldly, had hurt her. He'd known that and it'd killed him. But he'd done it. He'd wanted to make sure she understood there was no going back. At twenty, he'd had plans. He'd do something with his life. As soon as he got things squared away with his mother and sister he was going to get out of this hellhole. Get a job on a real ranch somewhere, maybe Montana or Texas. Maybe even check out the rodeo circuit he'd always dreamed about.

But life had hit Finn in a big way. Seventeen years later he was in exactly the same place he had been then. Right down to selling popcorn at the Mine Shaft.

He drove home, feeling unsettled and horny after seeing Liz. The same feeling he'd had on all his drives home after seeing Liz. Pulling the Jeep into the driveway of the farm, he saw a dim light in the picture window. The sight pulled Finn back to one night that stood out from the others.

He'd been with Liz at the beach, had gotten in her pants, had almost gotten her in his, when she'd called a halt to the evening. He'd dropped her off, grumbling about it being time she grew up, which she pretended not to hear. He'd pulled the Jeep into the driveway of the farmhouse to see a lone dim light shining as it was now.

He'd gone inside to find his mother at the kitchen table. Not a surprising sight for any other kid, but the fact that his mother was home on a weekend night before midnight was indeed shocking to him. Then he'd seen the glass in her hand, the half empty bottle of whiskey on the counter, and the rough-looking man entering the room from the bathroom, and Finn's surprise was replaced with concern.

"Where's Phoebe?" he asked immediately. He didn't need his sister to see their mother drunk. He certainly didn't want Phoebe to see Linda throwing herself at some stranger. He'd taken great pains to shield his sister from the frequent sight.

"She's staying in the trailer with your grandmother," his mother answered. Her eyes were looking at the man, her lips turned into a lustful smirk that the man returned with a low chuckle. As if Finn's concern about his sister reminded Linda that she was indeed a mother, she asked, "Where ya been, honey?"

He knew the endearment, in fact, the question as a whole, was only asked for the benefit of impressing the man who stood in the kitchen doorway, undressing Finn's mother with his eyes. Finn knew she couldn't care less where he'd been.

Hell, she didn't even know if he was home most nights, because she sure wasn't. He was home, though, making sure that Phoebe was taken care of. His grandmother was a huge help, but Gran and his mother rubbed each other the wrong way and Gran stayed in the trailer when Finn's mother was around.

Disgusted by the man's obvious lust, and his mother's attempt at feigning maternal concern, he lashed out at her. "Why do you care where I've been? You couldn't give a shit about me or Phoebe. Just as long as you've got a bottle and a man, you're happy."

He turned to leave, but his mother could give as good as Finn. In fact, that was where he'd learned to hurt, at his mother's knee.

"You were with that prissy Hampton girl, weren't you? That's why you're home so early. Had to get Miss Goody-Goody home before she turned into a pumpkin?"

He whirled around, meaning to answer, but stopped at the venomous look in his mother's bloodshot eyes.

"When are you going to get it, Finn? You ain't ever going to be good enough for the Hamptons in this world. That girl is just sowing some wild oats with you. She's slumming. And you'd better wake up and smell the coffee if you think you mean anything more to her than a wild, bad boy who can get her off. She may heat up nice and cozy when you're alone, but it will be a Charles or a Biff that she ends up with." She rose from the table, still holding her glass, nodded to the man to follow her, and unsteadily walked from the kitchen to the stairs.

He slammed out the door and slept on the couch of the trailer, trying to drown out his mother's words. Trying to escape the truth of them that rang in his ears.

Shaking off the long-ago memory, Finn left his Jeep and approached the farmhouse. He tried to ignore his mother's words as he thought about the coincidence of running into Liz after all these years.

Maybe he hadn't been good enough for her then. Hell, maybe he still wasn't. It mattered then, it didn't now.

Now, Liz was back for a short time, and she wanted him. Of that much he was sure. He'd been caught off guard seeing her but she'd taken the lead, obviously recovering from the shock of seeing him much faster. Next time he'd be on surer footing.

He was looking forward to Wednesday, and looking forward to *anything* was a feeling he hadn't experienced in a long time. Even though pretty much everything else in his life had turned to shit, it looked like he might get one thing he'd always wanted.

To sleep with Liz Hampton.

—⁓—

When Lizzie woke the next morning, she immediately did the same thing she'd done every morning for the last three years. She rolled over onto her right side, slid her hand under her pajama bottoms and down to her tummy. Then she measured it. Her tummy. Or, by now, what was left of her tummy.

Three years ago she'd decided she was ready to begin the next chapter of her life, one that would include losing weight and being open to the idea of real intimacy with someone.

She'd been a size ten in high school and though she'd probably never see that size again, three years of excruciating dieting and exercise had gotten her close. Now, the real work was ahead of her.

This morning, her tummy pooched out just slightly. Probably from her mother's creamed chicken the other night. The pooch wasn't an amount that anyone else could notice, but Lizzie did. She noticed within a centimeter if there was a change, just by the measurement of her hand from hipbone to hipbone. It was a minor miracle that she could even touch each hipbone across the span of her hand from wrist to fingertips. At her heaviest, her hand curved around fat and stopped before her fingertips even reached the mid-way point.

Slowly—achingly slowly—her belly had receded and her fingers curled less and less to become the straight digits they now were.

She'd have to be careful this trip, especially with her mom's cooking. She couldn't let loose like she was on vacation, not if she'd be here for the two months she'd mentioned to Finn. She'd come too far to have a two-month back-slide.

She thought of her upcoming date with Finn and her hand left her tummy and did a quick scan of her body as she rolled onto her back. All her parts seemed to be in the right places and would probably pass an inspection. And if not, well, it was only Finn. That was the whole point of the plan…trying out the new body on someone she could walk away from. She knew that was possible with Finn—she'd done it before.

She looked at her alarm clock and saw it was past ten. She couldn't remember the last time she'd slept so late. It must be the fresh Copper Country air and the walk home last night.

She went through her mental calendar once again. It was the second week in June. She'd allotted two weeks to find out where Finn worked and lived. Katie cut that down to just a few days with her connections at the *Ingot*. Another week to make contact with Finn. One more week to ask him out, and probably two to three weeks of seeing him before they would sleep together. She added another week on for additional sex if she so desired. It didn't occur to her to add in any time for what Finn may desire. Then back to Detroit.

Back to her business. Back to her future.

All totaled, eight weeks, give or take, to find a man whom she hadn't seen in eighteen years, dazzle him, sleep with him, get to a comfort level with her new body, then leave town.

Lizzie loved a plan.

It was a testament to how serious she was about her plan that she was willing to leave her office in the very capable hands of her staff for that long.

By asking Finn out the first time she saw him, she was already four weeks ahead of schedule. She wouldn't announce her possible early return to her assistant, Sybil, when she called the office this morning. No sense saying she'd be back sooner than she expected then have something go wrong with her time line. Better to give herself a buffer.

As she had her morning coffee, she made her check-in call and checked her email. Sybil told her everything was fine and it would be appreciated if she could limit her calls to at least every other day, preferably weekly. Lizzie laughed at that, and Sybil sighed, realizing the futility of the request. Sybil also told her that Pete Ryan had called. Nothing important, he had just wanted to check in, but was surprised to learn that Lizzie was in their mutual hometown area.

She wrote a note in her ever-present notebook to call Petey later that day. She could easily text him, but if Petey had called, that meant he wanted to talk. He probably wanted to commiserate about the Red Wings' loss in the playoffs. She knew he had a couple of charity appearances this week, ones she'd set up for him. He'd probably head up for the remainder of the summer. Since starting in the NHL, Petey had spent all his summers back in the U.P.

She couldn't wait to see him, even if his first night home would inevitably be her playing designated driver while he got smashed and bitched about "those fucking pussies", meaning, of course, the Colorado Avalanche. Her junior prom date, and her first client when she opened her own shop, she counted Petey as her closest male friend.

After touching base with her three account executives on upcoming events that their clients were scheduled to attend, she signed off and decided to take Sybil's advice and try not to call every day. She had an incredible staff, and much as she'd like to think she was indispensable, they were more than able to hold down the fort. Besides, now that the Stanley Cup had been decided, the only active professional sports in progress were baseball and golf. Hampton Public Relations handled only two baseball players and no golfers. Professional golf was the next arena Lizzie wanted to enter, but that would have to wait. It wasn't an election year, so no politicians for clients right now. If she had to be gone for this long, now was as good a time as any.

She hadn't taken a vacation of any length in the ten years since she'd started her own firm. A short trip home to see her parents and Katie and Alison. A quick flight to Florida to see her twin brother, Zeke, when he was stationed there. That was it. She hadn't felt cheated, though. Her job allowed her to go to some of the best sporting events in the country, in some of the best locales. And so much of her job involved social events that she never felt the need to "get away from it all" as many professionals did.

She loved what she did for a living. She was good at it. If she could just get this sex thing handled, she'd feel like she had it all. She'd be a freakin' perfume ad!

She threw on a pair of sweats and a tee-shirt and walked from her parents' old Victorian home on the east side of town, near the bridge, down the hill to Bob's Mobil to get the papers. The Detroit papers wouldn't arrive until later in the afternoon— the drive to this remote area was so far—but she could get the Milwaukee papers.

After giving her change, and a couple of extra ones, to Help Hannah, and responding in kind to Bob's curt "Lizzie", she left the station.

Bob's Bible verse today was *"The Love of Money Is the Root of All Evil"*. No one had seen how it'd gotten there.

—⁓—

By ten that morning, Finn was three hours into what would be another sixteen-hour day.

Two of the kids who picked for him in the mornings didn't show, so he was out with the twelve- and thirteen-year-olds picking strawberries in the north patch. He only had six kids working for him right now, but in another month, during peak season, there'd be twice that many.

Joining him this morning were a few townspeople who were picking some of the first berries of the season. There were also a few industrious kids who would pick several quarts to sell at a roadside stand for double what they paid Finn. And a couple of tourists who wanted some local color and thought picking their own berries to put on their shortcake back at their hotel would be a quaint story to tell back home. Probably from the city. Though that could mean either Chicago or Detroit. The western corner of the U.P. was equidistant from both.

His son, Stevie, was in the field too. Except for his mother's Finnish blond hair, Stevie was the spitting image of Finn at fourteen. He could only hope to give Stevie an easier life than he'd had.

He hadn't been ready for fatherhood at twenty-three, hadn't been ready to admit that Montana or Texas was never going to happen, but he thought he'd adapted pretty well. His unrealized dreams had never turned to resentment toward his son. Not from the first moment he'd held Stevie. It may have been unplanned, but once that baby boy was in his arms, Finn could never think of the pregnancy as unwanted.

He knew he shortchanged Stevie by spending so much of his time with Annie, but it just couldn't be helped right now. He wasn't going to try to change that. He'd just have to figure out how to better spend his time with Stevie. What did they call that? Quality time? Yeah, he'd spend more quality time with his son.

He looked over to see Stevie throwing a garter snake at one of the girl pickers. She shrieked in terror and ran through the rows of berry plants, causing the tourists to stand too quickly and dump the quarts of berries they'd already picked onto the muddy ground.

He better get started with that quality time. But when? He was booked solid between the farm, the theater and Annie. Now throw in Liz—though he really didn't plan on spending all that much time with her—and he didn't know where he'd find the time to keep Stevie on the straight and narrow.

He watched Stevie's mischievous grin turn to innocence as the boy felt his father's gaze. He'd find the time somehow.

—⚬—

"Last one, I promise," Lizzie said as she modeled what had to be the sixth outfit in contention for her date later that evening.

They were in Lizzie's childhood bedroom, once again talking about boys and clothes. Springsteen played on the CD player and her mom had left some lemonade on the desk. The identical scene had been played out hundreds of times before.

"Yowza, that's hot," Alison said in a mock low growl of appreciation over Lizzie's scantily clad body. She wore a red miniskirt and white halter top.

"Definitely says you're ready, Lizard," Katie added.

Lizzie gave the outfit a quick glance then started taking it off right away. "Nah, not the look I'm going for. Besides, I'd be too worried my boobs would fall out of the top."

"And that would be a bad thing?" Alison teased.

"What look are you going for?" Katie asked.

"It's got to be a tiny bit sexy, but more clean cut than anything else."

"Not exactly the way to get a guy into bed, Lizard, clean cut?"

"We're not talking about just any guy," she said as she put her bra back on after taking off the halter top that demanded she go commando. The bra's sturdy underwire harnessed her plentiful bosom and put her back in her comfort zone. "Finn always liked the idea of me being a good girl. I think the women and girls he knew were all a little slutty; dressed kind of tarty. His mom sure did, though I only met her a couple of times. I think my button-down oxfords and preppie attire really turned him on. I think…I think he liked the idea of the bad boy and the good girl."

"Are you sure you want this guy to be your first foray back into sex?"

"That's why he's so perfect. He's the most down and dirty guy I ever knew. If I can get through it with him, enjoy it with him, get over my body issues with him, it'll be a breeze with someone as refined and cultured as Davis."

"Be careful, Lizard—books and covers and wolf and sheep's clothing and all that," Katie added.

"Yeah I know, but I'm not some silly virgin you know."

"I don't know, what is the statue of limitations on virginity? Maybe the hymen grows back without use for fifteen years."

Lizzie laughed at Alison's remark. "Yeah, maybe Finn can finally get his wish and take my virginity after all. So, ladies, now that you know what I'm going for, what'll it be?"

"I'm thinking the white sleeveless with the khaki shorts," Katie said.

"Yeah, I guess that's what I'd go with too," Alison weighed in with.

"Really? You think I can get away with a sleeveless blouse?" Lizzie asked. The outfit had been her favorite, too. A white cotton, collared, sleeveless button-down blouse with khaki walking shorts and low sandals. Tiny gold hoop earrings and a thin gold chain were all the jewelry she would add. Casual, yet classic.

"Of course you can wear sleeveless."

She looked in the full-length mirror one more time at another outfit. She gave it a quick glance, as she did with the other five outfits she'd tried on for her friends.

"Why do you do that?" Katie asked.

"Do what?"

"Look in the mirror for about five seconds per outfit. You obviously care what you're going to wear tonight or else you wouldn't have us putting our two cents in, but you hardly give it a second glance."

"If it were me, I'd be standing in front of the mirror for a good twenty minutes with each outfit, turning every angle, sitting down in the outfit, the whole nine yards. You barely look at it," Alison added.

Lizzie shrugged. "It doesn't matter how long I look in the mirror, I don't see myself anyway, so why bother. I can get the idea with a quick look. Besides, that's why you guys are here, to back me up." At Katie and Alison's puzzled looks she tried to elaborate. "I mean, I *obviously* look in the mirror when I get dressed or do my hair or make-up, but…when I look in the mirror, I see parts, not the whole. It only takes a second to check on the parts that I know may be troublesome, so I look at those quickly and, if they pass inspection, then it's a go."

"What do you mean parts, not the whole?" Of course something like this would fascinate Alison the psychologist.

"I only see myself in parts…when I look at myself. I can't see me, just my parts. I've become very detached from my body image. I've had to, or I'd have gone crazy."

"I'm not getting it," Katie said. "Put the outfit we picked back on." The women waited as she stripped out of the last outfit she'd tried and put on the white blouse and shorts once more.

There was no modesty or embarrassment while Lizzie was only in her bra and panties. Not with the these women. Never had been. Never would be. Even when she was twice the size she was now. Even when Katie had felt that her body was betraying her by crying barrenness. Even after Alison had her appendix removed and there were bandages and scars. Since kindergarten, really. It was a sense of security that Lizzie took for granted.

Once she had the shirt and shorts on she turned to Katie for further instructions.

"Okay, now turn to the mirror and quickly tell me what you see."

It only took seconds for her to look and answer. "Arms. Not as tan as I'd like, stretch marks underneath, I'll have to hold my arms close to my sides. No high fiving," she chuckled, imagining greeting Finn with a high five. Definitely not his style.

"What else?"

She glanced again to the mirror. "Bust. The buttons don't gap across my boobs. That's good."

"What else?"

"Tummy. The pleats of the shorts lay flat, they don't pull even when I put my hands in the pockets."

Alison joined in, "What else?"

"Thighs. The shorts don't cling to my inner thighs or accentuate my saddlebags."

"What else?"

"That's it."

"What do you mean that's it?"

"That's it, that's all I see. Arms. Bust. Waist. Thighs. All sectioned off like that."

Lizzie caught Katie and Alison exchanging looks.

"Don't read too much into it. It's just the way I look in the mirror, nothing else."

"I don't know. Seems to me you could make a case for the fact that you divide yourself into parts," Alison said, putting her analyst's cap on. "It's all very Gestalt. The whole is less than the sum of all parts. Something like that. I forget. I always thought he was full of crap anyway."

Lizzie waved Alison off. "You do the same thing, everybody does, you just don't realize it." She noticed her friends once again giving each other dubious looks. "I'll tell you one other thing about this outfit."

"Yes?"

"The shirt is tucked in and I'm wearing a belt."

"So?"

Her voice cracked with emotion. Emotion she'd tried to silence with Ding Dongs for so long. "I haven't worn a shirt tucked in with a belt in fifteen years." She turned her head, but not before her friends could see the moistness in her eyes. Damn, she didn't want to cry. Not now. Not when she had her first date with Finn tonight. She pretended to brush her hair away from her face and caught the dreaded tear.

Katie was not quite as subtle and openly let a few drops fall as she whispered, "Oh, Lizzie."

Lizzie caught Katie and Alison's glances in the mirror and decided the spotlight had been on her long enough for one afternoon. Turning the tables, she asked, "So, Al, any prospects out there?"

Alison shrugged. "A new prof in the civil department at Tech has been sniffing around a little bit."

Katie perked up. "Really? Since when?"

"Just a couple of weeks ago. Of course with classes out now, I probably won't see him for a while, so it'll probably turn out to be nothing."

"You're not teaching any summer classes?" Lizzie asked as she put her gym shorts and tee-shirt back on, bringing the fashion show to an end. She put the winning choice over a chair and collected the runners up from the bed. Katie and Alison were lying cross-wise, their legs dangling off the side of the canopy bed that she had slept in since the sixth grade. She moved Alison's legs to get a top that had been cut in the first round, put it on a hanger and back in the closet.

"No, I'm not teaching this summer. And my patient load is pretty light right now, so the summer's looking pretty carefree."

"Is this prof teaching this summer? Will he be around?" Katie inquired.

"He is teaching a couple of classes. Being new, he drew the short straw."

"Where does he live? Has he ever been married? Kids? Where's he from originally?"

Alison put her hands up to stop the barrage of questions. "Whoa, Kat, slow down. I don't know any of that. Oh yeah, he's from Baltimore originally."

"And he's spent a winter here? And he didn't leave? The snowfall didn't scare him off?"

"As far as I know he's planning on teaching next fall."

Lizzie finished hanging up the last of the clothes. "Anything we can do to help land this guy? You two are helping me out with my plan. I'd gladly help you out, Al."

Before Katie could say a word, Alison cut them off. "No way. Let's just handle you right now, Lizard. I have a feeling that this twisted plan of yours will keep us all on our toes for the next few weeks."

"What do you mean twisted? This is a well thought out, succinctly planned mission which will be executed on time and in full."

"Yes, General Hampton," Alison said with a salute.

"Oh, shut up." She picked up a hairbrush and threw it at the other two, which Alison easily deflected then handed to Katie, who began to brush Alison's hair. It was a routine that had begun in fifth grade.

As if reading Lizzie's thoughts, Katie said, "Gosh, the more things change…huh? I half expect Zeke to come barreling in here and scream at us to turn the music down. Or your mother yelling 'Elizabeth, Ezekiel, behave yourselves'."

Alison and Lizzie both smiled, remembering all the time the three of them had spent in this room doing pretty much the same thing they were doing now.

Katie continued on with her thoughts, "Hey, where is Zeke now? Still on float?"

"Yep, still on float. I think the carrier's due back soon. You know the Navy, you get about forty-eight hours' notice as to when anything will happen. My mom and dad are ready to go as soon as they get the word. They're going to fly to Jacksonville to meet the squadron when it flies in. It's this big ritual they do after a float this long; all the wives and girlfriends go to the base and meet the jets with champagne. Anyway, with Zeke not seeing anybody right now, my parents wanted to make sure he'd have someone there when he landed, so they're going down. They just don't know when, yet."

"That's nice of them," Katie said as she continued brushing Alison's short, glossy locks.

"Yeah, it is. I did it, let's see, six or seven years ago. It's pretty cool. Those Navy pilots know how to party."

"Hey Lizard, if it doesn't work out with this Davis guy back in Detroit, you should have Zeke introduce you to his fellow pilots."

"Good God, no! I've been to their parties, I've seen the women they like, I am definitely not trophy girlfriend material."

"Oh, I don't know, you put that mini with the halter back on and you could definitely pass," Katie said.

"I don't know why I even bought that one, it's so not me. I think I was just so thrilled that I could fit into it. I don't think that baby's ever going to see the outside of my closet."

She watched the two women she loved most in the world, with the exception of her mother, and felt a sense of calm and serenity come over her that she hadn't felt in years. Maybe she never had. So many new feelings and emotions had surfaced in the last three years that her only way to deal with them had been to quickly acknowledge their presence then politely ask them to leave, assuring them that they'd be welcome some other time, when she was better equipped to handle them. When that day would be, Lizzie couldn't say.

She knew she sublimated emotions with food, she didn't need Dr. Phil to tell her that, but allowing said emotions free reign was another thing entirely.

She'd get there; it was just taking a while. She considered herself a work in progress.

Three

___

√ Meet Finn at Commodore
√ Do Pilates tape to make up for mom's dinner last night
√ Call Sybil

FROM THE BACK BOOTH of the Commodore, Finn watched Liz walk in. He got out from the booth and waved. He noticed the stares she got from a bunch of the guys as she walked past.

His chest filled with pride. His Liz, all grown up.

God, she'd turned into a beauty. Her long, pitch-black hair was swept from her face with a headband. It swung loose behind her, showing a teasing glimpse from around the side of her waist as she moved. She'd worn her hair very short when they'd dated, and he'd thought that looked great on her, brought out her eyes, but this…this was sexy as hell.

The body of the girl he'd known had developed into that of a woman. Her hips swung with tempting fullness and her lush breasts were framed by a crisp white shirt that she had unbuttoned only once. That was Liz, never giving it away. Only a lucky few got to see what was going on underneath. On every level.

Finn had been one of those lucky few. He'd known the softness of her skin past the second button. Known the deeper thoughts that went past her friendly exterior.

It'd been a huge hassle getting free to be here, but seeing her made it worthwhile. He hadn't outright lied to Annie, but he'd certainly omitted some facts. Even saying something as innocent as having dinner with an old friend who was in town for a short time would have sent Annie into a tailspin. If she whiffed the smallest scent of Finn's true feelings toward Liz, she would have gone into a full-blown tantrum.

The thought jarred him. Just what did he mean his true feelings about Liz? This was just going to be a one-shot deal, right?

He continued to watch as Liz stopped at a table halfway through the restaurant. A man got up from his table and pulled Liz into a huge hug, then held her out at arm's length, as if soaking in the sight of her. Finn's eyes narrowed as he had a flash of jealousy. It quickly left when he got a better look at the white-haired man who hugged Liz. He was sixty if he was a day. Certainly Liz wasn't into old men.

A fleeting notion of just what kind of men Liz was into went through him. Why would she have never married? She was into guys, right? She sure had been back then.

But that can sometimes change. Was that the reason she'd never married? She'd switched teams? Nah, she'd definitely come on to him the other night at the Mine Shaft. It'd been a long time for him, but not so long that he didn't know when a woman wanted him.

Still, a sense of dread eased its way into his neck. Liz was so nice, she'd be the type to give you a hug and want to catch up with someone she hadn't seen in so long. Maybe he was wrong and that's all this was to her. A chance to catch up with an old boyfriend, then back to Detroit to her lesbian lover. Although he'd definitely file the vision of Liz making love with another woman away to pull out some lonely night, he didn't believe it to be true.

His doubts were eased as Liz finally made it to their table and flashed him a killer smile.

Her smile was warm and genuine, like Liz herself, but it didn't say, "Gee, it's good to see you." No, the smile Liz flashed said, "I want to eat you up with a spoon." Which suited him just fine, and he hoped to fulfill her unspoken wish by the end of the night.

"Hey there," she said as she reached him. Calm, cool, like she saw him every day. He half expected her to comment on the weather or some such bullshit.

There was an awkward second, and they both looked at their feet while they wondered if a hug, handshake, or a simple smile should be their greeting. Then their eyes met. Eighteen years fell away and it was his Liz, whose eyes had always seen him with an integrity and strength he could only hope to aspire to.

His Liz, who didn't even realize that she was above him in all things, but looked at him with an adoration which both humbled and aroused him.

Always had.

He guessed it always would, because there she was looking at him in the same way, and all of Finn's thoughts about keeping this thing casual went out the window.

He pulled her into his embrace and held her. Just held her. Her arms encircled his waist and she stepped closer to him, laid her head on his chest, and breathed in the scent of him. She'd always done that. It'd made him self-conscious at first, wondering if he hadn't showered off the smell of horses entirely before their dates.

She breathed in deeply once more then pulled away, looking into his eyes. A small, teasing smile played on her face. "You still wear Brut. I didn't know they even still sold that stuff."

He nodded, mesmerized by her. By her smile, her apparently stellar sense of smell, but mostly by her memory of him. He had meant enough to her that she remembered his scent. They had only dated for a few months eighteen years ago and she remembered how he smelled? Had anyone else in his life ever known him like that? He wasn't sure that even his ex-wife would know him if blindfolded. Hell, his childhood dog probably couldn't even sniff him out.

"But no horses? Don't you still have horses?"

"Huh?" His moment of self-pity made him lose her drift.

"You always smelled of Brut and horses. But, no horses tonight. Do you still have them?"

"No. No horses. I sold them all." He didn't elaborate. How could he even begin to tell her about the horses? How his heart broke and the last of his dreams drifted into the dust that the trailer hauling away his joy kicked up. How he'd had no choice, not really, but the day he signed the bill of sale, a little piece of him had died.

He had precious few pieces left.

It was as if she knew he couldn't talk about it, seemed to sense the precarious place he was in just thinking about the loss of his horses.

Still entwined in his arms, Liz once again gave his waist a squeeze, and all Finn could do was hug her again.

It wasn't a friendly hug. It was a hug of lovers.

One could hope.

It seemed like forever, but was probably only seconds, before he got hold of himself, broke the embrace, and seated her across from him in the booth.

"So I always smelled like horses, eh? Nice of you to tell me. You know, I *would* shower before I'd pick you up," he teased.

She lowered her head and laughed. That deep, gut-busting laugh that he'd recognized after years apart. She raised her head, her black hair falling back into place, and her soft hazel eyes met his as her laughter died away, leaving her mouth in a sweet smile. "It's good to see you, Finn. I'm glad I...ran into you." Her eyes darted away, as if admitting it was more than she wanted to reveal.

He reached across the scarred wooden table, carved with lovers' names of long ago, and took her hand. It was cool and soft and fit into his larger one with ease. "I'm glad, too, Liz. Hell, at least one good thing came of working at that godawful job. Imagine the odds of you coming into that theater while I was working."

"Yes, that was quite a coincidence." She ducked her head again, not meeting his eyes. Something he said seemed to register with her and she asked, "Why would you say 'imagine the odds'? Aren't you there most nights?"

"Well, I've been there a lot lately, but I've only been back at the theater for six months."

"Oh, not since when we dated?"

Did she really think he'd done nothing but hawk popcorn to kids for the last eighteen years? God, what kind of loser did she think he was? And if she did, why was she out with him? He tried to mask his disappointment in Liz's low opinion of him.

"No, Liz, I haven't been working at the Mine Shaft all this time. Believe it or not, I was able to tear myself away from the glory of concession stands for a few years." He chuckled as he said it, but Liz picked up on the anger in his voice.

"Well, I didn't assume anything. Anyway, what would be wrong with you working at the Mine Shaft all this time? I always thought it was a dream job. See every movie, all the popcorn you can eat…what's not to like?"

"Yeah, for a sixteen-year-old kid, maybe." He was grateful she didn't mention that he'd been twenty when he'd worked there.

"So what *have* you been doing all these years?" What was probably mere curiosity in her tone sounded like accusation to Finn, and he inwardly bristled. He didn't have to justify himself to Liz Hampton or anyone else. The choices he'd made were ones that were thrust upon him, and he figured he'd probably do them all again if he had to.

Except for Dana. He'd definitely choose differently there. Of course, Dana hadn't really been a choice at all. More like a sentence handed down from some unknown jury.

He let the feeling slide as a waitress approached their booth to take their drink order.

"Bud in a bottle," Finn said and Lizzie nodded her head, indicating the same for her.

He picked up the menus between them and handed one to Lizzie. "Do you want to order right away?"

She pushed her menu to the side of the table, away from her.

"No, I'm not that hungry. Maybe we could just have a beer and talk for a while? Get something to eat a little later?"

"That's fine. Whatever you want." He made eye contact with her as he said the last, trying to get them back on track. Back to where they were after their initial hug, not to the weird place that bringing up the horses and his working at the theater had taken them.

"Whatever you want, Liz." He dropped his menu and took her hand again. He emphasized the "whatever", trying to make his intentions known. It'd been a while since he'd flirted, but he figured it was like riding a bike.

He must not have lost his touch completely, because he saw a slow blush rise from her neck to her cheeks. The color made her look about sixteen years old. And innocent. Still innocent. It had driven him crazy with want back then, and if the tightening in his groin was any indication, it still did.

The waitress approached, carrying two bottles. She put down their drinks, realized they wouldn't be ordering any time soon, and quickly left.

He took his beer in his free hand and tapped the neck of it against the top of Lizzie's bottle in a toast. "Here's to getting to know each other again,"

"Yes. Here's to getting to know each other again." She raised the bottle to her lips and drank. No sissy sip for his Liz. You can take the girl out of da Yoop, but you can't take da Yoop out of the girl. No sir, she took a good-sized gulp that left her sexy lips wet. He could barely draw his eyes away from them.

He tried to focus on what she'd just said. "To tell you the truth, Liz, I'm surprised to hear you say that."

She looked confused. "Say what?"

"Say that you're glad to see me, that you look forward to getting reacquainted. You know, we didn't end on such a good note." His voice was cautious, feeling her out.

"That's true, but it was a long time ago. We were just kids."

"Yeah. Kids."

"Besides, I forgave you a long time ago. Life's too short to hold grudges," she said with a conviction that almost sounded rehearsed.

"You forgave me? For what?"

"For dumping me because I wouldn't sleep with you."

"That's not how I remember it, Liz." His voice was soft, controlled; his eyes held hers.

"That's exactly how I remember it. What's your spin on the whole thing?"

"First of all, I don't 'spin' things, that's for you big city folks. Second of all, I didn't dump you because you wouldn't sleep with me. I broke up with you because you were *just about* to sleep with me."

She took in his statement, mentally chewed on it, then spat it out at him. "That's bull. I wasn't about to sleep with you."

"Oh yeah, you were."

The normally articulate Liz could only come back with, "Nah-unh."

"We were close, Liz. Remember? Your resistance had just about crumbled. It wouldn't have taken too many more nights down at the beach to get you to cave."

She looked away from him and took her hand back, as if stung. Stung by the truth. She wouldn't admit it, but she knew he was right.

"You're right." She said it so quietly, he wasn't sure he'd heard her.

"What?"

She looked back at him, her cute little chin held up high. "I said, you're right. It probably wouldn't have taken many more nights at the beach. I was getting pretty desperate by the end of those evenings."

He couldn't help but let out a little snort. "*You* were getting pretty desperate? I think we well established that the rumor you could die from blue balls was untrue. Never had a man gone home so unsatisfied so often and been able to walk the next day."

She winced, as if feeling the pain that he would endure on those nights. No way she could imagine how bad it had been.

"I didn't understand then how much…ah…pressure you felt when we'd be together."

"Pressure? Jeez, Liz, you had me hard from the moment I'd pick you up right through to dropping you off. Gran never could understand why I'd shower right before a date with you, then need to run to the shower as soon as I got home. Thank God for loud showers and lots of soap."

Her curiosity won out over her embarrassment and she asked, "Lots of soap?"

As always, he was amused by her innocence. "Lots of lather, makes the hands very slick, able to…you know…a lot quicker." And, as always, he wanted to educate her, but not be too crude with her.

He knew the moment she got it. The pink on her neck and cheeks turned a crimson red. "I don't know what to say. Do I apologize for that? Sending you home in that state?" She had a teasing lilt to her voice and he was happy to see that he hadn't turned her off with his blunt talk. On the contrary, her eyes seemed to shine.

"No need for apologies, I know that you went home pretty stirred up, too. I made sure of that."

"Yes I did, and I…" She cut herself off.

"You what?" She shook her head and Finn put a coaxing tone in his voice, "Come on Liz, it's just two old friends talking. You what?"

"I'd go home pent up, and I didn't even know how to take care of myself like you did." He slowly smiled, but was blown away when she added, "Then."

The thought of Liz taking care of business herself made his cock jerk. Damn, but he'd like to see that.

Slow down, boy, don't scare her off.

"So, wait, let's back up," she said. He dragged his mind from the image forming of Liz on white cotton sheets, her black hair a stark contrast on the pillow, her hands moving down her own body as he watched.

"Back up where?"

"You said you broke up with me because I was about to sleep with you. I grudgingly acknowledge that's true. So why break up with me? You were about to hit the jackpot."

"I never thought of your virginity as some prize to win, like a stuffed animal at some carnival game."

She raised an eyebrow in disbelief.

"Well, okay, maybe I did."

She gave him a small smile. "So why, then?"

"I don't know? I guess I had some misguided notion that you'd hate me later. Or that I'd be bringing you down to my level or something. You'd just turned eighteen…what can I say, I was a twenty-year-old kid! I was totally fucked up."

She took that in and slowly nodded. She seemed to understand. Or she was letting the point go for now, he wasn't sure which. He decided to get clear of these dangerous waters before he went down a final time. She must have thought the same thing, because she was the one who ultimately changed the subject.

"Is your grandmother still living?"

He nodded while he took another swig of his beer. "Yes. She's getting up there, but you'd never know it from her attitude. She's a great lady, I owe her more than I'll ever be able to repay." His voice turned soft, almost tender, as it always did when he spoke of Gran.

"I always liked her."

"She liked you too."

"We only met a couple of times." She seemed dubious.

"She liked you. She thought you were good for me." There was a long pause as they both let that sink in.

"So, what have you been doing these past eighteen years? You were going to State, right?"

She nodded as she drank from the beer bottle and he was again mesmerized by the sight of her moist lips wrapped around the head of the long neck bottle. He shifted in his seat and put his napkin in his lap.

After she swallowed she answered him. "Yes. State. I lived with Alison and Katie." At his blank look she elaborated, "They were with me at the movie the other night?" He nodded in comprehension and motioned for her to go on as he took a drink from his beer. "I got my degree in communications, moved to Detroit, where I got on with a public relations firm. Four years later I opened my own firm. It's doing pretty well."

He put his bottle down, sat back, and said, "That's it?"

Four

—∿∿—

√ Leave Petey another voice mail
√ Email Zeke
√ Call Sybil

LIZZIE WAS SLIGHTLY MIFFED. How dare he reduce her life's work to "that's it?" How could this guy possibly know what kind of courage and determination it had taken her to break free from the stability of an established firm and hang her own shingle?

But then, what did she expect from a guy whose main job consisted of scraping candy off theater floors? No, that wasn't fair. There was obviously more to Finn's story.

But for now the spotlight was on her.

"Well, I'd hardly say 'that's it'. Opening my own firm was a pretty risky step. I did have some friends who I knew would come on board as clients, but still…" She was cut off as he held up his hand for her to stop.

"Whoa. I didn't mean to diminish your professional achievements. I'm not surprised that you're doing well for yourself. In fact, I would have been surprised at anything less than you owning your own business. The 'that's it' meant you didn't say a word about anything other than business. Surely there's some personal life stuff to tell after all these years?"

"What do you mean?" she asked. She took just a second to

bask in how matter-of-fact he was about her being successful. Like there was never any doubt in his mind.

"Well, you said the other night that you never married. Were you engaged? Do you have children? Live-in boyfriend? Tell me something about *you*."

How could she possibly explain to him what the last fifteen years had been for her? The feelings of shame that putting weight on had brought her. Blocking out feelings. That opening her own business had been a distraction of sorts so that she wouldn't have to deal with anything personal. How do you relate the stuff that took you the last three years to figure out over a bottle of Bud?

You don't. She'd just tell him something smooth and be done with it. He had no more interest in knowing about her foibles and triumphs in the past than she did of knowing his.

But she *was* interested in Finn's past. Why he married at twenty-three?. Why he was divorced. And what had happened to his horses?

But that wasn't what this was about. This was purely a means to an end. The end of celibacy. The beginning of the future.

Instead of trying to explain the unexplainable, she answered, "Uh, that would be a no on all of the above."

He waited for her to go on, and she sighed, knowing there was no choice. "Never met the right guy. Too busy with work. You know, the usual reasons a woman my age is still single." She rambled the words out, as if she knew them by rote. And she did. People she met asked her that question a lot in the last three years.

She'd never been asked it during her years of obesity.

"Yeah, okay, I guess." He let it go, but only for now. There was a look in his eyes that made her think he didn't buy her simplistic explanation.

Eager to get him off the subject of her personal life, or lack thereof, she asked, "You said you were divorced seven years ago? So, only married that once, then?"

"Believe me, once is enough." There was a bitterness in his expression that she thought looked foreign on him. Or at least the Finn she used to know. She guessed a bad marriage could do that to you.

Come to think of it, he did look...harder. Of course, a seventeen-year span would age a person, but the Finn she'd known, though saddled at a young age with much responsibility, was still full of dreams. The man in front of her had definitely seen many tough days and they showed on his face.

He still looked good to her.

It wasn't a classically handsome face, though he possessed the chiseled cheekbones of a male model. His nose was crooked from a fight in eighth grade. There was a tiny scar through his eyebrow that he'd received when trying to take a whiskey bottle away from his mother at seventeen. Both experiences he'd told her about on a blanket at the beach, one with laughs, the other with tears.

His blue eyes, now serious and knowing, were light and teasing years ago. His mouth was firm and drawn tight, like he grimaced frequently, but his lips were still full—and tempting.

He looked as though the years of a hard life had caught up with him.

She didn't care. For her purposes she need only to be attracted to him, not to understand him. And she was absolutely attracted to him.

Sitting across from him, sparring with him like they used to, she knew she'd made the right choice. Finn was the one to bring her out of hibernation. He was sexy. He wanted her. She knew she'd enjoy their time together. And, most importantly, she'd be able to walk away from him.

"So, no plans to remarry?" she teased. He'd made it perfectly clear in his tone that one would be his limit.

"No way. What about you, ever think about it?"

She shrugged. "Sure, I'm open to it. Actually, I've become more open to the idea in the last few years. My business is in a good place, I've got great people who work for me. I'm able to slow down and smell the roses, as it were, so, yeah, I guess I'm looking."

She thought she saw a flash of panic in his eyes, but he kept his cool and only nodded at her summation. She waited a second or two, then let him off the hook. "Relax. I'm not looking tonight. Or for the next two months."

He let out a breath that he probably didn't even realize he held. He fastened his steely blue gaze on her and asked, "What *are* you looking for tonight, and for the next two months?"

This was it. The moment of truth. Lay her cards on the table and see if he plays. She leaned forward, her breasts resting on her forearms, her eyes locked on his. "No strings. No commitments. Just some laughs, some fun, some good old-fashioned messing around."

He seemed taken aback at first, then leveled her with his aw-shucks smile and said, "Then, Elizabeth, I'm your man."

—⚹—

They didn't order dinner. They had one more beer each, which they nursed for the next hour. The conversation turned to mundane things. Neither of them wanted to spoil the evening with more personal talk. After all, it was looking like they may begin a purely sexual, short-term fling, why bring anything personal into it?

Finally, Finn paid the bill, over her argument that since she asked him out, she should pay. "Not while I'm still breathing does a woman pay on a date with me," he snorted.

They left the restaurant. The air was warm and there was no breeze, which was unusual. The sky seemed to sparkle. Because it was so clear, with no pollution at all, the stars shone much brighter here than they did in the city. The downtown area of both Houghton and Hancock ran parallel to the man-made canal, with the back entrances to the businesses situated on a bike and jogging path that ran alongside the water. She could faintly hear the waves from the canal as they gently lapped against the seawall. She was taking in the stillness of the night when Finn asked where her car was parked.

"Just around the corner, in the parking deck."

He only nodded, took her hand in his, and started in that direction. His hand was rough with calluses. You didn't get hands like that from making popcorn. His fingers entwined with hers as he glanced over at her. His pace quickened and she had to nearly jog to keep up with him. She was excited, too, and could feel the tension building between them.

"Which car?"

"The black Navigator." She pointed to the vehicle, parked in the corner by itself, in a dark part of the small lot.

"Big city girl like you should know better than to park in the corner, out of the light."

She giggled, a sound that made him grasp her hand a little tighter. "I do know better. And believe me, in the city I park by the entrance and under a light, but that's what I love about being home, I don't have to do those things. I even left my car unlocked."

He gave her a frown. "We're not totally immune to crime, you know. No need to be foolish."

"I wasn't being foolish. I was just putting my faith in my fellow Yooper."

His frown vanished. They reached her car and he pulled her around to the passenger side. He edged her against the passenger door then disengaged their hands and placed his on her waist.

Oh God, her waist! Of course he'd have to go for her worst area first. She tried to gauge if there were any rolls or handles where his hands were placed and came away feeling as confident as she could with a body that hadn't been out of the garage in fifteen years. *Only driven three times, folks, by a little old lady who always drove the speed limit!*

If she placed her hands up on his shoulders, raising her arms and lengthening her spine, it would elongate her waist. Kind of like a yoga move. She did it, barely taking the time to notice how strong and firm his shoulders felt.

Her hands went around his neck as he took a step closer to her. "Seventeen years. It's the longest I've ever waited to have a woman, that's for sure."

She looked up at him and smiled. "You weren't waiting for me, Finn. I'm willing to bet you haven't thought about me once in all that time, so don't give me that."

"You'd lose that bet. I thought about you plenty for the first few years. Then, well, you know, life kind of happens and your priorities shift."

She laughed. "You mean taking me to bed wasn't a lifelong priority for you? I'm hurt."

His smile went right to her gut. Maybe a little lower. He stuck a workboot-clad foot between her sandals and nudged her feet apart, creating a nest for himself between her legs, which he flew into like a homing pigeon. "Oh, it was a priority all right, it just slipped a few notches on the list."

"Yeah, like a thousand notches." She put a slight pressure on his neck, coaxing him even closer. The heat of his body in front of her a stark contrast to the cool metal of her car along her backside.

"Well, E-liz-a-beth, you're right back at the top of the list now." He lowered his head and nuzzled her neck. She let out a soft sigh, luxuriating in the touch.

"I hate to disappoint you, but even though I never married, my virginity's not up for grabs any more."

His head shot up. "God, I hope not! First of all, I'd never believe a woman who looks like you could remain a virgin till thirty-five. Second, I'm not twenty years old any more, where the idea of being someone's first is exciting. I want my woman to know what she's doing. I don't want to have to break anybody in."

He leaned back in and brought his mouth to hers for their first kiss in seventeen years.

Her first kiss in *fifteen*.

How had she thought his mouth looked hardened? It was anything but. His lips, soft and moist, gently wisped over hers. She opened her mouth under his and felt his immediate response. He angled his head to get better contact and his body moved into hers, connecting them with a current that seemed to electrify them both.

"Oh God, Liz. Yes." His hands left her waist and held the back of her head, tilting it backward, as his tongue teased her lower lip.

Riding a bike. Riding a bike.

She flicked out her tongue to engage his. It was all the encouragement he needed. His tongue swept deep inside her mouth, tasting of beer, tangling with hers, trying to sample all of her, as if his tongue could remember her taste.

Her hands left Finn's neck and swept to his chest. She had to tightly wedge her hands between their crushed bodies to feel him, but her determination was strong. She wanted her hands on him. She moved them down to his waist so that she could place her breasts against his chest. They felt heavy and aching, and it was almost as if Finn's broad chest could give them more support than any underwire could.

His breath hitched when he felt her breasts against his chest. It was as if he remembered that she was a whole woman, not just a soft, wet mouth.

She didn't think it possible for the kiss to become even deeper, but she was wrong. His gentle lips turned hungry and she responded in kind, meeting his every demand. Her head leaned against the window of her car and he must have felt confident enough that it would not budge to let his hands roam down her body. His right hand swept around her back where it began to smooth over her spine. His left hand went right to her breast.

That was the Finn she remembered, no pussyfooting around, take what you wanted. This was one part of her body that he could play with as much as he wanted. They weren't cute and perky, but her breasts were full and lush, a breast man's dream. And Finn had always been a breast man. Though years of gravity were quickly catching up with them, they'd still be in okay shape for another couple of years. For the next two months at least.

Plus, it felt so damn good. His hand kneaded and molded her, pushed her up and squeezed. She voiced her approval with a quiet moan and a roll of her hips.

His hand at her back moved down to her butt and pulled her tight against him. The denim of his jeans was no barrier for his raging erection and the heat of it seemed to burn through Lizzie's cotton shorts.

"Liz, you feel so good."

"Mmm, you too. Oh—" she squeaked as he found her nipple. It wasn't difficult; the kiss alone made it pebble and harden against her white blouse. His thumb rubbed circles around the sensitive nub and for just a moment she didn't obsess over thoughts about his hand on her ass, and if he could feel cellulite through panties and shorts.

A car door slamming across the parking lot broke their kiss and Finn laid his forehead against hers, catching his breath. He looked over her head, over the roof of her car, to see someone in the lot getting into their car.

"Not here. I can't do all the things I want to you here. Let's go." He started to move her away from the door so that he could open it.

"Where do you want to go? We can't go to my parent's place—they're home right now."

He looked away, towards the water. He watched it for a few seconds, contemplating. He placed his hands on her shoulders and gave a quick kiss to her nose. "Let's go to the beach, that place was always lucky for us."

"Not as lucky as you would have liked," she said, laughing. She moved around to the driver's side and got in as Finn did the same in the passenger seat. He stilled her hand as she went to put the key in the ignition.

"Our luck's about to change, babe."

She started the car and pulled out of the lot and onto the main drag. The beach was in Hancock. Her side of the canal. As they approached the bridge, they saw a group of boys walking across on the pedestrian walk.

Finn slammed his hand down on the dash, startling her.

"God damn that kid! Liz, you better pull over. I need to get out," he spat out, his anger evident.

"Here? Right here on the bridge?" She got into the right hand lane, and slowed down.

He glanced in the rearview mirror. "Yeah, right here. There's no one behind us, just stop and I'll hop out."

She didn't know what to think. What just happened? Had he realized in the time it took to drive to the bridge just how flabby her ass had actually been and decided to jump ship? "Are you coming back?"

He let out a huge sigh. "No. Not tonight. It's okay, I can walk back to my car from here. I'll call you tomorrow. Your parents still in the book?"

At her dumbfounded nod, he added, "I'm really sorry. I didn't want our night to end like this."

"Then why is it?" She steeled herself for the worst, all thoughts centered on her body, and his evident disgust with it.

"See that group of kids up there? The one with the Lions ball cap is mine, and he's an hour past curfew." He left the car and shut the door in one sleek movement. He hopped the barrier to the pedestrian walk and headed to the unsuspecting kids.

To his son.

Finn's son.

A horn honked behind Lizzie, bringing her attention back to the road. She crossed the bridge and headed, not to the beach, but to her parents' home.

As she turned up the hill at Bob's Mobil the Bible verse seemed to shout at her.

"As for you, be fruitful and increase in number, multiply on the earth and increase upon it."

Apparently, Finn had followed that advice.

Five

—⁘—

√ Google if they still make Brut
√ Pick-up more suntan lotion
√ Call Sybil

"HE HAS A SON? Why did we not think of that?" Alison asked.

"I know—duh. I can't believe I didn't think of it before. And it never showed up online—although not much on Finn did. Of course he has a kid, nobody's married for that long and doesn't have children."

"Some people are," Katie quietly whispered.

Lizzie was awash with contrition. "Oh God, I'm sorry Kat, I wasn't thinking."

"Step A: Open mouth. Step B: Insert foot," Alison said.

"No, no, it's fine, really. I know you didn't mean me. And you're right, there aren't a whole lot of marriages out there that last that long and don't produce offspring. Especially in the U.P., home of long winters and large families."

The women were on the lawn at Alison's camp. In the U.P., all cottages, cabins, summer homes of any kind were called camps. It was something that Lizzie had tried explaining to her friends in Detroit to no avail. They couldn't help but picture a ramshackle place with some logs and lots of tarpaper. That was not the case with Alison's place.

When she'd moved back to Hancock to take her position at Tech, Alison renovated and winterized her parents' camp on the canal, just outside of Houghton (a fact that the Hancock contingency never let her forget). It was a small, darling Cape Cod, very cozy and just right for one person. It was on the water, which was idyllic for three months of the year, and a heating nightmare for the other nine.

Alison's two sisters were older, married with children, and lived in Chicago and Buffalo, so she was the only one at home. She'd been a change-of-life baby and her elderly parents were to the point where they would soon need to have someone nearby. Her taking over the camp seemed like a perfect solution for the entire family.

Katie lay on a blanket on the ground, wearing a skimpy bikini, looking gorgeous. She was on her stomach and had untied the straps from her top to minimize tan lines. Her white-blond hair was tied back in a ponytail.

Lizzie and Alison were both in tankinis and had pushed the tops up to get sun to their tummies in the privacy that Alison's camp provided.

Lizzie and Alison lay on chaise lounges, which they had dragged off the deck of the camp and down to the lawn to be closer to the water. The camp was about thirty yards away from the water. On the right corner of the lawn was the sauna house, which contained a sauna and a changing room.

"I mean, a kid! I don't even like kids. I'm horrible with kids, always have been. I remember every Saturday night when you guys would be babysitting and I'd think, no way, not me."

"Maybe it's time to throw in the towel on this plan of yours, hey Lizard?" Katie asked.

A sense of panic at giving up everything she'd planned overwhelmed her. "Why would I throw in the towel? So he has a kid. I can work around that." She reached for her totebag to pull out her notebook, but realized she'd left it up on the deck. Damn.

Katie rolled over and tied her swimsuit top together as she

and Alison exchanged looks.

"Are we back to that again? You guys not behind me in this?" Lizzie asked.

"It's not that we're not with you, it's just that we're concerned," Katie gently said.

"Listen, why don't you forget about this plan of yours, go back to Detroit, start something up with this Davis guy, and just take it slowly sexually. I know it's been a while for you, Lizard, but it's like riding a bike. It'll all come back to you."

Lizzie shook her head. "No, I can't risk it. Not with someone who's so perfect for me as Davis."

"Risk what? That it won't be good the first time together? It seldom is. That's what building a relationship is all about," Katie said.

Lizzie rubbed her hands up and down her thighs, liking the glide of the suntan oil against her skin. Her voice cracked as she said, "I might not get a second chance."

Katie and Alison kept quiet, sensing there was more. Damn women who knew you better than you knew yourself.

She took a deep breath and began, "About nine years ago I met a man. He was working on a political campaign for one of our clients. He came on pretty strong." She stopped. Alison and Katie had "so what?" looks on their faces. "You have to understand, at that point, men weren't coming on to me at all, let alone strongly."

"I find that hard to believe. Sure you were really big, but you were—are—a very confident woman who created her own business and surrounded by tons of me—politicians, athletes, movers and shakers," Katie said.

Lizzie smiled wryly. "When was the last time you saw a professional athlete or a politician with a huge fatty on his arm?"

"Hey, there are men out there that like that. Chubby chasers, I think they call them."

"Alison!" Katie chided.

Lizzie half-heartedly laughed at Alison. "I suppose there are, but they weren't traveling in the circles I was."

"So, this guy was coming on strong…" Katie said, leading Lizzie back to a story she didn't want to tell. Had never told the two women to whom she told everything.

"Right. It really shook me at first. But when he asked me out, I said yes. We went out a few times. On our third date…"

"Ah yes, the pivotal third date," Alison said knowingly.

"What? What's the third date?" Katie asked, not having been on a third date in seventeen years.

"That's usually the date that 'it' happens," Lizzie explained.

"That's when you fuck," Alison said at the same time.

Katie frowned at Alison and motioned for Lizzie to continue.

She took a sip of her lemonade, another deep breath, and continued. "Well, it went really well. We went back to my place. Things got pretty hot on the couch, we took it to the bedroom… and…and…" She stopped. Katie and Alison waited. Lizzie tried to just get through it. To recite what happened as if it hadn't been her in the room. Hadn't been her who'd suffered the incredible humiliation. "When we undressed, he lost his erection."

"Jesus," Alison said as Katie gasped.

Katie collected herself first. "There could be a thousand reasons for that," she said. "He could have had too much to drink. He could have been tired. Lots of reasons. It's happened to Ron. He was too tired."

Lizzie had told herself that at the time of course. And the next day, as she ate an entire Pepperidge Farm white cake. But she knew the truth. "It wasn't that he *couldn't* get it up, Kat. He was rock hard on the couch. I had him in my hand, I knew. It was when…when…when he saw me that he…he…"

"Became a limp dick—both figuratively and literally," Alison said. Lizzie could have kissed her friend for lightening the moment.

"What did he say?" Katie asked.

"What could he say? He was embarrassed, tried to assure me

it wasn't me. But not too convincingly."

"Well, of course not. Because if it's not you it's him, and no man's going to admit that," Alison said.

Lizzie shrugged. "Whatever. We kept our distance and I put the thought of men and sex out of my mind." She took another sip of lemonade, leaned back onto the chaise and tilted her head to the sun. "Until I met Davis Cummings," she said quietly.

"Yes, Davis Cummings," Alison said. "Don't think that we didn't put together you're mentioning this new guy in the Red Wing's front office and you starting to lose weight."

"He was what got me thinking that there was something missing from my life, I admit. I mean, I meet this guy and on paper he's perfect for me. And I knew I didn't have a shot at being with him. So I start thinking about my life and what I'd accomplished and what I'd missed. That's when I decided to get my life back.

"Nothing may ever happen with Davis. And that's okay. I didn't lose weight for him, I did it for me. He—or the thought of him—may have been the impetus. But if not Davis, then someone else."

"So, again, why Finn?" Katie asked.

"Because with Finn, if we get naked and he goes soft, it will hurt, but it wouldn't be the same as if it were Davis or someone who I really want a future with."

Katie and Alison seemed to accept her answer, or at least decided to give her a reprieve. Her thoughts returned to that long ago night when a man's lack of erection robbed her of her sexual self-confidence.

She let the sun pound down on her face and allowed herself to just…feel bad. It was a relatively new practice, and one she hadn't quite mastered. She was anxious for the sauna to be ready so she could sweat all these damn emotions right out of her.

—❧—

It took five days before Finn called. Five excruciating days for Lizzie, wondering whether her plan was dead before it had even truly begun. Wondering if she should call him. If she *could* call him. It had taken her thirty-five years to ask a man out, where would calling someone who hadn't called you after a date fit in with *that* timetable?

When he did call the following Monday, it wasn't with explanations or apologies, just an invitation for her to join him Saturday at his strawberry farm. They agreed on late afternoon and he said he'd do something on the grill for dinner.

"This is it, I can feel it," she told her friends. "Dinner at his place, it's going to happen Saturday."

"What about the son? How does he play into all this?" Katie asked.

She'd thought about that of course—wondered if the son would impede her plan. But Finn's asking her to his place could only mean one thing. And she was certain he wouldn't want his son around for that. "Maybe the mom has him most of the time. Or maybe she has him on the weekends and Finn has him during the week." She shrugged and pulled her tablet from her bag. "I don't know, but I'm sure he won't be in the picture Saturday night." She flipped the pages until she came to the checklist she'd started when Finn had called. "I scheduled manicure and pedicure appointments already. Is there any place around here I can get a bikini wax?"

She spent her time until Saturday hanging out with her mom and dad, who were still waiting by the phone for word to come about Zeke's squadron arriving.

Afternoons were spent at Alison's place trying to get more sun on her Michigan winter-white body. "I know it doesn't cover up the stretch marks, but they don't seem to glow as much when they're tan."

"Oh, Lizard, they're not that bad," was Alison's weak reply.

"You'd think that when you lost weight the stretch marks you got when you gained weight would go away, like it was reducing itself or something. Some kind of karmic reward. But nooooo, I get them when I gain and I get them when I lose. It's a double dose."

Her office was running smoothly, with the exception of one of her clients being pulled over and being charged with a DUI. At Lizzie's insistence that she fly back to Detroit to handle it, she was met with a strong refusal from the account executive who handled the client.

"I've got it under control. I need to handle this so that LeVar and my other clients know they're in good hands with me."

"Okay, James, you're right, it's your show to run. Just remember, the public will forgive a sinner as long as he admits he sinned. I have a file of already prepared statements for something like this. Cybil knows where it is if you need help with it."

"Oh that's right. The file of prepared statements for events you have no idea are going to happen?" James teased.

"Don't laugh, you're using it now, aren't you?"

James laughed. "You got me there."

James had worked for her from the start and was just as good at the nuts and the bolts of the business as she was. Her forte was, as it always had been, just plain being nice. She had a winning way with people and when she decided to woo a client, it was really no harder than shooting fish in a barrel.

In fields such as politics and professional athletics, filled with barracudas and back-stabbers, her genuine congeniality was a breath of fresh air. Besides, she'd always been a firm believer that you caught more flies with honey than vinegar.

The next day, when she read the write-up in the papers and online, and saw the coverage on *SportsCenter*, Lizzie couldn't have been more proud of James and how he'd handled the situation. LeVar had come forward, admitting his mistake and enrolling himself in an alcohol abuse program. The public felt his sincerity and proactive responsibility were admirable. As much as they could with this type of story becoming way too frequent.

Only Lizzie and James knew what a pain in the ass LeVar was and how he'd bellowed for hours that he wasn't going into any "fucking twelve-step pussy program." James did the math for him of the dollars he'd lose if the Lions didn't re-sign him when his contract was up in a year. Or the salary lost from game suspensions by the NFL if he didn't voluntarily seek some kind of treatment. LeVar reluctantly conceded to James' plan of action. Lizzie sent a box of cigars to James at the office with a note telling him how well he had done and how proud Hampton PR was to call him one of their own.

After playing a long game of voice mail tag, Petey Ryan finally got a hold of her. As she'd expected, he spent the first ten minutes of their conversation talking about evil triumphing over good when his Red Wings went down to the Avalanche in the Western Conference finals of the Stanley Cup playoffs.

"And then, to totally piss me off? They go on and win the fucking Cup."

"I'm sure that's why they did it, Petey, just to piss you off." She could almost see him in his plush living room in Bloomfield Hills, which she'd helped decorate. He'd be pacing back and forth, phone in one hand, a Styrofoam cup in the other which he'd use as a spittoon for the tobacco he was undoubtedly chewing.

"Fucking A they did! Hey Lizard, what are you doing in da Yoop?"

"Just a little R & R."

"You don't take R & R."

"I do now."

"All sorts of changes in you, hey Lizard? Hot new bod, long hair, new lazy-ass attitude."

Petey could always crack her up. She was so glad they had remained friends after they'd dated for a short time in high school. He was probably her best friend in Detroit. She loved being in his company, he was like a favorite pair of sweats that you'd put on the second you walked in the door at the end of the day. It was almost like having Zeke close by, he and Petey were so much alike. She missed him when he wasn't around. Being on the road so much during the season, and spending his off-season in the Copper Country, most of their conversations took place on the phone.

"I do not have a lazy-ass bone in my new bod and you know it."

"God, I love yanking your chain, Lizard, it's so damn easy." His voice became faint at the end and she knew he was turning his head to make use of the spittoon. At least he turned his head, and didn't spit right into the phone. Chewing tobacco was a dirty, disgusting, and tremendously unhealthy habit, but many of the Yooper guys she knew, and lots of other hockey players, indulged. Petey's voice returned. "Hey, Zeke back yet? Thought maybe I'd fly to Jax before I headed up there."

"Not yet. My parents are waiting by the phone. They're going to fly down as soon as they have a hard date. They expect the carrier back to Virginia within the next three weeks, but the squadron usually flies off and back to Jacksonville a week or so before that. At least that's what happened the last couple of floats."

"Oh, well as long as your parents are going to be there. I just wanted to make sure someone would be there for him when they come in." Although on other sides of the bridge during high school, Zeke and Petey had formed a deep friendship when they both attended Tech; Petey to play hockey and Zeke to get his engineering degree before he joined the Navy to become a jet pilot.

"I think he'd probably prefer for you to be waiting for him. It would be a whole different kind of welcome-home party with you than with my parents." She could hear his laugh on the other end. She'd been with Petey and Zeke out on the town many times. The combination of two good looking, rugged men, one a professional hockey player and the other a jet pilot, sent Lizzie scurrying from the elbows that were thrown her way as women tried to get near them.

Babe magnets. Total babe magnets.

Petey grunted on the other end of the line. "That's for sure… a whole different kind of party. Maybe I'll wait and take a detour to Jax when I leave the Yoop and head back for training camp."

"When are you headed up?"

"In a couple of weeks. Remember, I've got that thing at the Joe with the team next week."

It wasn't an event her firm had orgainzed, so it was lower on her radar. "Oh, right. Well, I can't wait for you to get up here, it's not the same without your foul mouth giving Katie apoplexy." Katie hated profanity, a fact that led both Petey and Alison to use it as much as possible in her presence.

"Ha ha, very fucking funny. Just have the sauna hot and the beer cold."

"Always, Petey, always."

Six

—ᵐᵐ—

√ Get bikini wax
√ Get ingredients for cookies
√ Send cigars to James

LIZZIE PULLED HER SUV into the driveway of Finn's farm. The picking was done for the day and the fields behind the house were empty. In fact, the whole place looked empty. She knew that Finn, his son, and his grandmother lived here, but there was almost an eerie feeling of desertion.

The house had definitely seen better days. It was an old two-story farmhouse complete with a veranda that wrapped around three sides. Lizzie was surprised to see that what would have been a wide entrance for steps leading up to the porch was replaced by a wooden ramp. Was the grandmother now in a wheelchair?

The house's white paint was peeling and a couple of the black shutters had come off their hinges, but you could see it had been a magnificent building in its prime. It really wouldn't take much to restore it. She wondered why Finn had let it go. She knew he wasn't the lazy sort. He'd spent hours working with his horses when they'd dated, then would work at the Mine Shaft in the evenings.

The horses.

Her eyes swung to the right, to the barn, and saw more neglect. Yes, that's what it was…the entire place looked neglected.

Only the trailer, to the left of the main house, refuted the idea that the farm had been deserted. His grandmother must be living there. Or maybe they had a boarder? Though the paint was also peeling, the trailer had a homey look to it. There were window boxes full of blooming petunias in glorious purples, pinks, and reds. White and pink alyssum lined the entire perimeter.

The fields, at least, had the appearance of hard work and attention. The strawberry plants looked healthy and plentiful, even from where Lizzie stood. There were two strawberry fields behind the house, separated by the area Finn must have used to train and work with his horses. Wooden gates linked three separate corrals, the final gate leading beyond the fields and to the woods. Overgrown trails led off in several different directions. There were two more strawberry fields on the other side of the road on land also owned by the Robbins family. One was as thriving as the two others, but the fourth lay fallow.

Finn had gotten rid of his horses, an occurrence Lizzie could hardly believe. His home showed an overall neglect. He'd taken the job at the theater six months ago. Something had happened here. Things were not quite right.

A movement at the front of the first field caught her eye. Someone who'd been crouched low now stood. He had his back to her, but she was able to tell who it was. The son. She hadn't planned on that.

She'd assumed they'd be alone tonight. But thinking about it, it did seem unrealistic. What was Finn supposed to do, send a seventy-year-old woman and a teenage boy out on a Saturday night with a "don't come back till morning" warning? Or maybe they had set up a signal? If there's a quart of strawberries hanging on the doorknob, don't come in?

She smiled to herself as she imagined an overflowing quart of berries with a piece of old yellow yarn tied to two sides, hanging like a pendulum from a rust-tinged doorknob.

She reached inside her SUV to the passenger seat and

grabbed her purse, a bottle of wine, and a container full of her world-famous chocolate chip cookies. She didn't make them much anymore, she wouldn't allow it, but she'd wanted to bring something for her dinner contribution besides the wine.

When she'd measured her tummy this morning she'd been pleased, so she figured what the hell, and went to the kitchen with zeal. Of course, after eating the equivalent of a dozen cookies in dough, her good feelings about her body drained out as quickly as she drained the huge glass of milk that accompanied her indulgence.

After that, the skin-tight knit top and short shorts she'd planned to wear were sent skulking to the back of the closet, as if it were their fault Lizzie couldn't control herself around chocolate chip cookie dough. Instead, she chose a loose, French blue three-quarter-sleeve buttoned blouse, and a khaki skirt that fell to her knees and had buttons its entire length.

Having gotten some good sun these past few days, she'd been excited about the shorts and ready to show off some thigh, but she couldn't help envisioning the dough passing through her system in record time to adhere itself directly to her inner thighs and saddlebag area. The shorts were history.

She still looked okay, she surmised, if not a little more conservative than she had planned.

Balancing her offering, she shut the door to the Navigator and headed to the house, her flat sandals choosing the grass rather than the dusty walkway. The noise made Finn's son turn. Though they were over fifty yards away from each other, Lizzie saw the boy's eyes slowly trail up her body in much the same way his father had done the first night she'd seen him at the Mine Shaft.

The boy was lanky, with none of Finn's power in his physique. Knowing zilch about the growth development of boys, she wondered if he'd fill out later, or if this was to be his basic build. His hair was lighter than Finn's, almost a towhead blond, so abundant in the Finnish-laced Copper Country. Finn's mother was Finnish, Lizzie remembered. She wondered if his ex-wife was, too. She couldn't tell the boy's eye color from here, but his face was all Finn. Angles, cheekbones; what seemed hard and masculine in Finn seemed almost fragile in the boy.

She wondered for a moment if she could just pretend she hadn't seen the boy, but decided to get the inevitable over with. For Pete's sake, she was acting like an idiot. She could walk into a boardroom full of strangers and have them all liking her in minutes, she could certainly handle a teenage boy.

The boy's eyes, still roaming her body, came to rest. She wasn't sure if it was on the items she clutched, or on her breasts. She lowered her arms holding the wine bottle and the package of cookies to her sides and the kid's eyes stayed locked where they were. Definitely not on the items she'd brought. *Cheeky little thing.* The idea that Finn had probably been exactly the same way at that age made her smile.

She walked toward the field and the kid, setting the wine, cookies and her purse on the veranda as she passed the house. The smile was still on her face as she got to the boy. Oh yeah, she thought, as she noticed his startling blue eyes still staring at her breasts as she neared, he's gonna be just like his dad.

Knowing this, and knowing nothing about kids, she handled him as she would his father. "Hey. I'm Lizzie," she said for greeting, raising her chin in salutation.

He raised his chin to her for response. "Stevie."

The boy's glance returned to her Navigator, then back to Lizzie. She could see the pieces falling into place for him that she was the one his dad had been with when he got out of that vehicle on the bridge. That was something to talk about.

"You get it pretty bad the other night?"

The boy seemed startled by her comment. She probably sounded just like one of his buddies asking the same thing. "Oh yeah, grounded for a week," he told her, with almost a tinge of pride attached.

"A week, sheesh, that's tough."

"It wasn't that tough, it's already over, eh?"

That's right, that had been nearly ten days ago. Finn hadn't wanted to see her for ten days. She was extra glad now that she wore what she did; it felt a little more substantial, more armor-like than her previous choice. Still, he had invited her here, that had to mean something, didn't it?

A car pulling into the driveway drew both of their attention. Seeing who it was, Stevie walked past her, wiping his dirty hands down the sides of his beat-up jeans. "That's my friend and his dad, they're picking me up." He was already beyond her, out of the field and headed to the veranda where Lizzie now noticed a duffel bag and a rolled-up sleeping bag.

Stevie picked them both up and headed for the car as the driver waved out the window to Lizzie, obviously mistaking her for someone who was in some way involved with Stevie. "I'll drop him off tomorrow on our way to church, around ten, okay?" She waved in return and that seemed to satisfy the father in the car.

Stevie was nearly at the car when Lizzie called out, "Hey Stevie." The boy turned to her. "Your dad around?"

He nodded his head toward the dilapidated barn. "He's in there."

"Okay, thanks. It was nice meeting you."

"It was nice to meet you." His hand was on the car door now, and he stopped and faced her again. "Has Annie met you yet?"

"Who's Annie?"

A chilling, almost devil-like smile crept up his face, "Oh man, she's gonna have a cow when she finds out about you." He shoved his stuff in the car in front of him then climbed in. With one last wave, and Stevie still wearing that eerie grin, the car drove away.

The lights were on as she entered the barn, so it was easy to locate Finn. He was halfway down the length of the building. He stood at the gate of one of the horse stalls, his strong thigh raised, his workboot hitched over a low board on the gate entrance. He leaned slightly, his forearms resting on the top of the gate, one wrist on top of the other. The lean muscles of his back were tight against his dusty tee shirt that in another life had been a pristine white. His head was bowed slightly and his eyes were glued to the empty stall, not really seeing it.

He looked…defeated. Like a boxer on the ropes, not wanting to be beaten any longer. Her heart started to go out to him, but she quickly slammed on the brakes. Not on Finn. Don't give your newfound emotions to Finn. That wasn't part of the plan.

She may be able to put her heart on hold, but she did nothing to stop the physical yearnings that slammed into her as she watched Finn shift his weight and put his other foot on the wooden railing. The movement made his jeans, which were second-skin worn, pull tight across his backside. She was involuntarily licking her lips as he noticed her and turned to look at her.

Her gesture didn't escape him. "Like what you see?"

His arrogance was nothing new to her; in fact, it was one of the things she'd liked about him. Arrogance in a life mate would not be desirable, but a cocky guy was just the one you wanted when looking for a purely down-and-dirty, no-holds-barred, make-sure-you-have-a-safe-word sex partner.

"I do. Hay always makes me hot," she delivered her line in her best "Happy Birthday, Mr. President" breathy sexpot voice.

He chuckled and the thought of making him laugh, when only moments ago he had seemed so low, made her smile. The idea that maybe their little interlude would bring him some comfort, or even just a few laughs (though hopefully not when she was naked), made her feel better about the whole thing.

"I thought I was always what made you hot." He started to walk toward her, covering the distance of half the barn in only a few, lengthy strides.

"That's what I let you believe, to salvage your fragile ego, but it was always the hay, Finn…always the hay."

He was now only a step away from her, and just when she was about to put her arms out for the coming embrace, he stopped. "Well, I guess there's one good thing about being a hayseed, you get all the best women. Did I tell you how sexy long hair is on you, Liz?"

Lord, how this man could get to her. She could have been a schoolgirl as she twirled the ends of her hair that she had worn pulled back into a low ponytail.

Sure, she had played business games with adults. There, she was on sure footing. But here, playing flirting games…it seemed like a lifetime ago when she'd last done this. It *was* a lifetime ago. This was a new life. And this was why she was here…to practice.

Her hand rose and followed her hairline from her scalp all the way down. She swung her ponytail over her shoulder to land on her breast, where she began to smooth it down, almost stroke it. She watched as his eyes never left her hands and saw the corners of his mouth turn up in approval. Maybe this flirting stuff is like muscle memory. Even if you think you've forgotten it, your body recalls the motions.

"Thanks, it's relatively new to me."

"What is?" He was jarred out of his hair-watching reverie.

"My hair. Having long hair. I only started growing it out three years ago. I'd had short hair all my adult life."

"What made you decide to grow it long?" His gaze now moved to her face.

She hesitated, searched for words. "I just decided it was time to try some things in life that I hadn't tried yet."

"A little young to be having a mid-life crisis, aren't you?"

She chuckled, "Yeah, but growing my hair was so much cheaper than buying a red sports car." She remembered Stevie. "Oh, by the way, the man who picked up Stevie said he'd drop him off tomorrow at ten."

His body seemed to tense, but he just nodded acknowledgement of her message. "So, he was still here when you got here? Did you talk to him?"

"Of course I talked to him." What she really wanted to ask was *who's Annie?*

"What did he say to you?"

He mentioned Annie if that's what you're afraid of. And what's worse for you, Finn, it sounds like he'll mention me to Annie if he gets a chance. "Not much, it wasn't long before his ride showed up."

She paused, waiting for him to speak. When he didn't, she said, "Why didn't you tell me you had a son?"

It looked like he was going to deny that he'd kept Stevie from her, but then he shrugged. He went to the side of the barn where there were piles of empty quart containers and began to stack them. "I don't know. It just didn't come up at first, and then…"

She walked over to where he worked and began to stack some of the containers herself. He seemed to be putting them in piles of ten, so she followed suit. When he noticed what she was doing, he took her hands and led her away from the piles. "Don't Liz, these quarts are all stained up, you'll get yourself dirty." His eyes swept her body, but this time it was no sexual perusal, but almost a paternal look. "You look so nice and clean. Don't get that pretty blouse stained with strawberry. Believe me, it's hell to get out of clothes."

She wanted to protest, but was pleased at his thoughtfulness. He returned to the pile and kept stacking while she watched. Enjoyed watching. He was squatting, balancing on his haunches, and once again she watched the muscles in his back ripple as he reached for a discarded container.

"The kids I hire to pick in the mornings do this. They show up with lots of energy, but four or five hours bent over in the field gets them pretty tired, so by the time they put away the unused quarts, they pretty much just throw them in this general direction. They're good kids, though."

She watched as he quickly put the work area back together. He was putting the stacks on several tables constructed from wooden planks over sawhorses. The tables held empty quarts and several wooden carriers, designed to carry ten quarts at a time. The side of the barn directly across from him, to Lizzie's right, contained bales of hay piled high, a pitchfork, and three wheelbarrows, their paint chipped and peeling. The hay was to put on the bed of the fields during picking time, and to cover the plants after the season. The rest of the barn was empty, including the eight stalls, and once again she wondered what had happened to Finn's horses. She wasn't about to ask, though. One uncomfortable subject at a time.

"Back to Stevie."

"Right. I don't know." He finished his work and was at her side once again. He stood with his hands on his hips, his fingers just barely entering the tops of the pockets of his jeans. Wranglers, she noted. He'd always worn Wranglers and she had always hated it. Only real cowboys wore Wranglers. Nobody in the U.P., they all wore tried and true Levi's.

They sure did fit him well, though. She found herself drawn more to the fit of the jeans across his backside than the label that resided there. That may have been a first for label-conscious Lizzie.

"I'm certainly not hiding Stevie from you, it's just that, bringing kids into what I took our arrangement to be, didn't seem...necessary."

"And just what exactly do you take our...arrangement... to be?"

"I thought we made that clear the other night. Actually, I think you were the one who set up the rules of the game."

"You're right, I did. Still want to play?"

He raised his eyebrows in a "what do you think" way. He reached out his hands, intending them for her waist, but looked down to see their appearance seconds before laying them on her. Stopping himself, he stepped past her and beckoned for her to follow. "Come on, I need to clean up. Then, I'm going to feed you, and then..." He let the words hang in the air. He held the door open for her, then switched off the lights after she'd passed into the dimming daylight.

"And then?" Lizzie said, as she followed him toward the farmhouse.

"And then...I think you know full well what's going to happen then, E-liz-a-beth."

Seven

—⁓—

√ Pick up wine
√ Call Sybil

LIZZIE POURED HERSELF a glass of wine while Finn took a shower. He'd gotten her a glass and a corkscrew then hastily retreated upstairs. She could hear the water beating down from the kitchen. Old houses. Her parents' was the same, you could hear any water running from anywhere else in the house. The sound was comforting in a way.

The wine tasted good, but she intended on indulging in only one or two glasses. She was determined that this would not be a repeat of her previous bungled sexual encounters. No, she wanted her wits about her. She wanted to know what kind of touches from a man made her body feel good, and, more importantly, if she was capable of physical intimacy with a man.

It had been so long.

She moved from the kitchen to the living room. She'd only been in the house once, on their first date. The house hadn't changed much and she found her thoughts drifting back to that long ago night.

They'd gone to a movie, then planned to go the Commodore for pizza. As the movie ended and the credits were rolling, Lizzie and Finn rose to leave. He stepped back, into the well of his pushed up seat to let her pass, but as she did, he stopped her with his arm. When she turned to face him, she was greeted with a hunger in his eyes that both shook her to her core and ignited something deep inside her burgeoning woman's body.

"Elizabeth," he whispered as he brought his lips to hers. In her young life it was the sweetest first kiss she'd ever received. It was no more than a soft brush of their mouths. Amazingly, she felt no nerves, no embarrassment, and when he pulled back, as if to leave her, she entwined her arms around his neck and pulled him back to her. Back to her now open mouth.

It was to be that way for them throughout their short relationship. Finn always making the first move, and Lizzie always clinging for more. More, but not too much.

They'd gotten the pizza to go and taken it back to the farmhouse, where Finn assured her that his grandmother had taken his sister to Marquette for the day and weren't expected back until very late.

It had all happened so fast. The kiss at the theater, kisses in the car on the drive home, and more sweet kisses as he led her to the couch.

"Liz, you feel so good," he said.

"You too. You too." She let his hands roam at will as he settled her down, stretched her out then lay next to her, placing her in a cocoon of his body and the back of the couch. It was a tight fit, but that was the idea.

She'd dated a lot by the spring of her senior year in high school, but had a strict, self-imposed makeout code. Kissing on the first through fifth dates. After a month, second base. After three months, third base. After five months, she'd touch "it" for him. And that's as far as she'd gotten, as far as she intended to go. She knew she was desperately behind the other girls, behind even Katie and Alison, but it was non-negotiable. She was not losing her virginity in high school.

She had a plan. In her sophomore or junior year of college, she would meet the right boy. After several months together, the passion and love would be insurmountable and she would gift him with her virginity. After that, she could do as she pleased. Not intending to marry until at least twenty-seven, she would then be free to sample several dishes from the smorgasbord of men available to her. But not the first time. No, she wanted to be in love, and she wanted to be emotionally mature enough to know the difference between overcharged hormones and love.

Her makeout code was thrown out the window, however, as Finn gazed down at her on the couch. He didn't say a word, but his eyes held a reverence that startled Lizzie. That was the kind of look boys bestowed upon Katie. Lizzie was the girl they'd punch on the arm with good humor. But Finn's eyes. Filled with a near-worshiping look that made her hands tremble as she took them to his face and cradled his cheeks.

She could stare into his eyes forever. Eyes that looked at her that way. Eyes that made her feel beautiful and wanted. As he rolled half on top of her, pressing himself into her hip, she became aware of something else that unveiled the level of his desire.

She should push him away and set the ground rules right now, then they could do some more of that wonderful kissing. This was their first date, after all, and they had only met last week as he sold her popcorn. Not being from the same school, and being nearly three years apart in age, he'd have no way of knowing about Lizzie's strict code unless she told him.

Her hands on his face, set to push him away, had a mind of their own and instead pulled him down to her neglected mouth. She slid her hands around to his neck and entwined one in his soft hair and the other across his back, which showed the result of the hard work he did mucking out stalls and grooming horses.

Of course she'd used her tongue when kissing before—she wasn't that green. But it had always been more of an acceptance of a boy's tongue in her mouth, which she would inadvertently brush with her own as she tried to keep out of its way. This was different; she wanted full participation. She wanted—no, needed—to taste Finn as he tasted her. She tangled her tongue with his, then pushed past it, into his mouth, finding warmth.

He angled his head, taking the kiss, and Lizzie's tongue, deeper. She responded with a soft gasp as his erection, fully hard now, began to press into her hip and started to slowly push back and forth. She was startled away from the thoughts of his hard penis, and how much longer she could enjoy the sensation before she'd have to call a halt to the whole proceedings, by a sharp pull on her tongue. He was sucking her tongue! None of the boys she'd made out with previously had done that—not even Petey Ryan, who was the most experienced of all the boys she'd dated.

Until Finn.

She pulled her mouth away, trying to catch her breath. His mouth never missed a step, gliding easily to her neck to continue his oral exploration.

Some level of awareness returned to her now that her mouth was unoccupied, and she was astounded to realize that her hips were grinding into Finn's with a rhythm that matched his. If it didn't feel so darn good, she'd roll him right off of her and onto the floor. But it did feel so darn good, so she just arched her neck to allow Finn's mouth better access.

He was unbuttoning her pink oxford blouse, pushing away the collar, trying to bare more of her neck. Now. She should stop him now. The idea drifted away as his warm tongue worked down the side of her neck. Her breath caught and her pelvis involuntarily flexed, pushing farther into him.

He pulled her blouse free from her cords to undo the remaining buttons, then spread the panels of cloth to her side, baring her. They hadn't turned on the lights in the living room, had been in too much a hurry to get to the couch, but the lights in the kitchen gave off enough glow for him to clearly see her. He stared at her tummy, her belly button just peeking over the waistband of her pants. He rested his hand on her warm skin.

Her white, cotton, utilitarian bra embarrassed her. It had never occurred to her to wear her nice bra—her makeout bra—the one with the matching panties that she'd bought for the prom last year and kept hidden at the bottom of her tee-shirt drawer.

The plain bra didn't seem to bother Finn; he barely gave it a second glance before pushing it up over her breasts. *He didn't even undo it!* No fumbling at the back clasp, trying to master it with one hand, then relenting and using both, as the few other boys she'd let go this far had done.

Her breasts, embarrassingly bountiful, stood at attention for Finn and she realized for the first time that they were tingling. She didn't remember that happening before. She glanced down to watch her nipples actually come to life under his intense stare.

"They're so pretty, Liz. *You're* so pretty." He managed to drag his eyes away from them to look at her as he said it. His gaze then fixed on her mouth and his head moved in. Instead of kissing her lips, he veered at the last moment, and took a taut nipple into his mouth and began to softly suck.

It was as though lightning struck Lizzie. No awkward fondling first, before a bumbling brushing of nervous tongue somewhere on her breast. Zeroing in on his target from the get-go, this guy meant business. Lizzie realized she was in over her head, because she could not—would not—make him stop.

Now his hands moved to her, and if she had thought she couldn't be wound any tighter, she was wrong. He kneaded and caressed her breasts, then moved one hand down to rest low on her belly, on top of her pants, while the other hand stayed, cupping the breast that was being laved so seductively by his magical tongue.

"It feels so…it feels so…" the usually articulate Lizzie mumbled like the silly schoolgirl she was.

"So goddamn good. It feels. So. Goddamn. Good." Finn finished her thought. His hips rolled on top of her and wiggled, trying to create a cradle for himself. As she kept her legs in place—together—her innocence made itself known. It didn't seem to deter him as he whispered in her ear, "Open your legs, Liz, let me settle in. Let me feel you. Let you feel me."

It seemed the most natural thing in the world for her to follow his request and her legs fell open, one sliding all the way to the edge of the couch, the other, nowhere to go, slid up the back of the couch.

Finn moved her hips over to the center of the cushion, allowing both legs to fall open. He nestled himself on top of her, and returned his mouth to her breasts, switching attention to her other side.

The stroking of himself against her was more obvious now—startling, really—as he had direct contact to the very core of her. And yet...and yet...it still wasn't time to put on the brakes. Not quite yet; she needed to enjoy this a moment longer, she needed to feel his weight on her, breathe in his deep, husky scent. *That wasn't Brut, was it?* Dads and grandpas wore Brut, not boys she wanted so desperately to keep sucking on her tender breasts. The mild recrimination left her as she deeply breathed him in again and the smells mingled and conjoined and became a fragrance she would forever identify as simply...Finn.

His head left her breast, and she tightened the hand that was buried in his hair to try to guide him back to her, but he had another goal in sight and raised his body up along hers to bring them face to face.

Her hands returned to the hold she desired, framing his face, hands along the hard planes of his cheekbones. His work-roughened hands brushed along her sides, up and down, his thumbs gliding along the underside of her breasts.

"I didn't mean to go this fast, Liz, really." His words were nearly choked out, his voice deep and gravelly with arousal.

"I know. Me neither. But..." She couldn't finish, couldn't explain it to herself let alone Finn.

"I know—but. It's pretty intense, though, eh?"

"Yah, eh." The heavy Yooper drawl just creeped out, and she was instantly horrified at her uncouth answer.

Finn only chuckled and dipped his head to give a chaste kiss to the tip of her nose. "My little Yooper girl." His blue eyes softened and perused every inch of her face, then came back to rest on her eyes beaming up at him. "God, but you're sweet, Liz. So sweet, so soft, so…clean."

Clean? What kind of girls had he dated, she wondered, taking his words literally.

He seemed embarrassed by his sentimentality, which she found sweet. He kissed her again. Softly at first, like the kiss at the theater, gentle and pure. But the kiss abruptly heated as Lizzie, deciding turnabout was fair play, sucked his tongue into her mouth. And continued to suck on it.

His hips began to rock again. Faster now, his hands settling hard on her hips, pinning her in place. He needn't have bothered, as Lizzie was going nowhere, meeting his thrusts with her own soft body.

His right hand slid from her hip to her waistband and started to unbutton her fly. Warning bells went off in her head, and she knew she was standing at the point of no return. Much as her body ached for some unknown release, she couldn't let this progress any further. She brushed his hand away, careful to place it back on her hip, not slap it away completely.

He gave her hips a gentle squeeze, conveying his understanding. "I won't push, Liz, but I want to make you feel good."

Not knowing how he could make her feel any better than she already did, she said nothing, just let herself bathe in the soft colors that wrapped themselves around her as he returned to her breasts, suckling her harder. His right hand began to move again and she stiffened, only slightly, but he picked up on it.

"Sshh, it's okay, Liz, I'm staying outside your pants. They'll stay zipped up, I promise. Okay?" He nuzzled her breastbone, breathing in the aroma of her cleavage. She was glad she'd spritzed some Love's Baby Soft right there earlier, never imagining it would get a close-up sniff.

"Okay." It was a whisper, a sigh.

"Mmmm, that's right, babe, we'll take it slow. But let me take care of you, Liz, I can do it through your pants."

Her mind reeled with images of what he could possibly do

to her through her pants and how this would "take care of her". Orgasms were something beyond her realm of sexual comprehension, a lofty image of things to come, later, when she was no longer a virgin and was proficient at sex play.

His hand, which had stopped as he explained himself to her, ran its way down the outside of her thigh, right along the grain of the corduroy, smoothing as he went down to her knee, then turned to the inside and slowly made its way back up.

The soft cotton of her Levi's rubbed the inside of her legs. His hips moved faster, nearly bucking against Lizzie, and her mind swirled at the vibration it caused coupled with the pulling of her tender nipples by his mouth. "Finn. Finn," she moaned. Her head rolled from side to side on the arm of the couch. She was just about to throw her damn rules out the window when she heard a noise, suspiciously like a door opening and closing, coming from the kitchen. "Finn. Finn," she repeated his name, but this time she took his shoulders in her hands and shook him.

"I know, Liz, I'll get you there." He was panting hard. Lizzie couldn't imagine where he planned on taking her, but they were going nowhere now because whoever was in the house was hastily making their way across the kitchen.

"No. Finn. Someone's here." When her words didn't permeate his one-track mind, she shook him again. "Someone is here, in the kitchen. I need to get my blouse on. You need to…stop."

As the words began to make sense to Finn, the overhead light snapped on. His head shot up, over the arm of the couch to see who was there. Whoever was in the doorway would be able to see the lower half of their bodies, but the arm of the couch restricted viewing of their heads or chests, which Lizzie profusely thanked God for as she stumbled to right her bra and button her shirt.

Finn stayed on top of her and monitored her progress, apparently willing to shield her body with his until the task was done, which she was grateful for.

"Gran. I didn't expect you back so soon."

"Apparently not." There was no censure in the voice, Lizzie thought. Maybe even mild amusement. Certainly a different tone than would have come from *her* parents should they walk in on the same scene. Was it the difference between her parents and this woman, or the fact that Finn was a boy to her girl, or that he was twenty? Regardless, she said a silent thank you that this woman was apparently understanding of the situation.

She peeked under Finn's arm, over her own shoulder, around the side of the couch to see a slight woman who didn't look old enough to possibly be Finn's grandmother. She was dressed in jeans (unheard of in grandmother-wear to Lizzie), a western-style shirt with snap buttons, and boots…cowboy boots.

Just as their gazes met, the older woman's warm and friendly, Lizzie's huge and terrified, a movement came from behind the woman that caught her eye.

A girl of about nine or ten stepped out from behind the grandmother and gawked at Finn and Lizzie, automatically processing what the naughty two had been doing. She was a towhead blonde, with cherubic, full cheeks and a mischievous mouth that curved into an "I caught you—I caught you" smile.

"Shit," Finn said softly. He looked down to see that Lizzie was covered. "Liz Hampton, this is my grandmother, Clea Robbins. And the little imp to the right is my sister, Phoebe."

Eight

—◊◊◊—

√ Get pedicure
√ Call Sybil

"LOOKS LIKE YOU'RE DOING some pretty deep thinking there, Liz," Finn said, jarring her back from wherever she'd gone. He had a pretty good guess where that was. To the only other time she had been in this room, the night of their first date. That night held special memories for him too, but he seldom let himself indulge in them.

She stood in the middle of the room, an untouched wine glass twirled between her fingers, her gaze far off, and a look on her face that he could only categorize as melancholy.

When he'd come downstairs, clean-shaven and newly showered and dressed, he didn't want to break her spell. So he indulged himself and just watched for a moment.

He still couldn't get over what a beautiful woman she'd become. Not surprised, but certainly delighted. There was nothing girlish about her now, but the quality that had first drawn him to her remained. An innocence about her, a healthy dose of pleasantness that at that time in his life had been so lacking in the people he knew. Hell, it still was lacking. Except for Gran.

Definitely a glass-is-half-full person, Liz had straddled the fine line between being incredibly nice and giving, and letting people walk all over her. He'd never thought that balance was possible, and often bristled through life rather than being taken for a chump, but Liz pulled it off.

As she came out of the past, she met his eyes and gave him a deep, "I'm glad I'm here" smile, which he speedily returned.

"No. Not deep thinking. Just remembering." She didn't say what she'd been remembering, but he knew.

"That was a pretty intense night. Quite a first date." He approached her, looked at her wine glass again, and decided to get himself a beer. From the kitchen he could still hear her reply.

"I didn't know I could get that carried away with someone I'd just met. I didn't realize it was physically possible to get that turned on that soon."

Finn's grip tightened on the beer bottle as her words washed over him. "I didn't either," he admitted as he reentered the living room to find her settled on the couch. He plunked down beside her as she let out a laugh of disbelief.

"Come on. No way will you make me believe you didn't get that randy that soon with the girls you dated. You'd been sexually active for six years."

He frowned. "I never should have told you I'd lost it at fourteen. You wouldn't let go of that."

"Well, I didn't know it that night. You didn't tell me that till later." She took a small sip from her wine and watched as he took a satisfying gulp from his bottle of Bud. "What do you mean 'I wouldn't let go of that'?"

"I mean that the idea that I had so much more experience than you both scared you and excited you." He stayed on his side of the couch, but stretched out his legs, still encased in denim, but cleaner jeans than he'd had on in the barn. She had her legs crossed, her tan and shapely calves poking out from the bottom of her skirt. The left one was crossed on top of her right, and she gently swung that leg, causing her sandal to slide slightly down her foot, so that it was dangling from just her toes. Finn found himself hoping the damn thing would just fall off already. What, was he becoming a foot fetishist now?

"Yes, I guess it did. It was obvious, even from that first night, that you knew what you were doing more than any boy I'd dated before." There was a small smile on her lips and he imagined she was being drawn back to that long ago night on a couch right in this same spot. The smile disappeared and her brow furrowed. "But you're right. Knowing you'd 'done it' for so long…" Her voice trailed off.

"What, Liz?" his voice was gentle, coaxing. What made a frown, however slight, cross her open face?

"Every time you'd drop me off after I'd shut you down again, I'd panic that tomorrow I'd get the call. The 'sorry this isn't going to work out' call." Her voice was light, and the small smile returned to her mouth, but didn't reach her eyes. And there was still that damn furrowed brow.

"And then you did. Get the call," he said quietly.

"Yes." Her shoulders shrugged, as if her next words would be light, but he could read her. Always too sweet to let other people know she was hurting.

"Liz." He waited until she met his eyes. "I *am* sorry."

She started to raise her hand, into some sort of brushing-aside wave he guessed, but then her hand dropped back to her lap. Her head was nodding, more to herself than to him, as if it were important that she get this out. "I knew it was coming, knew I'd get the call any day, and yet…I was devastated. I was just so… devastated." She watched him, but he got the impression that she had voiced the words more to herself than to him, as if finally coming to that conclusion.

He tried to speak, but what could he say? Besides, the lump in his throat wouldn't allow any words to form.

Her voice had almost dropped to a whisper. "That's the first time I've ever said that to anyone. That I was devastated. It's the first time I ever truly admitted it even to myself." She came out of her thoughts and smiled at him, her voice light once more. "And of course it would have to be to the one who devastated me. Sorry,

Finn. Water. Bridges. It was a long time ago. A bad case of teen angst, that's all."

Should he tell her again how sorry he was? Should he tell her how he'd regretted his decision the moment after he'd made the call? Should he tell her that he thought about her on his wedding day? And how at the birth of his son, he thought that the woman holding his screaming, wiggling, bundle of a baby should have been her?

Would it matter? *Did* it matter? He supposed not. And honestly, he had no intention of laying a lot of stuff on her and scaring her off. She was here a short time, and he was going to finally be with her. He'd had enough shitty stuff happen in his life, wasn't he entitled to a little bit of goodness?

With a sigh and a lets-change-the-subject voice, he said, "Are you hungry, Liz? Should I start the grill?"

"No, I'm not that hungry. Let's wait on dinner."

"Okay, we can wait, but I *am* feeding you tonight. We never did end up eating anything that night at the Commodore. I'm starting to think that you don't eat."

The force of her barked laughter surprised him. Was it laughter, or disbelief…it had a touch of scorn in it?

"I eat. Oh, believe me, I eat." It was said with force, and disgust.

Oh, one of those. Another one of those crazy diet-conscious women who think they're too fat when they obviously aren't. Sure, Liz was no stick, but she had the curves and fullness that becomes a woman. At least it had always been becoming in a woman to Finn. He loved holding a woman's full hips and ass when he pounded into her.

"Okay, you eat. Though I have yet to see it."

"Maybe I'm just a cheap date," she said, the defensiveness gone from her voice, replaced by a light teasing.

"My favorite kind."

She laughed. That Liz laugh that he loved. He got up and went over to the shelves on the far wall. A boombox was on one shelf, surrounded by a stacks of CDs. "Music?" he asked, although he had already set his beer down and was pawing through the discs.

"Sure, what have you got?" She didn't move from the couch to join him. Instead, she put her wineglass on the coffee table in front of her, slipped off her sandals and pulled her legs up onto the couch, curling them underneath her, tucking her skirt around her legs.

He watched the graceful movement with the appreciation of a man watching a woman do something so innately female. He turned his back to her and continued to pick through the CDs. "Waylon and Willie," he said.

"Ugh! Country?" she said, laughing.

Jesus, would he ever tire of hearing that laugh? It was beckoning him to her, like the call of the sirens, so he quickly found the CD he was looking for, loaded it, and returned to the couch, this time sitting closer to her.

As he moved, she berated his taste in music, as she had done on previous occasions when they'd dated. "You're still in to that stuff? Come on Finn, grow a little," she teased.

"Hey, country music has become huge, very mainstream. I can say I was ahead of my time."

"Mainstream country has hit the U.P., I'll give you that. But you were never mainstream, Finn, not in music, or anything else." Before he had a chance to wonder if he'd just been criticized or complimented, she continued. "I bet you don't have a Faith or a Carrie Underwood in that pile. It's probably stuffed with Willie, Waylon, and Johnny Cash. Oh, maybe you've gone daring and hip and added a little George Strait."

He smiled. She wasn't wrong. But she didn't know what else he'd added to his tastes. She would in a second. The CD finished its roll of the disc to the songs he'd selected in sequence. The identifiable strains of Springsteen's harmonica opening to Thunder Road came through the speakers.

Her head snapped to attention. "Bruce? You listen to Bruce

now?"

Her surprise made him smile. "Someone a long time ago got me turned on to him."

"I didn't think you were even listening, you used to bitch up a storm when I'd put him on."

"Yeah, well, I guess I was listening. I got some of his stuff, the ones I'd heard with you. But no, I don't listen to him a lot." He didn't tell her that he found himself reaching for the Boss when he was feeling low, feeling sorry for himself, wanting to sit in the dark of the living room after Stevie had gone to bed and Annie was asleep. He'd grab a beer, put on some Springsteen, and just sit on the couch in the dark room and brood.

He'd never made the connection before, but it seemed so glaringly obvious to him now. Listening to Springsteen reminded him of a better time in his life. Reminded him that there were people in the world who had seen him for more than just a shitty husband, or a struggling father. They had seen a glimmer of possibility in a young Finn, someone who would see his dreams through.

Liz leaned back into the corner of the couch. The corners of her mouth turned up as she hummed along with Bruce. He watched the perfect bow of her upper lip. He could barely remember Gran's birth date, or even his own phone number, but the shape of Liz's mouth seemed imprinted on his memory forever.

He placed his hands under her bent knees, and eased her legs from underneath her to straighten over his lap. She let him take her legs and push her back farther into the couch. He cupped her calf, then ran his hand down to her ankles where he began to rub her feet.

"That feels wonderful, but I should probably be doing that to you. You're the one who worked all day. I'm on vacation, I'm permanently relaxed."

He didn't mention the hum he felt flow through her body. He wouldn't call that relaxed. He'd call that...aroused. He sure as hell felt the same way.

"Don't worry, you can do plenty of rubbing on me." He was greeted once again with her laugh, but this time it was low and throaty.

He slid her skirt up her legs to the top of her thighs, freeing her legs so she'd be able to move to the next place he wanted her. Her eyes followed his movement, and when his hands stilled, she looked up to his face. Met his eyes. Shared his hunger. She licked her lips, an unconscious movement, which sent Finn into action.

Taking her by the waist, he lifted her from her sitting position, turned her and settled her across his lap. Her hands came out looking for balance and landed on his biceps. She sat straddling him, face to face.

It all exploded after that.

Her hands slid up his arms and locked behind his neck as his mouth crashed down on hers. She met him with every thrust as his tongue explored her. She tasted of wine, chocolate, vanilla, and…summer.

She started to rock against him and he slid his hands up her thighs, taking her skirt all the way with him so that there was only the barrier of her satin panties against his jeans. She gasped as her sensitive skin found the seam of his denim, and his cock rallied to show her his response. The room had grown dim as twilight had come upon them, but he could see her face clearly when he pulled away from her mouth.

Her hazel eyes glowed, sparkled. Her mouth was wet and already swollen from his hungry kisses. She took her hands from behind his neck. As he hoped she would do—as he *needed* her to do—she cupped his face in her hands and looked deeply into him. Into his soul, or what was left of it.

"Finn," she whispered, so softly he wasn't sure he even heard it. But he felt it.

Her eyes were full of compassion and redemption and second chances, all of which he needed, and none of which he sensed she was able to give him. Fine. He'd take whatever else she was offering. By the way her hips were moving against his hard dick, he was pretty sure what that was.

He took her hands from his face, unable to take the feelings her gesture raised in him. This was not about redemption or new leaves or healing old wounds, for Christ's sake. This was about getting laid, pure and simple. About getting this damn blouse off of Liz and burying himself in her lush breasts. His fingers stumbled over the buttons, but he got them undone.

They were larger, and fuller now, of course. Having lost their girlish perkiness, they hung lower. But still spectacular. There were small silver marks in her skin at the top sides of her breasts. He pulled aside the straps to look at them more closely, the only light in the room now streaking in from the kitchen. He felt her stiffen as she followed his glance and her hands left him and started to pull at the sides of her shirt, as if to cover herself.

Not knowing what had made her suddenly shy, he placed his hands over hers and stilled them before she could cover up. "No, Liz, let me look at you. Your breasts, so womanly, so…" He didn't finish, couldn't, because his mouth was full of the soft, jiggly flesh that overflowed the cups of her bra. Also satin, and a pristine white, just like the panties. There was a lot of material to the bra—to cover a lot of breast. But there was also a lot of flesh peaking out over the lacy top of the cups, and that's what his hungry mouth feasted on.

It wasn't enough. Not when he could feel her nipple tightening just below his chin. He peeled the cups down, hooking the material below her breasts, becoming as much support as the underwire, and lifted her bared breasts to his waiting mouth.

As he clamped down on her aroused nipple, he was assaulted with memories. Of this woman as a girl, in this room, writhing as he suckled her. Her hands holding his head to her as she was doing now. Her hips moving then, too, but that night, in her innocence, she hadn't known why. Now she did, and he guessed by her rhythm that she'd learned a thing or two about pleasure since that night.

It was too much, he needed to be inside of her. At the very least he needed to be on top of her.

He rolled her to their sides, then rolled himself up, tucking her underneath him. Her skirt, now tangled around her waist, was no hindrance as she opened her soft thighs for him to settle himself on top. His mouth returned to her breasts, wet and flushed. He was glad he'd shaved again when he'd showered. The thought of putting stubble burns on her unsoiled flesh was unbearable.

He was just about to readdress those little marks when he felt her hands pull on his shoulder. "Finn. Finn." He didn't find it hard to believe that she was so hot so quickly, he knew he was.

"I know, Liz. I feel it too." It was consuming him, this need to be inside her. He rocked against her. But she kept tugging on his shoulders.

"No, Finn. I think I heard a car."

That wouldn't be unusual. The picture window behind the couch faced the road and a loud car could occasionally be heard from inside the house. He tried to still and listen for the sound that had her spooked but all he could hear was the throbbing inside his head. And his cock.

"It's nothing." He returned to laving her nipples. He loved how the puckered flesh felt against his tongue.

Then he heard it too. But it was in the kitchen now. Another light flickered on and two unmistakably female voices drifted through the doorway to the living room. Two voices he knew. Shit. Shit. Shit.

"Not again!" Liz groaned as he thought the same thing. "This is so déjà vu," she said, once again mirroring his thoughts. She ducked her head under his chest and furiously began putting her bra back in place and reaching for her buttons. "I'm too old for this."

He grunted. "You and me both. This is unbelievable." He lay on top of her, once again protecting her until she was decent.

The light of the living room went on and he peeked his head over the arm of the couch. "Gran. I didn't expect you back tonight."

"Apparently."

"Annie's with you?"

"Of course. Where else would she be?"

"Shit," he whispered, and felt Liz freeze underneath him. A few seconds passed, he felt her take a deep breath, as if steeling herself for battle. She ducked her head under his arm, and peered out around the side of the couch.

"Hello Mrs. Robbins. You probably don't remember me. I'm Lizzie Hampton."

Finn could have kissed his grandmother. She didn't even seem to blink as she took in the scene. "Of course I remember you, Elizabeth, it's nice to see you again. And please, call me Clea."

"Thank you, Clea. It's nice to see you too, although I wish it were under different circumstances." She smiled at Finn's grandmother and the woman melted at Liz's friendly charm, just like everyone else. Gran waved her comment away and gave her a warm look of understanding. A sort of blood-brother look that he assumed only women could understand.

There was movement behind his grandmother and she stepped to her side to make way for Annie.

"Annie," Finn let out in a sigh.

Liz strained her neck to get a better look at Annie as she made her way around Gran. A mechanical "whoosh whoosh" preceded the rubber tires and spokes of a wheelchair that came to a stop. The inhabitant stared at Liz and Finn. His little girl, her eyes shining with tears and an anger that crushed him. "Oh Annie, honey, don't."

Liz took in Annie. Finn tried to see Annie through a stranger's eyes. She was breathtaking. An angel. White hair, wide blue eyes that a few tears had escaped from. Cherubic cheeks heightened in color by her rage and a wide mouth that was trembling

He felt Liz gasp beneath him. "Hannah? 'Help Hannah', Hannah?"

"I hate that damn name!" his potty-mouthed angel shrieked,

then wheeled herself through the living room. The bedroom door, which crashed open at the force from the bottom of her chair, crashed shut again as soon as she'd wheeled herself over the threshold.

After giving him a sympathetic look, Clea made her way out the door, to the trailer, leaving Finn and Liz alone once again. It wasn't the same. It would never be the same again.

"Liz, I'd like you to meet my daughter, Hannah Clea Robbins. Annie, to family."

Nine

———

√ Buy perfume
√ Call Sybil

HE WENT INTO ANNIE'S ROOM to help her get ready for bed, but his little girl turned away from him, not wanting his help. He tried to talk to her, but she tuned him out. Still, he waited to make sure she was able to get herself changed and into bed. When he came out of the bedroom, Liz had moved to the front door, her purse in hand. He grabbed his car keys and followed her out.

She was silent as they left the farmhouse. Finn didn't know if that was good or bad. "I'm going to go tell Gran I'm leaving for a while so she can come back to the house. Take your car and follow mine."

"Where are we going?"

He paused and thought. "To the beach."

She seemed startled at first, disbelieving that he'd still want to continue this thing, then she realized his intention was to talk, to explain this shocker, and she nodded.

Liz waited in her car while he rapped on the trailer and stepped up and in. His grandmother was in her kitchen, fixing herself a cup of tea. It was a scene he'd seen thousands of times. The normalcy of it comforted him.

"Gran, what happened at the camp? Why are you back?"

She placed the tea bag into her cup, then took the whistling teakettle from the stove and filled it, the steam billowing out around her.

"We couldn't stay. The counselor who was in charge of Annie's cabin broke her ankle tripping over some root or something just as foolish, and was taken to the hospital. They have a strict policy about the children-to-counselor ratio in the cabin in case of emergencies. I even offered to stay in the cabin myself, but they didn't seem to think me capable of getting four little girls in wheelchairs to safety in the case of a fire."

Finn smiled. His money would have been on Gran in case of any emergency. As a father, though, he guessed he was grateful that the camp had such a strict policy. It made him feel justified about the agonizing decision he'd made to send Annie to the camp in the first place.

"Was she okay until then?"

Gran nodded. "Yes. At first she was her usually snippy self, but some of the other girls had even bigger chips on their shoulders, if you can imagine that. When she saw she couldn't compete with them in the sass department, she settled down and started to enjoy herself. Then that klutz of a counselor had to go and fall and put the kibosh to the whole weekend."

"So, three other girls had to go home, too?"

"Two stayed, their mothers sleeping in the cabin with them, but there were only beds for five in the wheelchair-accessible cabins, so one other girl and Annie went home. We flipped coins to see who'd go." She sat at her kitchen table, bobbing the tea bag into the steaming cup.

"And did you win or lose the coin toss to be the ones to go home?"

She smiled. "Really, Finn, she was adjusting to it just fine. You did the right thing sending her, even if she did put up a holy terror about it. She made a big to-do about how lucky she was to lose the coin toss and go home, but she was pretty quiet on the ride back. I think she was disappointed, but, of course, she'd never let on."

"Of course not. Gran, I'm going to take Liz somewhere to talk. You think it's okay to leave Annie? You think she's really upset about not being able to stay?"

"I think she's probably more upset about finding you with a woman. Go, have fun, take your time, I'll check on her in a few minutes, make sure she's asleep. I'll stay over there until you get back. Stevie's at that sleepover, right?"

"Right."

Her keen eyes leveled on Finn. He felt like he was fourteen and trying to put something over on her. It hadn't worked then, no reason to think it would work now. "Yes, I thought I had the place to myself for the night, the whole night, and I invited Liz over. There, happy, old woman? I was trying to have a little female companionship."

She snorted. "About time, I'd say." She took a long sip of tea. "I'm just sorry it didn't work out."

"Me too."

"Well, I can get Annie going in the morning if you want?" The insinuation in her voice was clear. If he wanted to stay at Liz's, she'd cover for him.

"She's staying at her parents' place. Thanks for the offer Gran, but I'll be back in a couple of hours."

"It was nice to see Elizabeth after all this time, I didn't realize she was back in town."

"She's not. Not permanently. She's here for a couple of months. She came to a movie."

"Well, at least one good thing came out of that crappy job."

He laughed. "That's the exact same thought I had, although I think I used something a little stronger than 'crappy'."

"I'm not surprised." She took another long sip, measuring him as he still stood in the doorway. "Liz didn't know about the kids, did she?"

He shook his head. "She knew about Stevie, she met him tonight. But no, she didn't even know Annie existed, let alone…"

He looked away from her, as though the knick-knack shelf in the corner suddenly needed his attention.

"You may need more than a couple of hours with Liz. Don't worry, take your time. She was a good listener for you if I recall correctly."

"You recall correctly," he said and left the trailer.

He watched in his rearview mirror as Liz followed him to the beach. They'd planned on going there the night they met at the Commodore. They'd finally get there now, but it wouldn't be for the same purpose. When they'd both parked, he pulled a blanket out of the Jeep, took Liz's hand, and led her past the deserted public area to a small path on the other side of the dock. The path led to a secluded spot that they both remembered well.

They settled themselves on the blanket, Liz sitting up, hugging her legs to her chest, arms wrapped around them, watching the water from their hidden perch. Finn lay on his back, an arm thrown over his eyes, the other tucked under his head.

They'd sit like this for hours years ago, discussing everything, discussing nothing. Liz's excitement about going off to State in the fall. Finn's desire to take off for Texas as soon as Phoebe was old enough to leave behind. Horses, college, friends, siblings, parents, grandmothers. No subject was taboo, or even the slightest bit uncomfortable between them.

And now they sat, the silence deafening.

"Why don't you just start at the beginning," she softly prodded.

He'd tell her everything. Why the hell not. It wasn't like Liz was sticking around. And it felt freeing somehow, to be able to tell the story of his life to someone who hadn't seen it, someone who wasn't shaking their head in disapproval over every mis-step he'd made.

He put his other arm behind his head, creating a pillow for himself, and freeing his eyes to watch her. To gauge her reactions. "The beginning of why Annie's in a wheelchair, or the beginning of why there's even an Annie?"

"I guess the true beginning would be Stevie, right?"

"No, the true beginning would be Dana."

"Dana. Your wife."

"Ex-wife," he said.

"Right. Whatever. Go on." Her voice was still soft in the quiet night, but he sensed an agitation in it that wasn't there when she'd asked about his kids. Jealousy? Could she possibly be jealous over a woman she'd never met? A woman who hadn't been in Finn's life for years. The thought warmed him.

He took a deep breath and began to tell her about the past fifteen years. "I started dating Dana Paananen about three years after you and I dated. It was the summer after your junior year at State. The first summer you didn't come home."

"How did you know I came home the other two summers?"

"I knew." He waited for her to comment on that, when she didn't, he continued, "She was a lot of fun. A little wild. We partied a lot together, hung out, got drunk, had sex, you know, the stuff you do in your early twenties." He looked at Liz, but she still didn't say anything.

Hadn't she been doing the same thing at State? He sure had imagined she was. He'd imagined her with lots of guys. It was easier than imagining her with just one.

"Dana said she was on the pill. She wasn't. She got pregnant. We got married." He was precise, succinct, as if he was rattling off the sports scores, not the most pivotal time in his life. It was the only way he could do it and not totally lose it. Liz made him so raw, always had, and he was already on edge from their earlier physical contact. He knew if he hinted at the turmoil of emotions that he'd felt at the time, he'd be curled up in a fetal position crying for Gran in no time flat. Not exactly the image he wanted to project to Liz.

"Why would she say she was on the pill if she wasn't?" She turned from staring at the still water and looked down at him.

"She wanted to get married," he said, shrugging.

"Come on, people don't really do that. Purposely get pregnant to trap someone into marriage?"

"No, Liz. People *you* know don't really do that. People *I* know, it happens plenty." He let the harsh cynicism go from his voice. "It doesn't matter, really. Ultimately it takes two to tango, right? I could have used a condom, I didn't have to…"

"What? Trust the girl you were dating? Yeah, why on earth would you do that?" She gave him a soft, understanding smile, and turned back to gaze at the lake.

She never could take her eyes off the water, he remembered. What was she doing living in Detroit? Living in any city? She loved this place. He was just about to mention this to her when he realized they were still on him. Still digging into his past. *Okay, let's get that over with, then we can do Liz.* A smirk crossed his face as he let his imagination run free with the thoughts that "do Liz" could encompass. He was glad she wasn't looking at him anymore, couldn't see the horny smile plastered on his face.

Get it together, man! Your daughter's probably crying herself to sleep over the stress of this camp thing, then finding her father on top of a semi-naked woman. Your son's like a stranger to you. Gran was looking so tired lately, a phenomenon never seen by Finn before. You're a gazillion bucks in debt, and looking to be more so. And all you can think about is "doing" Liz Hampton?

He was jarred from his thoughts by Liz's soft, "I'm sorry, Finn."

"Don't be. It might have been under shitty circumstances, but it did give me Stevie. And, believe it or not, I love my son like there's no tomorrow."

She turned back to him. "Why wouldn't I believe you love your son? The way you took care of your sister, the way you looked after your grandmother? Of course you'd make a wonderful father. It would never occur to me to question that."

He was grateful for her honest words, clung to them like a drowning man clings to a life jacket. Which, in a way, was exactly what he'd become—a drowning man.

"Go on," she prodded, with both her tone and her body. She

nudged his hip with her foot, now bare, her sandals tossed aside, lying somewhere on the grass just off the blanket.

He snaked a hand out and clasped her ankle and held it. He ran his fingers over the ankle and up her calf, cupping the muscles and tendons. She let out a soft sigh. "I always felt like one of your horses when you did that to me. Like any minute you'd lift my calf and make sure I hadn't thrown a shoe."

He chuckled, realizing she was right—the caress was rote for him, the same one given hundreds of times to his horses. "No need to worry, Liz, I never thought of you as a horse. Other than wanting to ride you till you were all lathered up."

The belly laugh that he loved escaped her and she drew her leg out of his grasp, tucking it back with her other, under her skirt, winding her arms tight around them. "Not so fast, mister, you can't wriggle out of this one with suggestive talk. Spill."

He exhaled a deep sigh, sensing there was no escape. "Okay, okay. Where were we?"

"Stevie being born. You married to Dana."

"Right. Well, Gran and Phoebe moved into the trailer and Dana and I took over the farmhouse. She tried for a little while after Stevie was born, she really did, but…" He felt kind of cheesy; he didn't want to bad mouth the mother of his children, even if she was a treacherous bitch. But this was Liz, and he wanted—needed—to tell her the truth. Tell her what his life had been like while she'd gone off to college, started her own business, and had surely been surrounded by men.

"Well, it kind of finally dawned on me that Dana wasn't going to grow out of the partying phase."

"When did it finally dawn on you?"

"When she left a six-month-old Stevie alone so she could go to a bar." At Liz's gasp of disbelief he went on. "I know, I couldn't believe it either. Gran and I had gone to a parent-teacher conference with Phoebe and it was running behind schedule. Apparently the two hours we were gone was longer than Dana could go without a drink once she realized all the booze in the house was gone."

"Oh, God." Her voice was faint, but he could feel her concern. At least it wasn't pity, he couldn't bear that.

"Yeah. I tried to help her, but she didn't want to be helped. You'd have thought I'd have learned after my mom, eh?"

"Right. Your mother."

"I guess a case could be made for me getting hooked up with Dana in the first place because she was like my mother. You know, I couldn't fix her, maybe I could fix Dana? Classic enabler. All complete bullshit, but...whatever." He waved his hand in front of his face as if to dismiss the whole awful mess. "Anyway, I didn't— couldn't—leave her alone with Stevie anymore. Watched her like a hawk. Hounded her when she'd drink. After a while, she split."

"Where'd she go?"

"I don't know. I didn't want to know. I *still* don't."

"So, Annie has a different mother than Stevie?"

"No. God no, do you think I'd get hooked up with someone else and have another child so soon?" He didn't let her answer, was afraid to hear what she might think of him. "No, Dana came back, sober, said she wanted to try again for Stevie's sake. Stevie was three then. And I needed her. I hate to admit it, but the reason I took her back was because I needed someone to help. Phoebe, Stevie, the farm, the horses, it was too much for me alone. Gran was great, still is, but she raised me practically singlehandedly—I wasn't going to let her raise Phoebe and my son too if I could help it."

He waited for her response. He still felt guilty about not caring more about Dana. He figured she had sensed all he wanted from her was a mother for Stevie and resented him for it. Thinking about it now, Finn wondered if things might have turned out differently if he'd been able to feel for Dana what he'd felt for Liz.

Too damn late for thoughts like that.

Liz said nothing, he assumed waiting for him to go on, which he did. "We were okay for about a year. Not great, but okay. Then Dana got pregnant again."

"Not another lie about the pill?"

"No, she was on the pill, but what I learned later was a lot of mornings she'd be so hung over she'd either forget to take it or her stomach would be so bad, she couldn't hold anything down. It was stupid, plain stupid."

"So, Annie was born."

"Yeah." A single word, but his tone implied a joy and wonderment he could not put words to. The day he'd held her had been the happiest of his life. Where as Stevie had seemed a miracle, but so daunting, Annie had fit into his arms and nuzzled into him and it had felt liberating. It gave him a sense of purpose that he'd never known he'd been lacking. "She was so tiny, so perfect." His voice caught at the last, had a strangling quality, and he waited, trying to get himself under control.

Liz gave him some time, then said, "But she wasn't perfect, was she?"

"No. Not perfect, at least not physically. They didn't figure it out until she was nearly a year old and still hadn't rolled over or sat up. Her lower vertebrae had not fused properly and she was not capable of holding herself upright. She has feeling all over, thank God, so in theory she can walk. She can move her legs. They fit her for a brace that she wears all the time, even to sleep in, to keep her spine straight, and she's in a wheelchair—obviously."

"That's it? Nothing they could do? Seems like they'd be able to do something for that, some sort of operation or something."

"They can. They're going to, God willing." He snorted, sarcasm creeping in, "I guess I should say First National Bank willing."

"Huh? This is about money? That girl's been in a wheelchair for...how long?"

"Nine years. She turned ten last April."

"For nine years, and it's because there was no money for an operation? That's horrible. That's...that's..."

"Stop sputtering, little Miss Save-The-World. God, you haven't changed a bit, have you? That's nice...reassuring, I guess."

She was staring at him, wide eyed with indignation over the injustice done to his little girl. "They couldn't do the operation until her bones had matured to the point they're at now. They felt that an artificial fusing wouldn't hold during the growth period that happens from three to ten. They're not even sure if it will hold for the next eight-year growth period, but they feel if they don't do it now and she doesn't start using her legs, she may not be able to later. They'll probably have to do the operation again when she's eighteen or twenty if the fusing doesn't hold."

Lizzie let out a deep breath which sounded to Finn like relief. "Oh, okay. Where does Dana play into all this.".?

"She doesn't. Not anymore. The stress of Annie's circumstances made Dana's drinking—which I hadn't even realized she was doing again—come out. I told her I'd do whatever I could to help her stop, but she could not be drinking around the kids." He threw his arm over his head again, as if to blot out the whole tawdry doings. He wouldn't bore Liz with the ugly details of the numerous fights they'd had. "Phoebe had graduated and moved to Flint for work, so she wasn't able to help with Annie. Dana had to stay sober. And she couldn't, she just couldn't, so she took off. That's when we got divorced."

"Do you see her often?" She quickly amended herself. "Do the kids see her often?"

"No. Never. She came back once…she won't be back."

"How can you be so sure?"

"Because I paid her the money I'd been saving for Annie's operation to give up all legal rights and never see them again. Her idea, not mine."

"Oh, God."

"That was five years ago. When we first got Annie's diagnosis, we started saving for it. I have health insurance for the kids, which I pay through the nose for since I'm self-employed, but it won't cover the operation. It's a type of lumbar fusion, but this particular type is labeled experimental, so it's not covered."

"Rat bastard insurance companies."

He smiled at her show of empathy. "Exactly, though my language was a bit more colorful.

"Anyway, I started saving every cent from the farm that I could for the operation. I had nine years to get the money. At the time she was diagnosed the operation would have cost $50,000. Now, it's over four times that. But, it was doable. I took second jobs as soon as Annie got old enough to be left with Gran and Stevie in the evenings. I made some good investments with what I did save. A couple of my horses were getting good stud fees. I was going to have enough. Barely, but enough.

"Then Dana came back. She was making all kinds of noise about the kids coming with her, that they should be with their mother, that no court would give custody of a little girl in a wheelchair to a man. That she'd move them to Arizona where the weather would be good for Annie—like she had fucking asthma or something. Not even a clue about her own daughter's condition." His disgust was apparent.

Liz shook her head, making her ponytail swing. "This sounds like a bad Lifetime movie."

"I know. If it hadn't been happening to me, I never in hell would have believed it." He reached out and ran his hand down her hair, stilling the ponytail across her back. It lay between her shoulder blades, jet black against the blue of her blouse. "It was all a total bluff, of course, but I couldn't be sure. Couldn't take the chance. She knew I had some money saved. She suggested that she'd leave the kids for good if I gave her the money to start over."

"Blackmail, using her own children. You sure can pick 'em, Finn."

"Don't generalize, Liz, I picked you too, remember?" They both smiled at that, though neither one was looking at the other. "I can't forgive her. She made my daughter's life tougher than it needs to be. But...hell, I don't know...she was sick, an alcoholic...part of me felt sorry for her." He sighed. "The other part of me wanted to kill her.

"It was then that I knew I had to get her out of the kids' lives.

A woman who could demand the money she knew was going for her daughter's operation? It was worth it to me to give her the money and start saving again. But I made sure it wasn't just a first installment. I got a lawyer and made her sign over all legal rights to the kids and agree that she'd never come back to Houghton or attempt to see them. She was only too happy to sign, the bitch."

"Did the kids know what was happening?"

"No, thank God. She came to see me when they were in school, and we met the other times at the lawyer's office, away from the farm. They haven't seen her since she left when Annie was two and Stevie six. Annie has no memories of her and Stevie's are pretty fuzzy. You can't miss what you never had."

"Hmmm."

"What's that mean?"

She looked down at him. "Nothing, I guess. I just wonder if that's true. That you can't miss what you never had. I think you can. I think that those are the things you miss the most."

"Are you speaking from experience?"

She turned her head back to the water. "Yes, I think I am, though I never put it in those terms before."

"What do you miss? What did you never have that you miss?" He could almost hear the accusing tone in his own voice. Damn, he hadn't meant it like that.

"You think I've always gotten everything I wanted, don't you? You thought that back then, and you still think it now. Spoiled rich girl. Well, I was neither rich nor spoiled."

"I know that." And he did. Her father was a prof at Tech and her mother did something with one of the charities in town. They weren't rich, and she wasn't spoiled, but compared to Finn, she was the rich goody-goody that lived on the right side of the tracks. His own issues, he knew. Hell, there weren't even railroad tracks in the entire Copper Country, let alone between Liz and himself. Only the ones that he'd created in his head when he hadn't felt worthy of her. "I'm sorry, I didn't mean it to come out like that. But I am curious, what do you miss in life, Liz?"

She laid her cheek on her knees, turning her head to the side, away from him. "I don't know. Sometimes I can't put a name to it, it's just this fear that wraps itself around me so tight I can barely breathe. And all I can think of at those times are that I've missed something. Somewhere. I let something slide, something got through my grasp that I should have hung on to."

She lightened her tone, teasing, self-effacing, her good-ol'-Lizzie voice returning. "It's nothing that a pint of Ben & Jerry's doesn't cure."

"Liz." He reached up from the ponytail he was still stroking to place his hand on her neck, but she pulled forward, out of his reach. She pretended to wipe some nonexistent grass from the front of the blanket until he dropped his hand. She leaned back to her original position.

"So, you got Dana out of your life and you started saving again. Then what?"

"Well, that pretty much brings us up to now. We have a pre-surgery consultation next week in Ann Arbor. If that looks good, they're going to schedule the surgery, probably for this fall sometime."

"Finn, that's wonderful!"

"Yeah, in theory. I still can't even come close to paying for it even after taking out a mortgage on the farm and saving for the last four years."

He could almost see the light bulb go off over her head. "Your horses. That's why you sold your horses."

"Yeah."

"Oh, Finn, you loved those horses."

"You don't even realize what love is until something like this happens. It wasn't even a choice." He dropped his hand from her altogether and put it behind his head. "God, I can't believe I just said that. My life really is a bad Lifetime movie."

"How much are you short?"

"About a hundred thou. And another fifty thousand to get the farm out of debt."

"Wow."

"I know, not chump change, eh? I wanted to sell the farm, but in this economy, it wouldn't have gotten us much more than the mortgage did to put toward the operation. And it would have put us in the position of renting or buying something else anyway. Plus, at the farm, we've got ramps built for Annie, special shower, stuff like that."

She said nothing for a moment. He could see her wheels turning. She took a deep breath. he held his, sensing what was coming. "Listen, I don't have that kind of money, Finn. Most of my assets are tied up in my firm. But, if I moved some things around, cashed some investments in, I could probably come up with thirty thousand. Maybe forty. It's yours."

"No."

"Why? It wouldn't be enough, but it could help."

"No, Liz." His voice was unyielding.

"Finn," she started to say in a bargaining voice.

"Liz, no. I can't just take charity. It would take me forever to pay you back."

"That's okay."

"No, it's not okay. It's not okay with me. Not from you, Liz. Christ, you're the last person I want to take charity from." Damn, his voice was hoarse, full of emotion.

He watched her swallow, purse her lips, then seemed to accept his decision. She nodded. "Okay. But it's available if it becomes the deal breaker between getting the operation and not."

He knew he would do anything to get Annie her operation. Liz had given him a graceful out in case he needed her money later. "That's what's so different about you and Dana, Liz," he said.

"There's only one thing?" she teased. "After all you've told me, I'd hoped I'd be her complete opposite."

"Oh you are, you are. You're so honest and giving. Not like her at all. No hidden agendas, no behind-the-back plans."

She ducked her head, not looking at him. She never could take a compliment.

After a moment she asked, "So, what are you going to do? About the money?"

"When we're in Ann Arbor, I get to sit down with the bean counters and propose a way to pay for this thing for the next eighty years of my life. It's not looking good right now."

"They honestly wouldn't do the operation if you couldn't find a way to pay for it?"

"That's right. They run a business, Liz, they can't just be giving it away."

"That's what you get for going to the University of Michigan Hospital."

"I know the Spartan in you can't stand it, but you have to admit U of M has one of the best hospitals around."

"Okay, I admit it, grudgingly, but only because State doesn't have a hospital of their own. If they did, I'm sure it'd be better."

He laughed.

They sat for a minute. "You sound so matter of fact about all this, aren't you furious?"

"Not anymore, but I can show you the holes in the barn walls to prove I was. Fury takes up too much of my time. Time Annie needs me to spend on her. She has always clung to me, no surprise, really, with no mother, and having been in a wheelchair as long as she can remember. But now, as the idea of this operation gets closer, she panics if I'm out of her sight for very long. Gets real pouty when I have to go to the theater to work.

"There's this camp for kids like Annie near Munising. Gran wanted her to spend part of the summer there, getting used to being around other kids like her. She also thinks it might be good for Stevie. He really gets the short end of the stick because of the attention Annie needs. But…I just couldn't be away from her for that long. They went down there yesterday to spend the weekend, but—as you know—there was a change in plans and they're back."

He waited for Liz to digest all the stuff he was throwing at her. "She's never seen me with a woman before. None's ever come to the house. That's why the reaction tonight."

"You haven't been with a woman since Dana left?"

"I didn't say that."

He could see her mentally replaying his words. "Oh. Right. Just that you hadn't brought one around Annie."

"Right." He had to be straight with her. "But Liz, it's more because there wasn't one I wanted around my daughter. I'd…I'd like for you to meet Annie. Really meet her, get to know her, and Stevie of course, if you'd like that?" He waited for her answer, his breathing halted.

What the hell was he thinking? Annie was going to blow a nut. And Liz was only in town for a short time. Why was this so important to him, for her to get to know his kids? Damned if he knew, but he did know he wanted Liz to say yes more than he'd wanted anything in a long, long time.

"I'd like to get to know your family."

He exhaled a sigh of relief. "Good. Good. That's great."

They sat in silence for a few more minutes then, without saying a word, they both got up and made their way to their cars.

He didn't try to kiss her good night. That moment had passed and even he wasn't horny enough to force it.

He told her he'd call her the next day then followed her truck through Hancock until she turned up the hill at Bob's Mobil.

He noticed the verse on Bob's sign: *The Lord God said, it is not good for the man to be alone. I will make a helper suitable for him.*

At the beach, he'd been stoked that Liz said she wanted to get to know his kids, but suddenly, he wasn't so sure that he hadn't just made a horrible mistake.

Ten

—〰—

√ Google spinal fusion operations
√ Pick up burgers and buns
√ Have Sybil email past fundraiser information

"ARE YOU SURE it's not the grandmother? I mean, isn't that the old cliché, 'my grandmother needs an operation'?" Alison joked.

"Stop it, Alison, God, how can you be so heartless?" Katie chided.

"Years of practice?"

Her cynical friend made Lizzie laugh, and laughter was what she desperately needed right now. Finn and his children were due to arrive at Alison's place for swimming, saunaing, and burgers. Lizzie was eying the bowl of potato chips on the picnic table in front of her like they'd be the answer to her nervousness. Knowing better, but fearing she'd be unable to win a staring match with the salty temptation, she turned around on the bench and looked out at the water.

She watched the two men standing on the dock. Katie's husband, Ron, and Alison's date, a man Lizzie had never met named Brandt.

"Brandt seems nice, Al. Third date, eh? Just in time to bring him around to meet Katie and me."

"Yeah, well, don't be picking out your bridesmaid dress just yet."

"Too bad, I'm thinking taffeta and opera gloves," Lizzie joked then looked at the men again.

Brandt was shorter than Ron, and much thinner. His legs had obviously not been informed that it was nearing the end of June; they shone death-white from under his shorts. He seemed okay to Lizzie. Kind of boring, but okay. Probably able to keep up with Alison intellectually, which was a must. But Lizzie had the feeling he wouldn't be strong enough for her friend. And that's what Alison really needed, someone who could see through to the real Al, not let her sarcasm and cynicism push them away.

It was obvious to Lizzie that it was just a defense mechanism, but one that had been in place so long, it was as comfortable to Alison as second skin. Lizzie should know about second skins, the one she'd developed was just that, layers of skin. And fat.

Brandt was the civil engineering prof from Tech that Alison had mentioned when they were in Lizzie's room picking out an outfit. That day seemed like a lifetime ago, but had only been a little over two weeks. It was amazing what could change in so short of time.

Now there was Annie.

The one time she'd been to the farm since the night Lizzie had first met Annie had been a disaster.

Clea had made a lovely dinner of roast and mashed potatoes, that normally would have had Lizzie jumping for joy, but she couldn't even eat much under the intense interrogation of the ten-year-old. She half expected Annie to pull out a rubber hose and shine a spotlight in her face. "How long are you staying here? You *are* going back to Detroit, right? You knew my dad a long time ago? Did you know my mom? Why aren't you married? Why don't you have any kids?"

She tried to allay the little girl's fears of Lizzie encroaching on the her turf. But Lizzie found no articulate way of saying, "Hey kid, ease up, I'm only here to sleep with your father a few times—which, by the way, your mere presence has put seriously behind schedule—then I'm on my way."

The entire night was uncomfortable and forced, two things Lizzie had never felt around Finn. And she went home unsatisfied, again. Something she was very used to feeling around Finn.

She'd invited them here to Alison's thinking that she would at least have a home-court advantage when tangling with Annie again.

Ron and Brandt looked beyond Lizzie to the driveway. She followed their gaze and saw the Robbins family arriving. Finn was already out of the minivan that Clea normally drove and taking the collapsible wheelchair out of the back. Stevie had slid out the other side and went around to Annie's side to wait for Finn to bring the chair around. Finn unfolded the chair and, in one fluid movement, undid Annie's seatbelt, swept her in his arms, and placed her in her wheelchair. It was a flawless routine, practiced to perfection over years.

Stevie waited until they had cleared the minivan, then reached inside and grabbed a large duffel bag and a plate covered with tinfoil.

"Hey guys." Lizzie got up to greet the last arrivals.

"Hey there," Finn greeted her. He zoomed in for a kiss, seemed to feel Annie staring down the back of his head, and detoured to Lizzie's cheek at the last second. He gave a tiny shrug of apology to her.

Surely this man has had sex in the last seven years since Dana left? He must have some way of getting free. She just needed to be patient and let Finn figure it out. But when he raked his eyes over her like that, gazing in obvious appreciation of her tankini top and gym shorts that covered the bottom of her swimsuit, she hoped he'd figure out a way for them to be alone together. Soon.

After introductions were made, with beer for the adults and pop for the kids distributed, Katie led Finn and Annie to the dock where, with Ron and Brandt's help, all four were able to get the wheelchair to the dock's end. Alison was inside doing something in the kitchen. Lizzie and Stevie settled themselves at the picnic table, watching Annie and Finn.

Well, at least Lizzie was watching Annie and Finn. Stevie's eyes nearly bulged out of his head as he watched the bikini-clad Katie on the dock. Lizzie, remembering the torture of fourteen-year-old boys subjected to the sight of Katie in high school, felt sorry for the kid.

"She's spectacular, eh?" Lizzie asked him.

Stevie didn't even pretend not to know what she was talking about. "God, yeah. She's your age?"

"Ouch." It would never really go away, she thought, the pang she'd feel when men would ogle her best friend. Even a teen coveting Katie made Lizzie think about her inadequacies.

Sensing his error, Stevie started to backpedal. "I didn't mean it like that. You're pretty...but in a mom way, you know?"

Lizzie, knowing that Katie would kill to be looked at as a mother—to actually be a mother—thought there were injustices to everyone in the world, even the beautiful ones.

"Yeah, I know exactly what you mean." She needed to change the subject before she dove head first into the ever-taunting bowl of potato chips that she knew were lurking behind her. "So, did your dad drag you here today? Were you supposed to do something with your friends?"

He shrugged. "It's okay. Annie never gets to go to the water. She won't go to the beach 'cause she thinks everyone will stare at her, so this is good."

It dawned on her how much this boy had given up, would continue to give up, because of his sister. Out of the blue, she felt the need to touch Stevie. She scooted closer to him and meant to tousle his hair, but instead her hand stayed on his head. "You don't fool me, Stevie. You're a good kid."

She felt his head tense under her touch, then as she spoke it seemed to lighten, as if a huge weight had been lifted from it and the only thing keeping it attached to his body was Lizzie's strong hold.

He leaned in to her, almost a half hug, then, seeing his father's eyes on him from the dock, became embarrassed. He left the table mumbling something about changing into his swimsuit.

Finn's eyes followed his son, allowing her to watch him unnoticed. He was a contrast in skin tones, his torso darkly tan from working in the fields without a shirt. His back and forearms were strong and his muscles rippled as he adjusted the brakes on Annie's wheelchair. His legs peeking out of shorts were as white as Brandt's. Apparently, he always wore jeans while working outside. Her eyes returned to his chest, so lean and dusted with brownish hair that was turning lighter as the days, and the sunshine, increased. It was all she could do not to lick her lips with the fission of desire that shot through her.

She saw half-naked men all the time in the business she was in. And those men were professional athletes whose bodies were highly maintained works of art. But not one of them sent a shiver racing through her blood like looking at Finn did.

She got up and made her way to the dock just in time to hear Finn say, "The doctor said you need to strengthen your legs. This would be a great start." There was a determined look across Annie's face that reminded her of Finn's stubborn pride, but Lizzie also thought she saw a trace of fear in the huge blue eyes.

"I don't want to."

"Want to what?" Lizzie asked.

Katie explained, "We thought Annie might like to swim. We could take her out of her brace and put her in a life jacket and put one of those floaty things around her legs. Alison's got children's-size jackets in the boat house that belonged to her nieces."

"Oh, I've seen that done with paraplegics before, it's good exercise for them," Lizzie said.

"I am not a cripple! I can move my legs," Annie shouted.

Knowing she should feel chastised, but instead letting the kid push all her buttons, she simply said, "Prove it." She sounded like Alison, not good ol' Lizzie. She kind of liked it. Maybe Alison had the right idea all along, speaking her mind, damn the consequences.

The kid had spunk. Once faced with the dare, Annie allowed herself to be put in the life jacket, water wings around her arms, and a Barney flotation ring around her thighs holding her legs up. Alison's youngest niece was thirteen, at a point where Barney was only an embarrassing memory of youthful adulation. Like Shaun Cassidy was now to Lizzie. There was no telling how long the wings and Barney ring had been in the boathouse, but they held air. They also held Annie's limbs.

Katie, Alison, and Lizzie sat side by side on the end of the dock, dangling their legs in the cooling water, watching as Stevie and Finn administered advice and helping hands to a floating Annie. Lizzie could see the excitement and terror shining from Annie's eyes from her perch.

"Deeper. I want to go deeper," Annie demanded.

"It doesn't matter how deep ya are, ya dope, you can't stand up anyway," Stevie said.

That seemed to set Annie off even more. "Daddy, deeper!"

"We can't, honey, Stevie's up to his chin now, and we really need to have two people with you. This is fine, this is deep enough."

Without thinking, Lizzie lifted her bottom off the dock, slid into the water, and did a few quick strokes to get out to where the threesome floated.

When she reached Finn and Annie, Stevie quickly relinquished his position at Annie's feet to Lizzie and swam back to shore.

"Not her," Annie said to Finn. Not quietly enough so that Lizzie couldn't hear.

"Do you want to go deeper or not? Because there doesn't look to be any other takers to help." There were, of course. Everyone there, besides Stevie, would be happy to dive in and help, but Lizzie kept that bit of information to herself.

"I want to go deeper," Annie said, her voice small and tinged with resignation.

Lizzie gently put her hands on Annie's calves and followed Finn's lead as he took his daughter deeper. Stevie was right. For all intents and purposes, two feet of water or twenty would be the same to Annie, but there seemed to be a sense of freedom that shone across her face with each yard they moved from the shoreline. Lizzie realized that this might be the first time that Annie had not found herself bound to land in some fashion and her irritation with the girl was tempered with a new sense of empathy.

"Annie, what if I slipped off the Barney ring and held your legs up with my hands? I think Barney's springing a leak." A look of terror overcame Annie as she looked at the floaty ring and saw its rapidly decreasing size. "It's okay. You don't need it, I'll just slip it off and hold your legs myself."

Finn started to make his way from holding Annie's head in his hands to her legs, but the movement seemed to scare Annie even more and she began to struggle.

Lizzie put on her soothing tone, the voice she used when dealing with arrogant athletes. "No, Finn, you stay there. I've got your legs, Annie, see?" She slipped the ring off and threw it towards land. "There, who needs Barney anyway, he's so passé."

"Huh?" Annie said.

"He's old, out of style." At Annie's nod, she continued, "Okay. I'm going to raise my hands up to your fanny now, so you can kick your legs." She saw the look of panic from Annie, but didn't let herself look at Finn to see his reaction. "Your dad says you need to strengthen your legs as much as possible before your operation. Here…now…I've got you just as tight as before, just higher, that's all. Your legs want to float naturally, they didn't really need Barney at all. There, now let's just start slow."

The panicked look abated somewhat as Annie could see her feet and toes sticking up from the water. Lizzie watched her comfort level rise, and charged on. "Okay. Now just from the knees down. Bend your knees down, then up. If it helps, watch your toes. Make 'em disappear in the water when you take them down, then bring them back up so you can see them."

That was all it took. It seemed as if the little girl had been doing a backstroke kick all her life, she took to it so naturally. She quickly incorporated her entire legs. "Let go, Lizzie, let go, I can keep myself up."

"Of course you can." Lizzie let go and Finn had to step lively to keep up his hold on his daughter.

"Let go Daddy, I want to try it by myself."

"Are you sure?" He was reluctant to release her head.

"She can do it, Finn. Use your arms, too, Annie, that will keep your head up."

A small nod from the tiny head acknowledged her instructions, and Finn slowly eased his hand from under his daughter's head. Her head immediately went underwater and Finn jumped to put his hand back, but Lizzie swayed him with a curt, "No. Don't. She can do it."

Annie's head came back up, sputtering, and she immediately began moving her arms as Lizzie had told her. She began to move—jerking, awkward movements, but she was moving.

"I'm swimming! Daddy, I'm swimming!"

"I see, honey, I see. You're doing great." His voice was hoarse and choked up. Lizzie found she could not speak at all. She looked at Annie's face. The child's blue eyes shone with excitement and accomplishment. Finn's eyes. The thought made Lizzie's gaze shift from the little blue eyes up to Finn's larger, deeper eyes, which looked down at his daughter with a love so pure that Lizzie felt like an intruder.

His eyes turned to her. She couldn't read the emotion in them, but gave him a smile of understanding. He started to return the smile, then took a deep swallow and looked away, clearing his throat with a deep cough.

It didn't matter. Lizzie knew how he felt. If *she* felt this good about the kid swimming, she could only imagine what Annie's father must be experiencing.

He finally had Liz alone. Well, not really alone. The two other couples were right outside the sauna house at the picnic table enjoying an after-dinner beer. Annie and Stevie were in the camp, sacked out, watching TV, totally pooped after a day of water play and a filling dinner of burgers, chips, potato salad, and the cheesecake Gran had sent along. Happier than he had seen them both in a long time.

But here, in the blistering sauna, he had Liz alone. Finally.

Thoughts of her with Annie kept replaying in his mind. She'd been great with his daughter. He knew he would never have been able to be so unemotional with Annie; he would have caved at her first whimper. But Liz had gotten his daughter to swim. More than that, she had gotten a shriek of excitement out of Annie that he wasn't sure he'd ever heard coming from his daughter.

He felt an odd constriction in his chest. It was as if there was some kind of lightening, an easing. He didn't take too much time trying to figure it out, didn't want to figure it out, really. He was just…happy. It was an unfamiliar feeling. When was the last time he'd been as happy as he was right now?

Liz threw a bucket of water on the stove and the smooth rocks screamed and hissed as the steam rose.

"Jeez, you're going to kill us." He hung his head to try and breathe, and wondered if he'd seem like too much of a wuss if he moved down to the cooler, lower bench.

"Pansy-ass," she said, making up his mind for him. He stayed put on the top bench.

She arched her back up, lifted her arms to the ceiling, raised her face and took in the steam. He watched as her breasts jutted forward. He sat on his hands to stop himself from reaching out for her.

She was in her glory. Her skin, lightly tanned, was beaded with sweat. Her hair fell in wet masses down her back. Her lips were slightly parted. This would be what she'd look like when he had her beneath him. Sweaty, arching in obvious ecstasy. "You love this, don't you?"

"God, yes. The hotter the better. It does great things for your skin."

"Your skin is incredible already."

She breezed right over his compliment, as if not hearing it. *Or maybe not believing it?*

"God, I miss saunas. I mean, they have them at the gym, but it's just not the same. The ones there are electric. They don't get as hot, you don't get as sweaty or clean, and obviously there's no lake to jump in to."

"Which I'm about ready for, by the way."

"You're on." She got up and climbed down from the top bench to the cement floor and turned around to wait for him. She caught him looking at her ass and her hands went to her behind, tugging at the bottom elastic of her suit.

"Don't cover up on my account, I like when your suit rides up." She rolled her eyes at him and went out the door, Finn close on her heels. They slipped through the dressing room and out of the sauna building and ran the few steps to the dock. It felt so much better diving in quickly, not allowing your body to cool down from the sauna heat.

He grabbed her hand, both of theirs slick with sweat, and ran to the end of the dock where they both jumped in, their hands parting for Finn to do a cannonball and Liz to execute a perfect shallow dive.

The cool of the water shocked him. He heard a little yelp from Liz and knew she was feeling the same pins and needles he was.

She swam out a ways and he swam to reach her. When was the last time he'd been swimming? Years. He'd taught Stevie to swim when he was little, before Annie was old enough to know what was going on around her. As soon as she turned three, resentment would mar her cherubic face if Finn tried to teach Stevie things she wasn't able to do. So he'd either try to sneak his time with Stevie, or Stevie would miss out.

Not fair, he knew, but everything about the situation was

unfair.

He caught up to her and stood. The water was at her collar-bone, mid-chest on him. They stood for a moment, just looking at each other. He thought of her in the water earlier, with Annie, how she'd goaded his daughter into trying something that scared her. How Liz had jumped off the dock and swam out to them at the first sign of being needed. How her inexperience with kids seemed to fall away around Stevie.

How tempting her breasts looked swelling over the top of her swimsuit.

He couldn't stand it any longer. He placed his hands on her waist, pulled her close and bent his head, bringing his lips to hers. She didn't pull away, or pretend anything other than the truth. She wanted him as much as he wanted her.

Her lips burned on his. Her mouth could be scalding from the sauna, he figured, but knew it was more. She felt the same things he did, burned for him the way he burned for her. Always had.

He heard a quiet sploosh of water breaking as she raised her arms out of the lake and wound them around his neck, pressing herself into him. Steam rose off both their bodies, the contrast of their hot skin in the cool water creating a billowing cloud that encompassed them.

Her face, wet from her swim, shone in the moonlight. He nibbled her neck, following beads of water making their way down to her chest. A lone drop settled in the vee at her collarbone and he scooped it out with his tongue.

She let out a soft sigh and pulled his mouth back to hers. She took control of the kiss now, and Finn reveled in the reversal. She tasted of their earlier burgers and peppermint. She swirled her tongue into his mouth, exploring him. Her lips pressed hard into his as if she was trying to crawl inside him.

It mirrored how he felt. He wanted to be inside her, yearned to slip the bottom of her swimsuit off and take her right here in the lake. The water would make her skin as slick as Finn's attentions were surely making her.

Fearing he may actually do it, he said a silent thanks as they heard loud throat clearing and catcalls of "get a room" coming from the shore, bringing them both out of their lust-filled haze.

"Oh, God," Liz groaned and ducked her head to his shoulder. "I can't believe I just did that in front of everybody."

He felt a pang of pity for Liz, but then his pride raised its ugly head and he wondered if she was embarrassed to be caught kissing by her friends, or to be caught kissing *him*? He lifted her chin and looked into her eyes, wide hazel pools, still shining with the flare of passion that he'd ignited. "Believe me, I don't want an audience for what I want to do to you any more than you do."

He felt the tremor that went through her and his insecurity was put to rest. Nobody could fake that kind of response. She wanted him. Not some city-slicker business type. Finn could bring her to fever pitch in seconds. Let's see some BMW-driving, iPhone-wielding dickwad try to elicit the sounds from her that he did.

He smiled at her, gave her a quick peck on the top of her head, and started swimming toward shore.

He washed up in the lake, using the bar of soap and bottle of shampoo that perched at the end of the dock for just such a reason. Liz returned to the sauna for another round. He dressed and checked on Stevie and Annie. Exhausted from the day, Annie slept soundly. Finn took her out of her chair and carried her to a bed that Alison directed him to, then put her wheelchair in the minivan to save himself the trip later. Stevie watched some movie on HBO that he probably shouldn't, but Finn figured what the hell—a couple of buildings exploding and car crashes aren't going to scar him for life—so he left his son alone in cable heaven.

He sat with the others at the picnic table. Alison handed him a beer. They were okay people, Liz's friends.

The Brandt guy seemed to be nervous and he realized that this was a relatively new thing—Brandt and Alison. The guy was certainly more into Alison than she was into him, and Finn felt a pang of pity for the guy. It sucked when you were on the wrong side of one-sided emotion. He had been there, with Liz, but felt certain that if asked, Liz would think that she'd been the one who cared the most in their past relationship. It was easier to let her think that. Maybe not for her, but definitely for him.

He didn't get a good read on Katie's husband, Ron. He had gathered from Liz that they'd been married a long time, yet they didn't seem to have that comfort level that long-time marrieds had. Katie's eyes darted nervously to Ron as she spoke, as if gauging him for any reaction he may have. Ron seemed distracted, and looked at his watch often. Finn didn't think much of it, he didn't know them well, and after Liz left town, he probably wouldn't see them much again. A nod in Walmart or a hello at McDonald's—that would be the extent of their interaction.

Liz had obviously told Katie and Alison about Annie's operation, and that was the direction of their conversation by the time Liz finally got out of the sauna, fingers pruned and face red and glistening. He didn't take his eyes from her once as she made her way to the camp, taking refill orders and grabbing a beer for herself.

The soft cotton of her oversized tee-shirt hugged her body, still damp from sweat even after a douse in the lake and a shower. Her full breasts swayed as she walked, her hips seeming to have a rhythm of their own. He marveled at how natural she was. Curves and fullness, a sultriness that seemed instinctive.

He watched through the picture window as she spoke with Stevie for a while, then came back out and pulled a plastic chaise lounge over near the table. Finn got up from the table to help her, then sat down in the chaise himself, reclined, and pulled Liz down to sit between his legs, her back against his chest. He waited for her to accept their position, and when she easily did he was pleased. He pulled her hair out of the clip she had put it in, then realized she'd done so because it was still wet. Unable to do anything with women's hair—and he had tried innumerable times with Annie—he handed the clip back to her to put her hair back up. She did, leaning back into him. His arms circled around her waist, settling on her thighs. She took his beer can and placed it with hers on the ground beside their chair, then rested her arms on top of his. She squirmed her ass a little, finding a more comfortable position, though much more uncomfortable for him. She let out a sigh of contentment and joined the conversation.

"What are we talking about?" she asked. He hoped none of the others would remember that they'd been discussing his daughter and his lack of funds to help her.

Katie and Alison shared a look, then Katie said, "Actually, we were just discussing Finn's plans for Annie. About how to get the money for the operation."

"And what does Finn have to say about your prying?" She had a censure in her voice directed at her friends that he found admirable. She had to know that it killed him to have conversations about his failings as a father.

Just like his Liz to come to his defense. She always thought of him as an underdog, and perhaps he was, but he sure as hell didn't like feeling it now. "I was just telling them about the spaghetti dinner and pancake breakfast that the women at Gran's church are sponsoring."

The group was silent, no one wanting to say what everyone was thinking. That those two events wouldn't even pay for the charge of aspirin at the hospital, let alone an expensive operation.

"You know, I've been thinking about that…" Liz said. "I think I could pull together some sort of fundraiser fairly quickly. My staff is at a slow period right now with only baseball in season and no elections this fall where we have a candidate. They could make most of the calls from Detroit, and I could do the local stuff here."

"What kind of fundraiser? Another spaghetti dinner? Something like that?" Brandt asked before Finn could.

"No. Something bigger. Kat, throw me my tote bag, please."

He watched as Katie brought Liz's tote bag over to the chair they shared. Liz plopped it on her lap and dug through it. She came up with a tablet like secretaries use to take dictation. Actually, she came up with three. One, pristine and unused, got dumped back into the bag quickly. He could see that there was some kind of title written across the front of the tablet in red maker of the other two. He peered around her shoulder. One tablet was entitled "The Plan" and the other "Annie Aid".

She put The Plan tablet back in her bag and flipped through pages of the tablet marked Annie Aid. Finn had a sense of unease of what was in that tablet and how it may affect the rest of his—and his kids'—lives.

"I've spent the last few days making some quick calls, getting some ideas. Brainstorming with my mom. Making a few lists."

Alison laughed. "Lizzie, when *aren't* you making lists?"

Finn ignored Alison. He already knew Liz was a planner. He had been too, once upon a time. "What are you thinking of doing?" he asked.

"Something that will draw the entire Copper Country. I did some quick math; the three-county area is around 30,000 people. Say you can draw ten to fifteen percent of those to whatever event we plan. Charge thirty dollars per, that's a hundred grand right there. Maybe make a weekend of it, a couple other events, and we could make a dent in the loan on the farm, maybe even pay it off and put some aside for upcoming medical expenses. I'm assuming there'll be some physical therapy for Annie after the operation?" She turned her head to look at him behind her and froze when she saw the cold look in his eyes.

He felt like he'd been punched in the gut. So many emotions rushed through him. His pride was seething, he felt emasculated that this woman could sweep into town and in a few weeks possibly accomplish something he'd been attempting for years. And why would Liz put herself out like this? She wasn't trying to weasel her way into his life, was she? She had said no strings, and this seemed like a pretty damn big string that would bind them together.

Then he thought of Annie, and tamped down his feelings

of inadequacy and mistrust. Who cares how he got the money. This wouldn't be so much like a hand-out if people were getting something in return for their money. It certainly beat the idea of accepting Liz's money. The main thing was that Annie got the operation.

She was flipping through pages and Finn could see over her shoulder that there were pages of notes and phone numbers, checklists, some color-coded. That she'd been able to do so much in the few days since he'd told her about Annie astounded him.

No, nothing about Liz astounded him.

He forced himself to swallow, and unclench his teeth. "That's incredibly generous of you. You shouldn't take up yours and your staff's time and resources on my account. I'm…very grateful."

Lizzie sensed she was on thin ice here. How to accept Finn's gratitude but not make him feel like a charity case? She didn't want gratitude when she had him in the bedroom, she wanted him to take her with a fierceness and passion that she knew he possessed. She turned away from him, toward the others at the table. "You're welcome. But really, it's not that big of a deal. This is what I do. Plan events that my clients can attend and give back a little to the people who pay their salaries—the fans."

"Lizzie, it's a great idea," Katie said. "Surely you can get Petey to do something, help out?"

"He's going to be my first call. I just wanted to make sure it was okay with Finn before I got moving on it." Again, Finn nodded his assent, but remained silent.

She read through some of her lists to the group and when Petey's name came up again, Brandt asked, "Who's Petey?"

"Pete Ryan, he plays for…" Alison started to explain but an excited Brandt cut her off.

"The Red Wings, I know. You guys know Pete Ryan?" Brandt watched as the three women and Ron all nodded yes. "I've never heard him called Petey before."

Alison laughed. "Brandt, in the Yoop, everyone ends up with

an 'ie' or a 'y' at the end of their names if you live here long enough."

"How did you guys meet him?" The awe in Brandt's voice spoke of his fan status.

"He's from Houghton; we graduated the same year. Lizzie dated him our junior year in high school."

Lizzie felt Finn tense behind her. "That was a thousand years ago, we're just close friends now. He was my first client when I opened my own PR firm. He actually helped me get most of my original clients."

"And obviously you did great things for him, Lizard, if Brandt, a guy from Baltimore who doesn't follow hockey, knows who Petey is," Katie said.

There was a lull in the conversation. Katie and Alison could see Lizzie was in planning mode so they kept quiet. She scribbled some more notes in her pad. Finn was silent. Brandt seemed to digest the fact that the woman he was dating knew someone famous. Ron looked at his watch. Ron finally broke the silence.

"Come on, Katie, we need to go, I still have to go into the school tonight to pick up some papers."

They rose to leave and the others followed. "What kind of papers do you need from the school now? It's the end of June," Katie asked her husband.

"I need the roster of the hockey team. I want to call the boys this week and make sure they're working out."

"I better get the kids home, too," Finn said. He gave her a look of regret that yet another evening together would end with them apart.

Things were gathered and put in respective vehicles. Alison offered the use of the camp for Annie any time to strengthen her legs. Finn explained that he'd be taking Annie and Stevie to Ann Arbor this week.

Alison got a devilish look in her eyes. "Lizzie, why don't you go with Finn? You could go to the office, check in, get the fundraiser stuff rolling. Your condo is only a half hour from Ann

Arbor. I'm sure it'd be much more comfortable than some hotel room."

"Cheaper too…every penny, you know," Katie added, taking Alison's lead.

"Plus, you could help Finn with the driving. Unless your grandmother's going with you?" Alison directed the last part to Finn.

"Uh, no, she's watching the farm, dealing with the pickers, while I'm gone."

There was a moment of silence while Lizzie shot daggers with her eyes to her two best friends. "I'm sure Finn wouldn't want another person along."

"Actually, Liz, it would be really helpful to have a female along. Someone to help with Annie at the rest stops, stuff like that. Someone Stevie could hang out with the day we're at the hospital." There was a request in his voice, one she couldn't deny. She'd never been able to deny him anything.

Well, her virginity. Okay, one thing. And even that had been a close call. If he hadn't dumped her when he did, she was sure she wouldn't have been a virgin when she'd arrived at Michigan State.

And that had not been part of the plan.

"When are you going?"

"Day after tomorrow. Driving down Tuesday. Wednesday at the hospital. Drive back the next day. Three days total."

She mentally weighed spending more time with him against spending the same amount of time with Annie. Finn won out. "If you'd like company, I'd like to go along. We can stay at my place. The day you're at the hospital with Annie I can take Stevie to the office with me."

A look of relief washed across his face, "Thanks, that would be great. I'm swamped tomorrow with getting the farm ready, how about if I pick you up at your parents at eight on Tuesday?"

"That'll work."

As Finn went inside to gather up Annie in his arms and tear Stevie away from the television, Lizzie blasted her friends. "What was that all about?"

Alison and Katie looked at each other, a sure sign to her that they'd been discussing her behind her back. "We think this thing you're doing could go bad if you aren't careful, Lizard. That you could get really hurt. We want you to think of Finn as more than just a lab experiment. Spend some time with him. See him as more than a way to 'get your groove back'. Not just something to check off in one of those tablets of yours. If you can still have non-emotional sex with him and walk away after that, we'll stand by you and shut up."

She looked over her friends. "Hah! That'll be the day when the two of you will ever shut up about what I do." But she smiled as she said it.

"That's why you love us, Lizard," Katie said.

Lizzie laughed and put on her thick Yooper accent. "Yah, that's why I love yous guys, eh?"

Eleven

—⁂—

√ Call Tigers front office about clubhouse pass
√ Call Sybil, James and Petey
√ See list of things to do at office

SHE HATED MAKING the long drive to Detroit alone, but right now Lizzie would have gladly driven there and back—twice—if she could just have five minutes of peace and quiet.

It wasn't quite as bad as "Are we there yet? Are we there yet?", but it was darn close. She could tell Annie was nervous about the upcoming consultation, and she sympathized, but the kid was being particularly snotty today. Stevie chattered too, but stopped when he saw Lizzie rubbing her temples. Smart kid, Stevie. She shot him a smile of gratitude and he looked away, embarrassed. She guessed that pretty much everything embarrassed fourteen-year-old boys.

Finn seemed oblivious to it all, either very deep in thought as he drove, or so used to the non-stop bickering between his off-spring that he easily tuned them out.

They were nearing Lizzie's condo in Novi. She'd called Robin, her cleaning lady, and asked her to come in to tidy up the place and air it out. She also asked her to sweep the place for anything of a personal nature. When Robin needed more specifics, Lizzie hemmed and hawed then finally blurted, "Find any photos of me when I was fat that may be out, and hide them."

She'd spent the last ten hours—besides trying to ignore Annie—mulling over the ideas she had for Annie Aid. It would have to be big. It would have to be spectacular. They didn't have much time. And she would have to have help. Lots of help. She'd need to call in all her markers, even promise some favors out. But it was doable.

When they arrived the condo looked great. Robin had once again outdone herself. Fresh flowers were in the living room and kitchen and she'd even stocked the refrigerator with bread, milk, and juice.

They spent the evening in and ordered take-out from her favorite Chinese place. It felt odd to have to look up the number in the yellow pages; for years she had known it by heart—at one time she'd even had it on speed dial.

It always amazed her that something as inactive as sitting in a car or flying in an airplane could completely wipe you out, but it did. Annie and Stevie shared the guest bedroom and were both asleep immediately after Finn got them settled.

—◆◆◆—

After tucking in his kids, Finn found Liz in her office, putting sheets on the day bed, where he assumed he'd be sleeping. She had her computer on, and something was chugging out of the printer. The sound allowed him to enter the room unheard, where he admired her from behind.

He watched her bend over to fasten the elastic of the fitted sheet around the end of the mattress. His eyes narrowed as the denim of her jeans tightened across her ass, her hips full and tempting. God, how he wanted her. To topple her onto that day bed and strip her tee-shirt and jeans right off her ripe body. To free those spectacular breasts from her bra, feel them tighten, watch her nipples pucker. He got hard just thinking about it. Thinking about her.

But he knew it'd be another night of frustration. There was no way he was going to sleep with her with his kids in the next room. The kids were exhausted and he didn't think they'd wake up for anything, but he wanted to make Liz scream his name when buried himself deep inside her, so he'd wait. Again.

To divert his attention, and hopefully ease his hard-on, he focused on the printer. "What's that?"

She jerked away from the bed, obviously startled by his presence. She followed his gaze to the paper coming from her printer. "Oh. That's a rough outline of things I want to look into tomorrow for the fundraiser. And a map and directions for you from here to the hospital." She pointed to another stack of papers sitting to the other side of the desk. "And that's a list of outstanding issues at work I'd like to resolve tomorrow."

"Wow, are you always this organized?"

She laughed. "Always. It's both a blessing and a curse."

On the shelf next to the desk were two stacks of tablets. They were the same size as the two she'd pulled out of her tote bag at Alison's. One stack of tablets was clearly new, the pages lying flat, with no marks of any kind. The other stack must have been the "used" bunch. The pages on the bottom of the tablets were curled, some of the covers were bent, causing the whole pile to have an unbalanced look. He could only see the cover of the tablet at the top of the pile. In bold blue marker it read "spring clean-up".

Yep. A blessing and a curse.

He walked to the desk and turned the big leather chair around to face her as she continued to prepare the bed. He eyed the papers she'd printed out. "That's a pretty thick stack. You sure you have time for this fundraiser?"

She didn't look back at him. "Yep."

"I could take Stevie to the hospital with me if you'd rather. That was the original plan, anyway. I don't want him getting in the way."

She finished with the bedding and sat down, facing him. "No, I'll take him. We've got a pretty nice lounge, complete with a bunch of DVDs and video games. He'll be fine there."

He nodded. "Okay. He'll love that, he's been wanting a Wii

forever…" He didn't finish the sentence. They both knew how it ended. Finn couldn't afford to buy special gifts for Stevie.

Liz shrugged. "It'll be nice to see it be used by a kid for once. Usually it's our athlete clients who come in to the office for something and end up playing it all day. What time do you think you'll be done at the hospital?"

"The appointment's early, but there will be a lot of tests. I would think we'd be back here around five, five thirty, why?"

The printer silenced and Liz rose to retrieve the pile from the output tray. Her breasts brushed across his arm as she reached past him and they both jumped as though they'd been shocked. She flushed and took the last sheet of paper from the pile and perused it as she answered him.

"The Tigers are at home tomorrow night. I thought it might be fun to take the kids, if you and Annie were done in time."

It took him a moment to focus on what she was saying, his body still reacting from the graze of her breasts. "Would we be able to get Annie in okay?"

"Yes. Comerica Park has great wheelchair accessibility. Plus, I have a client who's on the team, he can probably get you and Stevie into the clubhouse after the game."

Stevie would love that. And Annie would love going to the game once she got over the idea of being stared at. He looked hard at Liz. "Why are you doing all this?"

She didn't pretend to misunderstand him. She knew what he was really asking. She removed one piece of paper from her pile and placed the rest back on the desk, then crouched down to rest on her haunches in front of him. She placed her hands on his knees, in essence to balance herself. Or maybe just to touch.

"Really, there's no ulterior motive here. I'm not trying to get to you through your kids. I'm not looking for anything more than what we talked about that first night. A few laughs, a few good times, a fun, summer fling. That's it. Besides, this fundraiser is not all about helping you and Annie. I'll be getting as many of my clients to attend as possible, and I'll have lots of news and sports media outlets made aware of it, too. I'll be playing up the altruism of my clients. This is a win-win situation."

"There'll be media coverage of it?" He hadn't thought about that. He was able to put his pride on the back burner for Annie in front of the Copper Country, but wasn't sure if he'd be able to do it front of the whole country.

"Of course, as much as we can drum up. I'll have Katie write something up for the *Ingot,* and I'll make some calls to the people I know at the AP and hopefully they'll pick it up. See, it will even be good for Katie's career. Don't worry, the focus will be on helping Annie, not on…"

How he couldn't provide for his own daughter? He kept the thought to himself. "Promise me there'll be nothing about Dana and giving her the money I'd saved."

She seemed shocked that he'd even suggest such a thing. "Of course not. How many people know about that anyway? We can just make sure those people aren't contacted for comment."

"Only you and Gran. And Dana, of course."

She squeezed his knee. "Thank you for telling me the whole story." She slid the piece of paper she held to his hands then rose up and stepped away from him. "I'm going to hit the sack. That's an outline of the fundraiser done on Hampton PR letterhead. It explains the expected revenue. Take it into your meeting with the financial people tomorrow, maybe it will help. If they have any questions about it, my office number is at the top."

She left the room before he could say thanks. Again.

—〰—

In the morning, as she and Stevie waited for James to pick them up on his way into the office, Lizzie looked around her condo. When she'd bought it six years ago it had been her pride and joy. A symbol of her success. At least in her professional life. As she looked around now, she realized her feelings had changed. She was still happy with it, but realized it missed something. Mess. It missed the messiness that living brought to a household. Granted, she'd been away nearly a month, but this was pretty much what it looked like all the time.

Her parents' house had a warmth and comfort that seemed lacking here. And Finn's house. Well, his place had a history and a clutter that screamed family. Generation after generation. It was something she hadn't even realized she lacked in her sleek and stylish condo. Yet, as she compared the two, the condo definitely came up short.

She certainly hadn't missed the city traffic while she'd been away, either. Being only five minutes away from anything was a definite advantage of small-town living. And the water. Only a short time away from the Copper Country and she already missed seeing water at every turn. She sighed and called to Stevie as she heard James pull into her driveway.

—ɯ—

Annie's consultation with the doctors had surpassed Finn's highest hopes. Her bone growth had progressed to the levels needed to perform the surgery. His meeting with the financial people had been successful too, thanks to Liz's statement of expected revenue. It was much easier to show them than the stack he'd brought of bank notices and mortgage payments due. The surgery was scheduled for October. The doctors wanted Annie to spend the time until then strengthening her arms and legs for the long road of physical therapy ahead.

He and Annie had beaten Stevie and Liz back to her condo, and when she and Stevie entered, he whisked her in his arms and buried his head in her neck. Stevie, sensing his fragile emotional state, went to find Annie in the bedroom.

He pulled her close, not trusting himself to look at her as he spoke. "It's going to happen. They're going to do the operation. And they figure a seventy-five to eighty percent chance of success. She could walk, Liz. My baby might walk." His voice was hoarse and quavered with emotion.

—ɯ—

Lizzie realized that Finn had never really given the whole thing much chance of happening. They had totally different mindsets. As soon as she'd heard of the situation, she began planning how it could work.

To be fair, she hadn't had years of disappointments like he had. And, of course, she wasn't emotionally involved like he was. It surprised her to find she couldn't speak quite yet, and she clung to Finn with a fierceness that contradicted her supposed lack of attachment.

He pulled away and looked at her with a gratitude and longing that made her wish for the years they'd never had together. His hard face softened and his eyes shone with want and need. He started to say something but the squeak of Annie's wheelchair interrupted him.

"Daddy, Stevie said we're going to a baseball game tonight. Are we?"

Finn looked at her for the answer.

"We can if you'd like to, Annie. I've got pretty good tickets and the guys are invited to the clubhouse after the game," she answered.

The little girl seemed torn. Lizzie could tell she desperately wanted to go to the game, but that would mean accepting a gesture from Lizzie, something Annie was loath to do. She had as much willful pride as her father.

"Will I...do they..." Annie's blue eyes searched her father's face, then turned to her.

Reading her mind, Lizzie said, "The ball park has great wheelchair access. We'll be able to park real close, too. Besides, I could really go for a hot dog."

—⁘—

At the game, as the kids gorged themselves on hot dogs, Crackerjacks and Mountain Dew—a usual no-no—Lizzie recapped her and Stevie's day at her office for Finn.

The highlight was when Petey Ryan had stopped by unexpectedly. Stevie could hardly believe he was meeting his idol, that Lizzie even knew Pete Ryan, let alone that he was there in the flesh.

She could have kissed Petey when he offered to take Stevie with him for the afternoon as he went to Joe Louis Arena to clear out his locker. Stevie came back to the office with autographs from a couple of the players as well as five rolls of half-used tape, a broken stick, and numerous other mementos that players were pitching. Proving the theory that one man's trash is another man's treasure.

Her staff once again proved their worth and took her plans for the fundraiser and ran with them. Phone calls to clients took up most of the day, with only one saying no to the fundraiser and only because his wife was due to have their first child on the same date.

She relayed the promising outlook to Finn, but she didn't tell him about everything that had happened at her office that day.

She'd had a very long meeting with her top account executives. Not surprised that things had been handled so well in her absence, she nonetheless gave them the praise they deserved. As if sensing her good mood, James, the obvious designated ringleader, pushed a folder across the wide conference table to her.

It was a presentation that the account executives had put together proposing a formed partnership in Hampton Public Relations. At Lizzie's shocked look, James said, "We love it here, Lizzie, we all want to stay, but we want to make sure there's room for us to grow. As partners, we'd have an investment in the future of Hampton PR. Read it when you have time. We don't have to talk about it now; there's no timetable attached to it. It can wait until you come back."

She'd leafed through the proposal while she waited for Petey to come back with Stevie. It was well-written, very sound, and could make her very wealthy down the road. Of course she'd have to give up complete control. Was she capable of that?

In some ways, she'd been like a reverse anorexic. Anorexics oftentimes feel they have no control in their life, so at least they can control their eating. It was just the opposite for Lizzie. She was such a control freak in her professional life that the one thing she allowed to get completely out of control was her eating.

Damn, now she'd have this partnership proposal dangling over her head while she was in the U.P. trying to seduce Finn. Though she knew that wouldn't take much effort if the way Finn's eyes followed her movements were any indication.

Lizzie knew she was pressing her luck, but as soon as Petey and Stevie came back, she pulled Petey into her office and said she had something important she needed to ask him. He narrowed his eyes at her suspiciously, but waved her on.

She told him about Finn and Annie, and Annie's operation. He said he vaguely remembered Finn being ahead of him in high school. As much as any die-hard jock would remember a guy who didn't even know how to skate—a mortal sin in the Copper Country. She told him more than she should have, alluded to the trouble with Dana, hinted at the looming mortgage on the farm. Then she told him where he fit in to her plans.

"You want me to what? Are you out of your goddamn mind?"

"Come on, Petey, it's not that big of a deal."

He snorted and plopped himself down on the leather couch that ran along one wall of her spacious office. "You want me to call members of the Avalanche and ask them to take their day with the Stanley Cup in the U.P. for a fundraiser? It's a big fucking deal, Lizard."

He was right. Petey would love for the Stanley Cup to be brought to the Copper Country, but only because he was on the winning team. His two stints with the Red Wings had been great for his career, but the Wings' Cup-winning run was during years Petey had been with the Islanders. Being thirty-six, ancient in the NHL, and never having won the Cup was Petey's hot button. Lizzie knew he was hanging on, trying to stay healthy, so he could skate that victory lap hoisting the Cup over his head before he retired.

"Just two of the Russian team members, Petey. Look, each team member gets a day with the Stanley Cup in the town of their choice, right?" It was a ritual dating back decades, one that Lizzie had always found charming. The Stanley Cup brought to little backwoods towns in Canada and the Midwest to bask in their local boy's heroics.

At Petey's leery nod of agreement she forged on. "The Avalanche has five team members who are Russian and are living in Denver, with no plans to take the cup back to Russia. I checked. If only two of them would give up their day with the cup so it could be in the Copper Country, it'd still be in Denver for three whole days. Surely they can manage with that."

"Yeah, it's doable, but why do I have to be the one to do the asking? I hate those fucking guys. Man, of all the teams…the Avalanche. Lizzie…" he whined. He was rubbing his big hands through his hair, and Lizzie knew she had him.

Petey could wrap himself in the label of NHL hardass bruiser, but he was a pussycat at heart. She'd known that since their first date when he'd taken her to see *Out Of Africa* and she'd heard him sniffling into his letter jacket when Robert Redford died. Knowing which heartstrings to pull, she'd been able to wrap him around her little finger ever since.

She soothed him, rubbing his back in a sisterly fashion. "I know you do, but I don't know any of them, Petey. Even if you'd just make the introduction call, I'll do the asking. I'm willing to give each of the five of them a year's worth of Hampton PR services at no charge."

He dropped his head in resignation, then looked up at her. "That's using up your staff's resources for a whole year, Lizzie. Are you sure you want to do this?" Before she could answer he held up a hand. "I mean, are you sure you want to get this involved?"

She feigned ignorance. "It's just another fundraiser, Petey, like the kind we plan all the time. This time it benefits a fellow Yooper, so I guess I'm trying a little harder."

He narrowed his eyes at her. "Trying harder for the kid, or for her father?"

She waved his question away with a flick of her hand then rose to get the phone and list of the Russian players from her desk and to put Petey to work, ignoring the look of concern that he leveled at her.

—॥॥—

The big foam finger poked Finn in the head for what seemed like the five thousandth time. "I swear, Annie, that thing hits me again, and it's going to be floating in Lake Michigan."

She giggled, a sound so rare to him that he had to turn around in his seat to confirm what he'd heard. "Sorry, Daddy. Stevie pushed me."

"Did not."

"Did so."

Before the verbal ping-pong could go any further, Liz broke in. "Okay, the turn-off's coming up. Everybody ready for Great Lake number two?" She was driving, giving Finn a break from the wheel.

The route home they'd chosen was her idea. She said she, Alison, and Katie had done it years ago when they'd spent a weekend at Mackinac Island. Within the course of one afternoon, they'd swum in Lake Huron, Lake Michigan, and Lake Superior, hitting three of the five Great Lakes.

This morning, as they'd left Liz's condo, she'd made everyone don their swimsuits under their clothes. She'd put several towels in the van with them, and unearthed the life vest Annie had worn at Alison's that she'd borrowed. She'd also purchased a new flotation ring, this one bearing Justin Bieber. They picke up McDonald's at Cheboygan and found a tiny public beach that Liz had Googled and GPSed on her cell phone, where they swam in Lake Huron and ate lunch.

He was amazed at her organization. Amazed, but not surprised.

—॥॥—

It took the allure of swimming in the second Great Lake of the day for Stevie to part with the autographed baseball that the Tigers had signed for him after the game. Even then, he put the ball in his seat, lovingly covered with the Tigers cap and tee-shirt that Lizzie had bought for both he and Annie. Along with the giant foam finger that was now liable to put someone's eye out.

By the time they reached Lake Superior three hours later they had gotten into an easy routine. Finn carried Annie to the water's edge, where he'd remove her brace, which Lizzie would take back to the van. She'd bring back the life vest, floaties, and towels. She'd lurk nearby, but she hung mostly with Stevie.

This would be their quickest swim, Lake Superior being by far the coldest lake due to its depth. A quick in and out, but they could claim they'd been in three Great Lakes in one day.

"It'll be pretty cool to tell your pals, eh?" she asked Stevie as they dried off for the final time. Finn was discreetly helping Annie change out of her swimsuit and into dry clothes. With her brace, it would be too uncomfortable for her to spend the last two hours of their trip in a wet swimsuit. The rest of them would just dry off as much as possible then throw shorts and tees on over their suits. They were from the Copper Country—with water everywhere you turned—so they were used to sitting on towels in their car seats in the summer.

"Yeah, but not as cool as telling them I met Pete Ryan." His mind continued on. "Or Avila and Verlander." The number of sports stars Stevie had met in the three days they'd been away from the Copper Country would impress even the most jaded teenager. The thought spurred on another one.

"Maybe your friends would want to help out with the fundraiser?" She wanted to get Stevie involved somehow. With the event being all about Annie, it was important for Stevie to get some attention.

He had that *"Oh. Oh. What's the catch?"* look on his face. "Help out how?"

"Well, if we get to do everything I've planned, I'll need about eighteen people to man a golf hole at the golf outing. We usually have little contests that people can buy their way into at each hole, you know, closest to the pin, stuff like that." Before he could get the "no" that was obviously forming on his lips out, she added,

"Of course, each golf group will have a sports star in it. Plus each celebrity athlete will probably want a caddy."

His blue eyes, his father's eyes, widened. "Deal."

Twelve

—w—

√ Ask Dad about exercise bike
√ Make dessert to bring to farm
√ See separate call sheet for Annie Aid

TWO WEEKS LATER, Lizzie pulled her Navigator into the Robbins' driveway. Which wasn't different than any other day since they got back from Ann Arbor, but today the back of her SUV was held shut with a bungee cord.

She waved Stevie over to help her from the field where he was picking berries. She had taken her mother's old exercise bike from the storage area in the basement and brought it out to the farm. She and Stevie carried it to the edge of the strawberry field nearest the house. She then went in to the house and met Annie's accusing stare as the girl sat in front of the picture window, obviously watching the happenings outside.

"What's that thing for?" she asked Lizzie.

"What do you think it's for?" Her voice matched Annie's petulant-child tone.

"I'm not riding that damn thing outside where people can see me."

"That's too damn bad, because that's where I'm going to be, and you really need to have someone near you if you're going to be on it." She went to the desk in the living room, sticking her tongue out at the back of Annie's head as she passed by.

She picked up her Annie Aid tablet from the desk, took her cell phone from her purse—which she then threw on a kitchen chair—and left the house. She could feel the little blue eyes burning a hole in her back as she went to the barn and got the milking stool she'd made her own and a couple of empty quarts and went to the first row of the field.

She plunked down the stool, placing her tablet and cell phone on the ground next to her. It was a routine she'd gotten used to since they'd gotten back from the hospital trip. She spent the mornings in the field, half-heartedly picking berries, whole-heartedly working on her tan, and keeping her fundraiser things nearby so that whenever she had a brainstorm she could jot it down, or even make a call or text and set the idea in motion. In the afternoons she went into the house, and after lunch, usually prepared by Clea, she set to work at the desk that Finn had cleared off for her.

Her plans were coming together, and she felt confident enough that everything else would fall in to place so that they'd be able to announce the fundraiser at the upcoming Strawberry Festival Community Dance.

The festival had always been a favorite—the little neighboring town of Chassell hosting not only all the area's population but a large number of tourists for a three-day weekend with a parade, events, and strawberries, supplied by the local berry growers, in any and every array you could imagine. Madge Goodson, the perennial Strawberry Festival Chair, unwittingly did a dead-on impression of Bubba in *Forrest Gump* reeling off all the ways to cook shrimp when she told of the myriad ways you could serve strawberries.

A Strawberry Festival Queen pageant highlighted the weekend—local girls sponsored by the fraternal organization where, most likely, their fathers or uncles were long-time members. The festival always culminated with a community dance. Kids ran around eating cotton candy and the adults gossiped and talked about the success or failure of that year's strawberry crop. Little girls in their best new dresses took to the floor for their first dance, standing on their fathers' shoes.

Petey was scheduled to crown the queen at this year's festivities. Maybe she'd have him make the announcement about the fundraiser at the same time. She wrote a quick note to call Madge and talk to her about it.

The festival was only a week away and Finn had hired extra pickers to bring in more berries that would be sold to the festival committee for the weekend. They picked both mornings and afternoons now. Most of the pickers were in the south field, farthest away from the house, and some were in the field across the road. Finn was deep in the south field with a wagon that he carted around to fill with the picked quarts. She waved to him when she saw him take notice of her arrival in the field. She couldn't see his expression when he saw the exercise bike, and she was glad, not knowing how he'd respond to her interference.

After only a few minutes, she heard the telltale sound of the screen door opening from the house behind her and the squeak-squeak of wheels as Annie made her way down the ramp and across the paved walk to the edge of the fields.

Lizzie got up and made her way to Annie, careful not to meet her eyes. She went around her and started to push the chair through the rougher terrain until they arrived at Lizzie's stool, conveniently placed next to the exercise bike. She stood behind the wheelchair, waiting for Annie to make up her mind.

"Those people picking in the field…they'll laugh at me," she whispered.

Lizzie's heart lurched. "No they won't. First of all, they better be busy working or your father's going to get all over them. And even if they do notice, they'll think, 'boy, that girl is going to have the best toned thighs in the whole Copper Country'."

She couldn't see Annie's reaction to that, but heard a soft exhale, possibly from a small laugh.

"Why can't I do it inside? Gran's there to watch me."

"Your gran has other things she needs to get done. This way you can get some sun as well." She hesitated, then added, "Besides, I'd like the company." She was surprised to realize that she spoke the truth.

She didn't waste any time, in case Annie chickened out. She motioned to Stevie a few rows over, who had been watching the entire exchange. As soon as he saw her beckon him, he speedily made his way over to them, as if he'd been on call.

She liked that kid more every day.

She also saw Finn notice Stevie's movement, then look to see Annie out in the fields. He dropped the handle to the wagon and started making his way in, but stopped when he saw Lizzie hold up a hand to stop him.

She knew it took every ounce of willpower Finn had to turn around and go back to the wagon and continue on. She knew his eyes would be on the three of them the entire time, but that was fine.

"Stevie, would you help me lift Annie on to the bike, please? And maybe you could pick in the first row with us for a while?" Lizzie didn't need to add that she'd feel better with another pair of hands and eyes near Annie while she was on the bike.

"Sure," he said, then started to release the footrests on Annie's chair. "Think you're going to give Lance Armstrong a run for his money, huh, brat?"

"Who?" Annie asked.

Stevie let out the exasperated sigh that only a wiser, much put-upon older brother can master. "Never mind. Okay, Lizzie, you take her left side."

Annie herself, thin as she was, was light as a feather. The cumbersome brace was another story, but she and Stevie managed to place her on the bike seat with minimal effort.

Lizzie'd told her father what she intended the bike for, and her father, being an engineering professor, spent a few hours last night widening the seat and cushioning it for better balance. He also added cups at the end of each petal, so Annie's feet wouldn't slide off. He must have found Lizzie's first bike—which was surely in the garage somewhere, as her father never threw anything out that had working parts of any sort—and put the bike's basket, horn, bell, and handlebar streamers on the exercise bike.

Lizzie thought of Finn and her own father. What daddies did for their little girls, never mind if their babies were ten or thirty-five. Her father hadn't pried or asked too many questions when she'd said what she'd needed, and yet he'd outdone himself.

"Are you comfortable?" Lizzie asked once Stevie had placed Annie's feet on the pedals and eased the cups over them.

Annie ran her little fingers over the circular bell on the handlebars, next to the grips. "What's this?"

Lizzie's heart squeezed when she realized that the kid didn't even know what a bike bell looked like. God, she'd missed out on so much. "It's a bell, you ring it to make people get out of your way."

The girl rang the bell loudly then stilled when she saw all the heads perk up in the fields and look around. Lizzie was afraid Annie would turn tail, but she began to turn her legs instead. She pedaled, tentative at first, then picked up speed. Lizzie'd had her father rig the setting of the bike to the lowest resistance. When Annie started pumping like she had indeed entered the Tour de France, Lizzie gently placed her hand on the girl's shoulder.

"Slower. Your legs will get better exercise if you go slower, but longer." She waited for the smart-ass comeback that was sure to follow. Instead, Annie slowed down her pace, and nodded her head in understanding.

Lizzie sat on her stool and resumed picking berries. After a while she shed her shirt to the tank top she wore underneath. Noticing that Annie was wearing long sleeves and jeans, she asked, "Annie, would you like me to take you in to change into shorts and a tank top so you wouldn't be so hot?"

"I don't have any shorts or tank tops. I only have the swimsuit that my dad bought me the day we went to Alison's."

She thought back and realized that she had, indeed, only seen

Annie in pants, even the day they drove back from Ann Arbor. She'd had her swimsuit on, but jeans and a long-sleeve top over it. Was it because Annie was self-conscious about her legs? Every ten-year old girl's legs were spindly and gangly, so how much worse could Annie's be? Maybe the brace was more pronounced under a tee shirt or tank top? Or was the reason she didn't have a more extensive wardrobe a lack of funds? To ask either question would embarrass Annie or Finn, so she said nothing, but made a note in her tablet to stop by Walmart and pick up a couple of pairs of shorts, some tee-shirts, and tank tops.

"Why are you always writing in those notebooks?" Annie asked.

She looked up at her. "Huh?"

Annie tentatively took one hand off a handlebar and pointed to Lizzie's ever-present tablet. She quickly put her hand back on the handle and resumed pedaling.

"They help me remember stuff," she answered.

"It doesn't seem like you forget much," Annie said.

That was true. Lizzie didn't really need her tablets to remember things. She had a steel-trap memory and went over plans and lists in her head nightly before going to sleep and in the shower in the morning.

Always a bit of a list maker, she knew exactly when she'd taken her planning to this extreme level. It had been when she began to lose weight. She'd started journaling everything she ate. A humiliating experience. But eye-opening. The lists had then morphed into eating plans. And then she'd found herself writing down everything.

The notebooks, tablets, lists, all became a security blanket for her. A benchmark of her weight loss. An emblem of success. And a safety net against backslides.

She couldn't explain any of that to Annie. She could barely explain it to herself. She just knew that the lists were a crutch she couldn't walk without. Yet.

She just shrugged, and that seemed to be answer enough for

the little girl.

They spent the better part of an hour like that. Lizzie picking, taking the occasional call on her cell phone. Stevie hovering nearby in case he was needed. And Annie pedaling. Lizzie was astounded at the girl's endurance, and wondered if she should put a stop to it before Annie overdid it.

Clea brought out fresh lemonade at one point and it provided Annie with a much-needed rest, but she refused to get off the bike, even for just the time it took to drink her glass of lemonade. Lizzie also decided to pick up a sports water bottle when she was at the store, one that would fit in the basket of the bike, so Annie could have fluids throughout her trek.

Clea, knowing Annie so well, did not fawn over the child's accomplishment, but gave a quick, "Looking good, Annie." She did, however, make deep eye contact with Lizzie and reach out to squeeze her arm before she returned to the house.

Soon, it was time for the pickers to take their lunch break, which was usually a couple of hours, most of them going to the beach with bags of McDonald's, taking a cooling swim, then returning for the afternoon pick. They were paid by the amount of berries picked, not by the hour, so they often took the hotter afternoons off then returned to pick in the early evening.

As they passed Annie and Lizzie, most of them said hello and gave words of encouragement to Annie. Lizzie could see the sense of pride in the girl's eyes. She had to be dog tired, and yet her pace seemed to pick up as the workers walked by. Her back rigid due to the brace, her head held high, her white-blond hair damp along her face from her exertion and the heat of the sun. The hinting pink of sunburn across her nose made Lizzie realize it was time to go inside.

Finn made his way in behind the workers and Lizzie got up and brushed herself off. "Time to stop, Annie, I need to go inside for a while. Besides, if you're going to be outside again this afternoon, we need to get some sunscreen on your face."

The idea of being outside long enough to actually burn was

obviously new to Annie. Lizzie could see the girl warring with herself internally. She didn't want to leave the bike, but she had to be exhausted, hungry, and in need of a potty break. Lizzie sure was. She tried to make it easier on Annie.

"I'll have Stevie put the bike in the barn, and we can do it again tomorrow morning, okay?"

That seemed to please her and Annie nodded. Finn was nearing them and began helping Lizzie disengage Annie from the bike. "My, my, my…my own little Lance Armstrong," he said.

"Just who the hell is Lance Armstrong?" Annie said.

Lizzie couldn't help but laugh as Finn chided Annie for her language, much like Katie constantly chided Alison. He lifted her and put her in her chair as Lizzie knelt to put Annie's feet in the stirrups and disengage the break. She looked up past Annie's glowing face to Finn's and her heart stopped at his expression. It beamed with affection. And this time it wasn't directed at Annie, but at her.

He mouthed a silent "thank you" and turned his attention to his daughter.

—⁓—

"No wonder you went into PR, Lizard, you always did plan the best parties. I'm starting to think that's all you do for a living."

Lizzie raised her head from her tablet that contained her notes and numerous lists for the fundraiser and accepted the glass of lemonade that Alison brought to her at the picnic table. She stuck her pen behind her ear, and took a long swallow of the sweet, icy-cold drink. "Mmm, thanks, Al, that hits the spot."

Finally registering what Alison had said as she'd approached, Lizzie answered, "This is definitely the upside to my business, that's for sure. You know how I love to plan things."

Alison chuckled. "Yeah, right down to the time line for having introductory sex with a man you haven't seen in years."

She took the ribbing good naturedly. "Anything worth doing is worth planning out several times over."

"Heaven forbid you ever do anything spontaneously."

"I do lots of things spontaneously. See." She flipped through her day planner and pointed to an imaginary entry. "I have spontaneity planned for next Friday from two till five."

They were at Alison's, catching up because Lizzie hadn't seen much of them in the two weeks since she'd been back from Ann Arbor. Katie joined them, bringing chips and salsa with her from the camp and plunking it down in front of the three of them. Lizzie only briefly looked at the snack, then resumed writing a note to herself about confirming the menu of the banquet with the caterer.

She grabbed her cell to make a call, but Katie placed her hand on hers and gently tugged the phone away. "Slow down. This can all wait a couple of hours. Talk to us, tell us what's been happening."

Katie was right, this stuff could wait. Or better yet, she could call Sybil later and have someone at the office handle it for her. She was getting better and better at delegating.

She caught Alison and Katie up on the time she'd spent at the farm. About Annie now riding daily on the exercise bike. She didn't tell the last part of the story to Katie and Alison as they sat on the dock, dangling their feet in the water. The part about the look in Finn's eyes as he'd thanked her. It'd be just like them to make a mountain out of a molehill.

Besides, there was no way Finn could love—or almost love—her. He had always seen her as a conquest, nothing more. She supposed that this fundraiser would cloud things for him. His pride was an animal all its own and he probably struggled with everything that was being done for him. For Annie, she corrected herself.

"So that's how you've been spending your days—playing trainer and getting your manicure totally ruined by picking strawberries—but how about the nights?" Katie asked, her voice sing-songy at the end.

"Have you fucked Finn yet?" Alison asked, getting right to it.

Katie bristled, as she always did at blunt language. "Al!"

Lizzie laughed at her girls. She knew Katie wanted to know the same thing, she just asked in a much more roundabout way. "No, not yet, and I'll tell you it had better happen soon, or I'm going to have to totally reconfigure my timetable." She threw that in for Alison's earlier lack of spontaneity comment.

Katie and Alison looked at each other and Lizzie waited to see which one would be the spokesperson. Obviously they had something they wanted to say.

It ended up being Katie. "I'll ask again. Are you sure about this plan? You're spending time with his kids, more time with Finn than you thought you would. That wasn't part of the plan."

"I appreciate your concern. But it isn't necessary. Look, I've spent the last three years really examining my life..." she started to explain.

"You've spent the last three years working really hard to become half the size you were, and beautiful, just beautiful," Katie emphasized, with just a hint of misting in her eyes as she took Lizzie's hand and squeezed.

Lizzie could take a compliment from Alison and Katie, because they were always her friends, in thin, thick, really thick, and then thin again. She was not nearly so accepting of compliments or encouragement from other people. Her staff knew not to even mention her diminishing size, because she'd brush them off with some self-effacing piece of humor, then be pensive the rest of the day.

"Thanks, Katie," she acknowledged, returning her friend's hand squeeze. She fingered the pages of her notebook; a talisman giving her strength to continue. "But during those three years, I had all that time on my hands that I used to eat with, so I did a lot of thinking," Lizzie joked. She joked about her weight gain and subsequent loss, but only she knew what she had gone through to not reach for a bag of Oreos after a stressful day.

Instead, she'd turned her focus onto herself. "The thought I kept coming back to is when and why I started putting on weight, it was a tree through the forest kind of thing for me, but I think I've got it semi-figured out. I started putting on weight our senior year in college, then it took off fast, so fast I didn't even realize it at first. Sure your clothes don't fit and you can feel the changes in your body, but you kind of stop paying attention to your body. The style was leggings and long sweaters then, remember? Those sweaters hid a lot of sins for a while."

Both Alison and Katie nodded, but remained silent. They weren't about to interrupt this stream of consciousness from Liz, she so seldom *really* opened up about herself. She was the keeper of other people's secrets—her own as well.

They had been there when she began putting on weight and Lizzie knew they felt helpless as they watched. What could they do? They'd mentioned it, at first in a teasing way, then in a we're-here-because-we-love-you-and-this-is-an-intervention kind of way, but to no avail.

"So, anyway, I've realized that my eating got out of control not too long after I'd become sexually active, which could be Freudian enough, but now I think that was a red herring, and the true trigger was not becoming sexually active but why I did it then, after waiting all those years, being pretty much the oldest virgin any of us knew. I mean, my God, Sparty's helmet was only a few months away from dropping!"

The women all laughed. Sparty was a statue on the campus at Michigan State of a Spartan warrior. Lizzie always felt he had been modeled after Michelangelo's David; strong, gorgeous, very virile. He held his shield in one hand and his helmet in the other. The legend went that if a virgin ever graduated from Michigan State, Sparty would drop his helmet. Lizzie had been close—she was midway through fall term of their senior year when Sparty sighed with relief that he'd hang on to his headgear a while longer.

"So, why *then*? It certainly wasn't because you had found true love," Alison asked. The guy Lizzie had finally relented with, Matt, was a guy from Hancock, someone Lizzie had known for-ever and was also going to State. They had been at a party, chatted all night like the old pals they were, gotten drunk, and went home together. Matt was shocked when he realized Lizzie was still a virgin, and tried to put the kibosh to the whole dealings, but a drunken Lizzie was adamant that tonight was the night.

They hadn't gotten together after that, neither of them had expected to. She then had two more encounters like that in the next five months. All had been friends she had grown up with, or had know her three plus years at State, trusted completely, thought of as brothers, and slept with one time. She felt nothing, either emotionally or physically, during any of it.

The first time with Matt she'd been pretty drunk. Drunk enough, she rationalized, that she had numbed out in her body, not feeling any sensations at all. The second time, she had drunk less, but was still numb. She tried again cold sober, but came away with the same feeling of inadequacy in her sexuality. She hadn't climaxed in any of the couplings, or if she had, didn't realize it, which in Lizzie's opinion may have been worse.

After the five month-long debacle she and to her two pals had dubbed "Bad Romancing in East Lansing", Lizzie subconsciously swore off sex and instead concentrated on the upcoming graduation and entering the real world. She thought of her future, what she would like to be doing, and where she would like to ideally live, but mostly, she thought about food.

"I think it was 'then' because a month earlier my mother had sent me a batch of clippings."

"So? Your mother sent clippings all the time, what was in this batch?" Katie questioned.

Lizzie's mother, Doris, had sent a thick envelope every month or so, filled with clippings from their local paper. There were engagement announcements, wedding photos, drunk driving arrest bulletins, scores from football games, reviews of movies that Doris thought the girls would like. Each clipping had a hand-written note with Doris's convoluted reasoning as to why that particular clipping was included. "Wasn't she in your class, or was it her sister?" would accompany a birth announcement. "This sounds like something you could do when you get out" scribbled around a job posting that inevitably would be something Lizzie either had no interest in whatsoever or was not remotely qualified for.

Alison and Katie teased her mercilessly whenever an envelope arrived, but were always found going through the clippings after she'd read and discarded them.

The clippings were never too exciting, but always seemed to come at a time when Lizzie would be homesick, or missing her parents, or feeling small and insignificant amidst her 40,000 fellow students, and the sight of the bulging envelope would brighten her day.

Along with online links to the *Ingot*, and near daily emails, Doris was still sending envelopes to Lizzie in Detroit, and she still got a smile on her face when she would receive them. Though now she recognized more names in the divorce announcements than the wedding column. And the birth announcements for her classmates were for their fourth or fifth child.

"This particular clipping was a wedding announcement for Finn Robbins," Lizzie quietly said. There was silence while Alison and Katie exchanged confused glances.

"I don't get it, are we supposed to yell 'eureka!' and everything becomes crystal clear? Twelve years of using Krispy Kreme as a significant other and three years of turning that around, and it's all because you saw a clipping of Finn Robbins's wedding announcement? I don't buy it," Alison said.

Alison wasn't dubbed "the smart one" for nothing.

"And maybe there's nothing to buy," Lizzie conceded. "Maybe it's all just coincidences, and I'm trying to psycho babble my way into one giant rationalization…maybe it just boils down to being really, really hungry for twelve years," she joked with a small smile. *That's right, always keep 'em smiling. Make them like me.*

"Okay, let's for the sake of argument say that his wedding announcement triggered your virginity loss, and *that* disappointment triggered the emotional eating, the eating spirals out of control for twelve years while you concentrate solely on the professional side of your life, becoming a mover and a shaker in your field and then one day, three years ago, you meet this Davis Cummings, have your epiphany and start to lose the weight. Have I got it?"

Lizzie nodded and watched as Alison ruminated on this.

"I don't know, Lizard. This plan of yours could so blow up in your face. Having sex with no emotional connection is what caused you to turn to food for solace in the first place. Do you think it's going to be so different if you have sex with Finn now?"

Lizzie didn't answer right away. She finally shrugged her shoulders. "I think it will be different, because I know what I'm doing now. I know my reasons for being with Finn. And it's not totally unemotional, I've always cared for Finn. I just know there's no future there."

Katie started to make a comment, but Lizzie, tiring of the analysis, quickly changed the subject. "Oh, I forgot, I'm naming the two of you as board members for the Hannah Robbins Foundation."

Katie and Alison exchanged glances then blankly looked back to her.

"Don't worry, you don't have to do anything, I just want to have a six-person board, it looks better. Finn didn't have anything set up in the way of a foundation or special status or anything for the money for Annie's operation. I set up the Hannah Robbins Foundation that all proceeds from this and any other fundraiser will go to. As long as there's a board of directors, the money is all accounted for, and about a ton of other legalities, the money won't be any tax burden to Finn."

"Who are the other board members?" Katie asked. She laid her lean body back along her towel spread out on the dock.

Lizzie looked at Katie's body with admiration, but didn't feel the familiar twinge of envy.

"Finn, me, you two, Margo at the bank, and Petey."

"Petey on a board of directors?" Alison laughed.

"Yep. I figured having a celebrity on it would make it look more legit. Not that there's anything not legitimate about the whole thing."

"The board just happens to be stacked with your friends, that's all."

"Exactly. Our first and probably only board meeting will be held near the keg during the Strawberry Festival Dance. Please plan on attending," she said, in her best call-to-order business voice.

"Oh, I wouldn't miss that for anything," Alison said, as Katie nodded in agreement.

—⚏—

When she got home that evening, she was surprised to find her mother packing. Lizzie sprawled across her parents' bed and watched as her mother pulled things out of closets and dresser drawers and threw them on the bed. When she noticed Lizzie, she seemed startled. "Oh. Lizzie, I didn't hear you come in. We got the call about Zeke. The carrier is due in seven days, the squadron into Jacksonville in four. Your father and I have decided to drive to Florida instead of fly. We'll spend a week or two with Zeke, then take a leisurely drive back. I've always wanted to see the Smoky Mountains, and your father's going to take his golf clubs."

"That sounds great, Mom. I'm just sorry I can't join you, but with the fundraiser and all…"

A concerned look came over Doris Hampton's soft face and she sat on the bed next to Lizzie. "Dear, are you sure this is such a good idea? You spending so much time with Finn Robbins?"

Lizzie was surprised. "I thought you liked Finn, Mom?"

"Oh I do, I do, or…I did," she took a deep breath and let it out. "Until he hurt you so badly."

Her mother remembered Finn more than Katie and Alison had. That's because she'd heard Lizzie crying in her room every night for a week after Finn had broken up with her. She'd seen Lizzie struggle with the heartache that she'd hidden from her two best friends. Doris was a mom, and moms knew everything and forgot nothing.

Memories flooded over Lizzie, but she quickly set them aside. "That was a long time ago, Mom."

"I know dear, but you know what they say…you never really get over your first love."

Lizzie picked her head up from where it had been resting on her forearms. "Finn wasn't my first love, we only dated a few months."

Doris reached out and smoothed Lizzie's hair back, just like she'd done as a child. "He wasn't? Then who was your first love, Elizabeth?" Her voice was as soothing as her touch and Lizzie realized that her mother wasn't asking a question, but making a point.

"He wasn't, Mom." But she could not give any other name to Doris to prove her mother wrong.

"Anyway, we'll be leaving in the morning. Water the plants on Tuesdays and Saturdays. Remember the trash goes out on Thursdays. I think we'll be back in time for your fundraiser, but if not, good luck with it. If you're still planning on leaving right after it, maybe we'll stop in Detroit on the way home if we're still on the road."

Lizzie's father poked his head into the bedroom just then and, seeing his wife giving instructions to Lizzie, offered up the only set of rules he had been giving to Lizzie and Zeke since his and Doris's first overnight trip when the twins were sixteen. "Remember the house rules, Elizabeth. No dope, no dopes."

Lizzie laughed a "yes, Dad" as her father retreated from the room. Her feelings for her parents were as warm and cuddly as the worn quilt she was laying on. "Mom, about Finn…"

Her mother rose from the bed and returned to the dresser to gather socks from a drawer, keeping her back to Lizzie. "Just be careful, dear. I think you were in love with him once. I'd hate to see you fall in love with him again, if it would turn out the same way."

She left the room and a stunned Lizzie behind her.

Was her mother right? Had Lizzie been in love with Finn

all those years ago? She had thought it was just hormones or teen angst and pride that had her crying for a week. She hadn't planned on falling in love until her twenties.

She couldn't think about this, not now. Not when she was so close to achieving her goal and getting back to her life. She tried to picture her office, her condo, even the face of Davis Cummings, and was not entirely surprised when no vision of them became clear. Instead, she saw a ten-year-old girl pumping the pedals of a bike for all she was worth, and the girl's father looking at Lizzie with fathomless blue eyes.

Thirteen

—๛—

√ Get folding chair, sunscreen, stuff for kids
√ Talk to Petey about Annie Aid
√ Call Sybil

THE WEATHER FOR the Strawberry Festival could not have co-operated more. A beautiful mid-July Saturday shone bright over the Copper Country and the tiny town of Chassell, host to the annual festival.

The day before, two trucks had come to the farm to pick up as many berries as Finn's pickers could deliver. The crop had been plentiful and everyone agreed that this year's berries were the sweetest anyone could remember.

Lizzie sat in a folding chair, the kind that came in a pouch that slung over your shoulder, with Annie in her wheelchair beside her. On the other side of Annie was Finn's empty seat. Lizzie couldn't believe that she was actually in a "soccer mom" chair. The thought seemed incomprehensible, and yet the reality was very… comfortable. They had arrived at the parade early, to get a good position for Annie's chair. It paid off, because they had prime real estate for all the festivities while those who were arriving now were relegated to the back of the four-person-deep crowd along the main drag of Chassell.

Finn was off somewhere seeing to what would be the last

piece of berry business he would have to conduct for the day. Stevie was across the street and down a little ways from Lizzie, but she could see him and his buddies as they elbow jabbed each other with guffaws and chuckles. She noticed Stevie didn't share in his buddies' merriment. She followed his gaze and came to rest upon three girls that looked to be about Stevie's age, but were dressed, and trying to act, much older.

Stevie's eyes never left the girl standing in the middle of the three. She was the tallest and, even at that age, Lizzie could tell the girl would be a beauty. She had on a spaghetti-strapped purple tank top that didn't quite cover her belly button, denim shorts, and flip-flops. Her blond hair was caught back in a tie-dye bandana. *Oh no, Stevie, don't fall for the pretty one, she'll break your heart.*

The girls seemed oblivious to the boys, but Lizzie had seen that act before. Had practiced it to perfection over the years with Katie and Alison. She bet that one of them would let out a fake yawn soon to project a "this is kid stuff, aren't we above it all" vibe for all to see.

As if on cue, the middle girl arched her neck back and put her hand to her mouth to stifle a yawn. Hah! The fake yawn never went out of style! A hair flip would surely have been in order if the girl hadn't been wearing a bandana.

Lizzie took comfort in witnessing the adolescent mating ritual. It wasn't much different from the games adults played.

The parade went on for over an hour. Every area high school band came through, along with all local elected officials. Finn and she were kept busy gathering up the thrown candy for Annie, who squealed with delight as they dumped new contributions into the increasing pile on her lap.

The queen candidates came by, each one in a separate convertible with the candidate's sponsor's banner on the side of the car. Finally, Lizzie and Annie found some common ground. They did what women through time did in order to bond—trashed other women.

"Do you think she looked in the mirror at that hair before she left this morning?" Annie would say.

"No. If this one's dress is any indication, there were no mirrors to be had in all of Chassell today," Lizzie would counter, and the two would giggle. Finn shot the two females a stunned look, but kept his mouth shut.

In a backward turn, which seemed fitting in the U.P., the grand marshal came last and Lizzie laughed when she saw Petey hamming it up in the back seat of a red convertible. He had to have just gotten into town, she hadn't even seen him yet. He was wearing his Red Wings jersey and holding a hockey stick like a scepter. Last year's queen was with him and Lizzie, noticing Petey's gaze on the young beauty, made herself a mental note to remind Petey that the girl was barely over eighteen.

After the parade, the streets were filled with tables and booths offering strawberry shortcake, shakes, pies, anything you could imagine. Having had their fill of berries, the Robbins contingency decided to head for home to let Annie rest and to get cleaned up before the queen ceremony and dance later that evening.

It wasn't hard to track Stevie down in the crowd. Lizzie found the girl in the purple tank fairly easily then scanned a twenty-yard radius looking for the boy. Sure enough, there he was, skulking behind a shortcake booth, eyes huge as he watched the purple tank girl enjoying a strawberry ice cream cone. Not wanting to embarrass the kid, she told Finn she'd round Stevie up then meet him and Annie back at the minivan.

She surreptitiously circled the booth until she came up behind Stevie. In her best secret-agent voice, while pretending she didn't see him, she whispered, "Psst, the eagle takes flight in five minutes. I repeat, the eagle takes flight in five minutes."

She saw Stevie's body grow rigid, then relax. "Roger that," he said under his breath.

She walked toward the minivan certain he'd be close behind. No way would he risk his father coming back to get him.

When they pulled up to the farm, Lizzie headed to the back

of her car, which she'd left there earlier, while Finn unloaded Annie's chair, then Annie. She grabbed three shopping bags from her car and followed them inside. She didn't acknowledge Finn's narrow-eyed glare at the bags as she walked past him into the kitchen.

Finn's grandmother had seen them pull up and made her way over from the trailer. "I have some fresh lemonade made if you'd like," she said, and went to the refrigerator and got an old-fashioned glass pitcher out while Lizzie automatically began pulling glasses out of the cupboard.

"That would be great, Clea, thanks. We're all probably parched from the sun, but the parade was great." Annie showed her candy payday to her grandmother, confirming Lizzie's review of the parade. Lizzie handed the beverages out to everyone as Clea poured. "Stevie, this is a pre-thank you gift for all the help you've been to me with planning the fundraiser. Having your friends volunteer for the golf outing will be a big load off. I'm giving it to you now, because I thought you might like to wear it to the dance tonight." She handed one of the bags to Stevie and set the other two on Annie's lap. "And this is for you Annie, for all the hard training you've been doing on the bike all week, and for agreeing to go up on the stage tonight when we announce the fundraiser."

That had been a hard-fought battle involving shrieks, tears and tantrums, not all of which had come from Annie. But Lizzie was adamant that the little girl show her angelic face when the fundraiser plans were announced. "Put a face to the cause, Finn, it's important. When the community sees her as one of their own, they'll be more likely to contribute," she'd said.

Finn had hated the thought, of course. It bordered on exploiting Annie to him, but Lizzie had cajoled, reasoned, and even begged and had eventually made him see the light.

The kids tore open the bags and Lizzie nearly swallowed a lemon seed when she saw the look of pure joy that crossed their faces. They held up the new, ultra-cool clothes that Lizzie had agonized over in the store. Annie got not only a new dress, but also matching hair accessories and sandals. She'd even found some tween lip-gloss and body glitter to go with the ensemble.

Stevie started to try on his new Red Wings jersey and khaki shorts right there in the kitchen, but Clea drew the line. "Not while you are so filthy, young man. Showers for the both of you before new clothing gets on those bodies."

It may have been the first time ever that kids raced each other to see who could claim dibs to the bathroom first. Annie pushed her wheels fast so she could block Stevie's entrance to the bathroom.

Lizzie realized she was just as sticky and filthy as the children, and got up to make her exit. "I need to get going, get cleaned up myself. I'll meet you at the rec center at seven?" She turned to Finn to confirm the time and was stopped cold by his hard stare.

"What the hell was that, Liz?" he asked, his voice bitter and accusing.

She knew what he meant, of course, had steeled herself for it. "Look, I know what you're going to say, but really Finn, Stevie has been helping me a ton getting volunteers lined up. And, frankly, we need Annie to look perfect tonight. It wasn't a bribe, or out of charity, Finn. Just a gift, that's all."

His face softened ever so slightly. "Don't try to buy my kids, Liz, it would be too easy because I can't give them much."

"Good God, do you think that's what I'm doing?" She started to laugh. "I'm not trying to buy your kids. Jeez, I don't even want to *rent* them. Trust me, it was a one-time thing, okay?"

He let out a breath and gave a curt nod, then got a teasing look in his eye. "Well then, what did you buy me to wear?"

Lizzie chuckled, raising her hands in a fending-off manner. "Oh no, I learned my lesson the time I bought you that shirt when we were dating. You wear whatever floats your boat, mister, I'm not getting involved."

It had been a valuable lesson for her to learn so young. Never buy a prideful man something he couldn't afford himself. She'd given Finn an expensive shirt that she thought would go great with his blue eyes and that she'd spent hours picking out. They were supposed to triple date the next week with Alison and Katie and their boyfriends and she thought that he could wear it then. He proceeded to read her the riot act about if he wasn't good enough for her as he was she should find someone else, who did she think she was anyway, miss high and mighty deigning to go out with a mere pauper, yada yada yada.

She never bought him another gift.

It was also the reason she hadn't pushed harder when he'd refused her offer to loan Finn money. She knew he would never accept money from her. She knew it was hard enough for him to swallow his pride and accept her help with the fundraiser.

"Well, thanks for the stuff for the kids. You didn't have to do it, though."

"I know."

Clea, who had remained silent throughout the exchange, now threw in her two cents. "I think it was a nice gesture, Elizabeth, and if nothing else, it got the kids to the bathtub without a major fight, so for that alone, thank you."

Lizzie smiled back at Clea. The older woman stood and placed the empty glasses in the sink. She had her back to Lizzie and Finn as she said, "You know, I don't think I'll be staying at the dance all that long tonight. I think after a while I'll bring the kids home with me. I think I'll even sleep in here tonight instead of the trailer."

Finn and Lizzie looked across the table at each other, knowing full well what Clea was saying. He didn't need to come home tonight. And Lizzie's parents had left for Florida.

They both leaped up from the table at the same time, Lizzie saying she really needed to get going, Finn murmuring something about checking on the fields before he showered. Both eager to get the afternoon out of the way and get on with the night.

—⚋—

Liz was waiting for them in the parking lot of the rec center. He pulled the van in next to her SUV and realized she held a brush and rubber band in hand, presumably waiting to see what

kind of havoc Finn had done on Annie's hair. Good thing, be-
cause he knew it wasn't pretty. Once Finn had Annie in her chair,
Liz sat down on the running board of the minivan and wheeled
Annie's chair in front of her and began from scratch.

"Daddy tries, but he doesn't know much about doing girls'
hair," Annie said.

Liz tore down the lopsided mess and brushed out the silky
white strands. "Well, I don't know much about girls' hair either,
but I can do a mean French braid. Actually, that's the only thing
I can do."

While Liz did Annie's hair, Gran and Stevie pulled up in the
Jeep. They'd decided to take two cars so Gran could take the kids
home earlier and Finn could take the Jeep to Liz's parents' place.
Gran and Stevie went into the rec center to get a table.

Finn leaned on Liz's Navigator, watching the two females
talk about the dress that Annie was wearing. How it brought out
the blue in her eyes, how it covered her brace, but still showed her
arms, which were now lightly tanned due to the tank tops Liz had
bought for Annie to wear while outside on the exercise bike.

Finn was more interested in Liz's dress than Annie's. Oh,
he thought his daughter looked like an angel in her new dress,
and had actually choked up when Clea had wheeled her out after
helping her change because Annie'd wanted to surprise him. But
he'd absorbed Annie's appearance on the drive to the Hancock
rec center. He was still trying to pull himself together from the
impact of Liz.

It was a black linen dress—shift, he thought they were
called—and was simple and elegant, just like Liz herself. Her tan,
now deep and dark, was highlighted by the black. The dress came
to just above her knees and her long legs were bare. She had on
black sandals with just enough heel to put her right at kissing level. She wore her hair up in some kind of twist that Finn thought
would come out easily enough later and allow him to sift his fingers through the glorious mass. A brush of mascara and a little
lip-gloss was all the make-up she wore. She didn't need anything

else. Tiny pearl earrings, a gold chain with a pearl pendant, and a pearl bracelet that hung down a little onto the back of her hand. Classy as hell, he thought.

Sexy as hell, he had always thought.

He almost wished she'd forgotten about that long-ago incident and bought him something to wear tonight after all. He didn't look too bad, though, he figured. New khakis that he'd bought to meet with the financial people at the hospital and his most presentable shirt, a white cotton button-down oxford. Hell, he figured he almost looked like the type of guy she normally dated. Except this outfit was not him at all. It stuck out in his denim and western shirt laden closet like a sore thumb. Which was kind of like them. He probably stuck out in her array of men like a sore thumb.

Too bad. Tonight she'd be crying out his name, not some Poindexter Howell III's.

She finished with Annie's hair and rose, closed the minivan door, and turned to Finn. "All ready?"

His eyes met hers and he relayed the hunger for her that he felt. "You have no idea how ready I am, E-liz-a-beth." He took her hand as he pushed the wheelchair with his other and was pleased to feel the shudder of excitement that went through her body when they touched.

She seemed to need to distract herself. Finn guessed he needed to also if he was going to wait till after the dance and not resort to nailing Liz in the restroom of the rec center. "Annie, are you all set? You look great," Liz asked his daughter.

Annie took in a big breath and released it, and nodded her head. Finn knew she was nervous about this. For a few minutes, when they announced the fundraiser, Annie would be the center of attention, a thought that no doubt terrified her. The level of her anxiety was made obvious when she gulped, then looked up at Liz and Finn, big blue eyes fearful, and asked, "They won't laugh at me, will they?"

He heard Liz's gasp but was proud of how quickly she recovered. "Why would they laugh? Because you're in a wheelchair? Big deal. If anything, girls will be so envious over how good you look they'll be ripping you to shreds over your great hair and cool dress and awesome tan, they won't even realize you're in a wheelchair."

It was the most fucked-up logic Finn had ever heard, but it did the trick. Annie got a huge smile on her face and turned forward, apparently more than willing to be the object of scorn if it was envy-based.

Women. Go figure.

He squeezed Liz's hand in silent thanks. "Speaking of envy over how good people look, you're going to be a target yourself tonight, Liz. You look beautiful." He was rewarded with an eye roll from Liz.

Damn, the woman had no idea how good she looked. Had some man done a number on her and made her question her desirability? Finn wished he could get his hands on that man—if there was one—and squeeze the life out of him for ever making Liz doubt herself.

A cold sensation passed through him and he prayed that it hadn't been him.

They weren't in the door more than a few seconds when Finn heard a female shriek and saw a blur of flowered dress heading toward them. "Lizzie Hampton? Oh my God, is that really you? I haven't seen you in four or five years. You look unbelievable! My God, I can't believe it's really you. I almost didn't know you."

Before Finn could discern what was going on, Liz told him to take Annie and find Stevie and Clea. She needed to do a few things, see a few people, then she'd meet up with them. Then she dropped Finn's hand and made her way to the woman who was bearing down on them and still going on about how great Liz looked.

Strange. He agreed that Liz looked spectacular tonight, but was surprised at the intensity from the woman.

The dance was being held at the rec center on the concrete that normally held the city ice arena. In the summer the ice was

melted, the boards taken down, and community dances and wedding receptions were held. Faint traces of paint remained on the
concrete floor, denoting the blue lines, face-off circles, and the red
centerline. It was an open room with a stage and dancefloor at the
center, two bars, one on each side of the room, a concession and
pop stand, and eighty or so circular tables set on every remaining
space of floor. It was typically the most attended gathering of the
year in the Copper Country, though Liz had boasted that her
fundraiser dance and auction would top it.

He had never been to this event. As a berry grower, he should
have, but he had never been much of a socializer and Annie had
always been adamant that she didn't want to go to so public an
event, so he used her as an excuse not to attend himself. Gran had
gone most years, representing the Robbins farm, and Stevie went
last year, but this was Finn's first time.

The same feelings he always got at these kinds of things overcame him. Like any minute someone would come up and ask him
to quietly leave, that he did not belong here. It was a community
dance, for Christ's sake, and he was part of the community, but
he had deep-rooted feelings of inadequacy that he wasn't sure he'd
ever lose.

He watched as Liz circled the room like the pro she was.
Hugs from everyone she knew, even from those who she was obviously being introduced to for the first time. More than one person
held her arms out from her, taking her all in, as Finn had done the
first night he'd seen her at the Mine Shaft.

My God, did the whole town share his feelings of lust for
Liz? He wouldn't be surprised, but he couldn't help but feel there
was something else happening with all the people gushing over
Liz. He'd have to remember to ask her about it later.

Thinking about what he wanted to do with Liz when they
were finally alone, he conceded that those questions could wait
until *much* later.

She was checking in with Madge Goodson, the one running the show tonight. She stopped and chatted briefly with each

of the queen candidates as they gathered around the stage, the crowning about to begin.

Finn saw her face break into a huge smile and followed her line of vision to Pete Ryan; the hockey star who was a friend and client of Liz's. He saw the moment Ryan saw Liz and the wolfish smile that crossed the athlete's face made Finn tense with jealousy.

Whoa, boy. She's only yours on loan. She doesn't belong to you, don't go all caveman on her and scare her away before you get what you want.

Still, his fists were clenched and only eased as he saw Liz, instead of stepping into Ryan's outstretched arms, punch him—playfully but hard—on his bulging biceps. She grabbed his jersey as he pulled away from her, rubbing his sore arm, and yanked him down to her so she could whisper something into his ear. Ryan's eyes went to the girl about ten yards away from him, the girl Finn recognized as last year's queen. He nodded at Liz, then put his hands up in a surrendering motion to her as she laughed.

That was about right; what man didn't surrender to Liz in some fashion? Lord knows way back when, he would have done anything to please her. *Anything but gracefully accept a shirt she had especially picked out for you.* Yeah, so he'd been an ass about the shirt, and probably would have been an ass if she'd bought him one today.

It hit home that Liz was all about giving. It was why she was able to pull off this fundraiser so effortlessly, or know exactly what his kids would need to feel special tonight. Or why so many people dropped everything to say hello when she entered a room.

Did a man who was so reluctant to receive, so distrustful of hidden strings, have any business being with a woman who personified giving?

She was whispering something else to Ryan now, and nodded her head toward Stevie where he stood with a pack of boys. Finn watched as the hockey player listened, nodded, then followed Liz's head as it swung toward a group of adolescent girls that huddled on the other side of the room. Again, Ryan nodded, accepted a squeeze on the arm from Liz, and watched as she walked away. Walked toward Finn. Ryan's eyes watched her stride to Finn's table, then he looked up and saw Finn watching him watch Liz. Showing no embarrassment, Ryan nodded to him and Finn gave a short nod in return.

Total guy thing. Without a word, Ryan had said, "You're damn lucky, she's a great girl" and Finn had sent the message back, "That's right, she is, and she's MINE." They both knew where they stood.

"Get everything handled?" he asked Liz as she sat at the table with Annie and him. Gran was off getting them all some refreshments and Stevie had left them to be with his friends since their arrival.

"Yep." She placed her hand on Annie's knee and gave a light squeeze. "Annie, when they get done announcing the queen, my friend, Petey, is going to call you up and he'll announce the fundraiser, okay?"

A determined look fought the terror on Annie's face and she nodded to Liz. "You'll go with me, won't you…" Before he could assure his daughter of his presence she added, "Lizzie?"

His heart felt like it had been lassoed and rustled to the ground. Stunned that his little girl didn't feel the need to cling to him, and overjoyed that the person she wanted near her for this momentous occasion was Liz. He looked at Liz to see if she had garnered the importance of this request.

Her eyes glistened. She pretended to fix her mascara as she gave Annie a nonchalant, "Sure, kid, I'll be with you." But he knew Annie's words had affected Liz as much as they had him.

Shit. This was not supposed to happen. A summer fling, that's what they'd decided, what they'd agreed upon. He didn't want to feel this deep connection with her. But he couldn't draw back now, not when they were so close to closing the deal, to sleeping together. Finally.

He'd get through this night, then they'd slow things down. Most of the work for the fundraiser was done, so Liz wouldn't need to be at the farm as often as she was now. They could spend the next month between now and the fundraiser just getting together for sex. No kids, no friends, no Gran, just the two of them, occasionally getting together to scratch the itch. Not even friends with benefits. Just benefits.

Yeah. Right. Like that was possible.

He sighed, accepting his fate. Who was he kidding? Keeping things to a minimum with Liz would never work, and wasn't really what he even wanted if he was honest with himself. He loved when she was at the farm. The work wasn't quite as back breaking when he knew there would be a few stolen kisses in the barn at the end of the day. He'd take every minute with her up until the moment she left for Detroit. Even that would be pure torture, to see her drive away from him, back to her life, her business and whatever guys might be waiting for her in the Motor City.

The queen crowning went smoothly, with Ryan playing his role to the hilt. Hugging and chastely kissing each of the contestants until only the winner remained. As he quieted the crowd and told them he had an announcement to make, Liz got behind Annie and made her way toward the stage. Finn rose to help, but she waved him off.

The stage had a ramp on either side, and Liz was able to easily wheel Annie to the corner of the stage.

Once the queen and her court had been escorted from the stage, Ryan stepped to the microphone. "I just want to let you all know about an upcoming event. Mark your calendars now. August eighth and ninth are going to be the most exciting two days the Copper Country has ever seen and it's all to help out my good friend, Annie Robbins."

Finn snorted from where he sat. Annie had never even met Pete Ryan.

What the hell, it was all about the surgery. He didn't mind putting up with a little phony emotion if it meant his daughter would someday be able to stand and walk. He watched as Liz wheeled Annie to the front of the stage then went back to the

curtains that served as the backdrop during the queen corona-
tion. She nodded to Ryan and yanked on a cord, which opened
the curtains.

Ryan put on his best "let's get ready to rumble" voice and announced, "Ladies and gentleman, it's my pleasure to announce…
Annie Aid!" The crowd, solely feeding off their hometown hero's
enthusiasm, began to applaud.

The curtains parted and a huge banner that read "Annie Aid"
shown behind. It listed the dates, and in two neat columns, one
for each day of the happening, summarized the events. Finn had
seen some of Liz's notes, but was floored by the sheer volume of
things that she'd been able to plan and organize on such short
notice.

"As you can see, we're having a celebrity golf outing on Friday, a barbecue Friday night. A dance on Saturday, and throughout the weekend you can have your picture taken with…" He
held the pause as long as he could before shouting, "The Stanley
Cup!"

The crowd burst into excitement. There was applause and
shouts. Finn realized how right Liz had been about the willingness
of the people of the Copper Country to pay to have their picture
taken with the Stanley Cup.

Ryan held his hands up to quiet the crowd. "And that's not
all. Each event will be attended by several members of the Detroit
Red Wings, the Lions, and the Pistons. There'll be Chicago Bears,
a couple of Patriots and yes, even a few of the NHL champion
Colorado Avalanche." The last was obviously hard for Ryan, and
Finn swore he saw the guy turn his head and roll his eyes at Liz.

As if she feared he may tell the crowd how he really felt
about the Avs, Liz strode to the microphone. "All proceeds go to
the Hannah Robbins Foundation. That's Annie to you and me.
We've got flyers with all the information at the doors. It's got the
website address with more information. Ticket sales to all events
begin on Monday."

She stepped away and gave the mic back to Ryan who said,

"Where's my good buddy, Stevie Robbins? Stevie, come on up here for a minute."

Finn sat, stunned, as he watched his son head to the stage. Clearly, Stevie had no more idea of what to expect than Finn did.

When Stevie reached the stage, Pete Ryan put his arm around him and said, "This is Stevie Robbins, a good friend of mine and Annie's older brother. Stevie was helping me clean out my locker at the Joe the other day…" He paused and let the audience, especially the kids in the crowd, absorb this bit of information. "And we got to talking about all the help we could use during the fundraiser. Stevie said he'd be glad to keep track of anyone who'd like to help out. So, if you'd like to volunteer to do something during Annie Aid, say, I don't know, caddy for a Red Wing or a Lion, you just let Stevie know and he'll put your name and phone number on a list and we'll be calling you in the next week or two."

The crowd took a visible step forward, as if they couldn't wait for the event to begin. Finn watched Liz's satisfied smile as she caught his eye from the stage. She gave a tiny thumbs-up to him and he felt like the weight of the world had just been lifted from him.

It was quickly replaced by the weight of his feelings for Liz.

"Whoa there, everybody, plenty of chances. If not tonight, there's a number on the flyer to call, or a contact us button on the website, so you can find out how you can help. Everybody relax, enjoy the rest of the Strawberry Festival and get ready for Annie Aid." Ryan wrapped it up and stood between Annie and Stevie, an arm around each of them.

Finn watched his son realize that though he'd just been assigned a chore, he would now be heralded by all his friends as Pete Ryan's personal buddy. The boy's smile could have melted the ice off the floor if it still remained.

His gaze then turned to his daughter, expecting to see terror and embarrassment. Instead she seemed to blossom right in front of him. She fed off the good vibes of the crowd and flashed Pete Ryan a dazzling smile that Finn saw as a harbinger of things to come.

Like they said, when you have a boy you worry about one boy, when you have a girl…you worry about *all* the boys.

Oh God, how would he bear it when men started looking at a teenage Annie? He'd happily learn to deal with it, though, if the looks his daughter received from boys years from now were filled with teen lust and not pity. Well, maybe not *happily* deal with it, but he'd learn to deal with it.

Fourteen

—⁓—

√ Get candles
√ Find out if they still make Love's Baby Soft
Call Sybil

ANNIE COULD BARELY keep her eyes open and did so from sheer adrenaline alone. Finn had danced with her, holding her hands up and swaying to and fro in front of her chair. After seeing how the feat could be accomplished, other men asked the little girl to dance and she quickly turned into the belle of the ball.

Lizzie herself felt like she'd danced with every man in attendance. Everyone except Finn. He had been surly every time she accepted a dance invitation, but hadn't asked her himself.

She could count on two hands the number of people in the Copper Country who'd seen her at her heaviest—unfortunately, it seemed like they all were here tonight. Lizzie tried to keep the couple of people who wanted to congratulate her on her stunning weight loss away from Finn and succeeded. But she couldn't miss the question in his eyes when a woman came up to her and said she hadn't known who Lizzie was until someone had told her.

Let him think she never came to town. Let him think that woman was senile with her inability to remember Lizzie. Oh, hell, let him think whatever he wants, after tonight it wouldn't matter.

She just needed to get him in the sack before he knew her

tale of obesity. He'd probably figure it out when he saw all the stretch marks, but she was counting on a very dark bedroom and enough distractions to prevent that from happening.

Not that she didn't think he wouldn't sleep with her if he knew she'd been fat. She just didn't want freak curiosity about her body to be a motivating factor. Or worse yet, a pity fuck. She couldn't bear the thought of that.

It was nearly eleven before Clea decided to take Annie and Stevie home. They had purchased pizza and other junk from the concession stand, which Finn and the kids wolfed down, but Lizzie, envisioning being naked later, turned down all food. Her tummy measurement this morning was the best she'd experienced since she'd begun the bizarre ritual. It was almost a pleasure slipping on the black linen dress.

She watched as Stevie said good night to the girl from the parade. She had traded in her purple tank and shorts for a sundress, also purple. Her signature color, apparently.

The girl had made a beeline for Stevie the minute he stepped off the stage with Petey, just as she'd hoped when she'd asked for the favor. She did a quick mental tally, adding up her favors column. She better be careful; too many more times of trying to impress Finn's kids and she'd end up owing the entire NHL.

The thought made her stop. Was that what she was doing? Trying to impress Finn's kids? Or worse, trying to impress Finn?

Why?

The reason she picked him for this experiment in the first place was because she didn't feel the need to impress him, had no stake in his opinion of her whatsoever. Right?

Before she could analyze it any further, Finn approached her where she stood by their table. He'd taken Annie and Clea to the van and had headed Stevie in that direction as the boy said a reluctant farewell to the purple girl. He had gotten Lizzie and himself both a beer but instead of handing her one, he set them both on the table.

"Finally, I can ask you to dance." He held his hand out to her and she took it. It was cool from holding the cup of beer, and was an extreme contrast to the heat that seemed to emanate from her.

She felt more anxious to finally be held by Finn than walking into any boardroom with a million-dollar proposal.

He led her to the dance floor where a song had just ended and the DJ was saying something about "slowing it down for the old folks". There were a few boos and catcalls from the remaining couples, none of whom wanted to be placed in the old folks category, but who were happy to have some slow songs played.

"Why couldn't you ask me to dance before?" she asked.

He brought them to the middle of the dance floor, hiding them amongst the sea of other couples. "I wanted to be able to get to Annie if anything happened. And, honestly, I wasn't sure what her reaction would be if she saw us dancing together. I just didn't want to chance a melt-down, not when everything went off so smoothly."

She placed her right hand in his and her left on his shoulder and followed his lead. "It did go pretty well, didn't it?"

He gently squeezed her waist. "Because of you." He pulled back from her so he could look into her eyes. "You know I'll never be able to thank you enough for all you've done. Even if the operation isn't successful, we'll know we tried everything we could."

She watched his blue eyes, met them, and said in a very serious tone, "I don't want your gratitude. I saw a chance to help and I did something. Something that will be very beneficial to my clients, by the way, so it was a good business decision. But make no mistake, it's not gratitude that I want from you."

She saw his strong Adam's apple move as he swallowed. She knew how he felt; she couldn't seem to keep her throat from closing up either.

His steady gaze remained on her. "What is it you do want from me, Elizabeth?"

"All I've ever wanted from you. All you've ever wanted from me. Just to…be together. Just for tonight, no past, no future, no kids, no friends…just us, Finn. Alone, with no limits, no good-girl tears, no cold showers of frustration. You and me together. Finally."

The song ended and segued into Willie Nelson's "You Were Always On My Mind". They remained on the dance floor, encircled in each other's arms, entranced by each other's eyes.

Indicating the song, she said, "There's an oldie."

Finn smiled, his strong cheekbones rising. "But a goodie," he finished for her. He put his head close to hers and hummed along with Willie, even sang a line or two.

She had a strong suspicion that he was trying to say more than he was able to with a little help from Willie. It could be just wishful thinking on her part. A giant rationalization so she wouldn't be jumping into the sack with someone who hadn't given her a moment's thought in the past eighteen years?

It was a rationalization she was prepared to live with when Finn said, "This song could be about us. For those first few years after we broke up, you *were* always on my mind. Probably longer than that, if I'm really honest. After I got married, though, it just didn't seem fair to think about you at all, even if it was only as 'the one that got away'."

She had no response to that. It was more than she'd ever hoped to hear from him. She thought she was more aptly the one he'd tossed back than the one that got away. She chastised herself for starving for the few crumbs he threw her way, but there it was.

Finn had thought about her, and that made her happy.

She slid her hand from his shoulder to the back of his neck. His skin was warm. One finger moved slightly into his wavy hair, and another swept softly just beneath his collar. His hand tightened again on her back. He dislodged their joined hands, taking them apart, and placed hers around his neck to join her left hand. His hand moved to her waist. Dancing like you did as kids, because you hadn't yet been taught how to dance like proper grown ups.

Most of her contemporaries still danced this way, the man's arms around the woman's waist, the woman's around the man's neck, just going in circles. No steps, no time or rhythm to keep. It allowed for much closer contact, and that was what they were after.

She pressed her body into his, physically approving with his decision to change their dancing technique.

"It feels so good to hold you like this." His breath grazed across her neck as he spoke.

She didn't trust her voice, could only nod her agreement. Her cheek nuzzled closer to his shoulder.

"We fit so well together. We always did, you were always a perfect fit for me."

"You know," she quietly said, "my summer fling's half over and I haven't even…flung yet."

Finn nuzzled her neck. "You know how bad I want to… fling you."

"Let's get out of here," she whispered as she pressed herself against him.

He didn't answer, only grabbed her hand and started walking to the exit, not even slowing when people tried to catch her eye to say hello.

He walked her to her Navigator then zeroed in for a kiss, but stopped. "Let's not start here, we always seem to be interrupted in parking lots. I'll follow you to your parents'."

Lizzie only nodded, her disappointment at not being kissed evident in her half pout.

He chuckled and gave her a quick kiss—on the cheek! "It's only a five-minute drive, Liz. You can hold out that long." He shut the door behind her as she got into the Navigator and turned toward his Jeep. She revved her engine and he turned around and waved at her, then got into his Jeep.

She pulled out of the rec center and headed through downtown Hancock, her mind racing to the moment when she and Finn would be totally alone—with no chance of interruption.

Always prepared—those rascally Boy Scouts had nothing on her—she'd prepped her bedroom once Clea had made her generous offer to free up Finn for the night. She supposed making love in her parents' king-size bed would be more comfortable, but Lizzie hadn't entertained that idea for more than a moment before discarding it and setting up the seduction scene in her own bedroom, unchanged in its decor since she'd left for college.

She'd added candles on the dresser against the far wall from the bed, wanting as little light as possible, but ready to be lit if Finn balked at total darkness. She'd changed the sheets from the floral ones her mother had put on to crisp white cotton, fresh off the line this afternoon. That was another thing she missed about the Copper Country, climbing in bed at night and drifting off to sleep amidst the smell of freshly hung sheets. She could just see the hissy fit her toney condo association would pull if she strung up a clothesline in the backyard.

She didn't think more was needed in setting her seduction scene. Finn wouldn't be looking for toys or whips, at least not tonight. No, tonight was all about fulfilling a promise. About recapturing something thought lost forever.

About setting free the past and looking to the future.

Obesity, poor self-image, and sexual hesitancy were her past. Lizzie didn't expound on her thoughts of what the future would hold. Her vision of that wasn't quite as clear as it had been when she drove to town just over a month ago.

Not only foregoing food at the dance, she also drank only water for the entire evening, wanting to have her wits about her. This was do-or-die night for her and she wanted no impairments.

The physical sensation she'd felt dancing with Finn still coursed through her body.

She thought of him saying how well they'd always fit together. She knew nothing was further from the truth. They might have fit perfectly physically—though they'd never gotten the chance to know if the ultimate fit was perfect—but they were different in every other way. He was rough and hard, had no use for the niceties that she so enjoyed. He'd seen the harsh realities that humanity and fate could dish out. She'd worked hard, but had basically had a very drama-free life—no major losses, no deranged ex-spouses.

No wheelchairs.

She wondered if she would have had the strength to go through what Finn had in his lifetime? She'd like to think so, but realistically the only challenge she'd been faced with in her life was losing weight. And even that had been because she'd been so weak in the first place that she'd become crazy fat.

She knew she needed to let herself off the hook for that, for the weight gain. She had gone to see an expert on compulsive eating when she was first starting to lose weight. She wanted answers, she wanted to pinpoint, she wanted to be able to say with complete confidence, "This. This is the reason I put on weight. Because of X, Y and Z." Once a culprit was clearly defined, it would be dealt with and disposed of.

But it wasn't that cut and dried, as she learned while working through the eating issues. The therapist was patient with Lizzie's need for an explanation but offered none. "You may never know why you became obese. You may just want to think of it as something you felt you needed at the time but don't any longer, such as a child needs a security blanket but then can discard it. Usually there's tears and tantrums and the removal of the blanket is painful and not done lightly, but once done, the child can then move forward."

"But if I don't know why, can I hope to change?" she asked. She was already losing weight and the thought of a backslide terrified her.

"Think of it as a journey that you are driving. Suddenly you realize you are going in the wrong direction, have been for some time. Do you pull over and spend hours trying to figure out why you went the wrong way? No, you turn the car around and start to drive in the right direction. Along the way, you start to think about the reason you got off course, but you do that as you're headed toward your destination."

It was a mini-breakthrough for Lizzie, and her progress took a positive leap. When she likened her obesity to a security blanket, the analogy made sense. The same could be said for her "epiphany". She simply no longer needed the shield that obesity gave her. Now, if she could just figure out what she had needed shielding from.

The obvious choice was sex, of course. But it was more than that.

She neared the turn to her parent's place. The radio played the Dixie Chicks singing an old Stevie Nicks song. Talking about fear of changing, and what you build your world around.

It felt like a light bulb suddenly going on above her head. The unnamable emotion that had hung on the fringe of her psyche the past three years suddenly had a name. Fear. That was what had her running to Taco Bell at midnight, undoing a great week of dieting. What had driven her to one step forward and two steps back.

Fear.

And it was because she had built her life around being fat. And that was changing.

She'd watched enough self-help shows to know the difference between body image and self image. How intertwined they can become if you let them, but how they are indeed separate entities. She had done a great job—maybe too great of a job—of not allowing her body image to rule her self image.

Her full relationships with her friends and her family. Her successful business. All accomplishments that led Lizzie to have a very healthy self image even if her body image lingered in the cellar.

But that body image had been her closest companion for fifteen years. It was who she woke up with, who she left in the car when she entered the office, who was waiting for her at the end of the day, and who she shared a pillow with every night. It was scary to say goodbye.

But say goodbye she must. And tonight with Finn would be the final wave to her old compadre.

Fifteen

—w—

√ Get new bra and panty set
√ Get rid of bedside lamps
Call Sybil

IT STARTED LIKE it had so many times before. The physical yearning, the need to be together, their differences swept aside as the attraction grew palpable. The setting was also similar. They had once been in Lizzie's bedroom when her parents had been gone overnight.

He brushed his hand across the flowery canopy. "I was only here that one night, but it's exactly like I remembered it."

She smiled, pleased he remembered something she would have thought to be insignificant to him. "That's because nothing's changed."

His eyes swept the entire room. "Really? That's nice, I guess. Something familiar when you come home to visit."

"I think so, too. Or I did. It's a little eerie though, I step through this door and suddenly I feel fourteen again."

A devilish grin arose on his mouth and his brows crinkled. "Funny, you stand in that door and suddenly I think you're *eigth-teen* again."

A small tremor of discomfort assailed her. "I'm not eighteen, Finn. I don't think like that anymore. I don't feel like that anymore. I'm not that naive anymore. And I'm certainly not that innocent anymore." It was as if she needed to impart full disclosure to him. He wasn't getting the sweet virgin he had so desired. Not to mention an entirely different body. She had told him so before and he'd been glad to hear it, but she wanted to drive the point home.

He crossed to where she still stood in the doorway, and placed his arms in the doorjamb, not trapping her, she needed to only step backward into the hallway to be free of him, but more as if encircling her. "I know. I'm no boy of twenty, and you're a woman who's been through eighteen years of living. And I'm sure we've both got the scars to prove it."

She thought of her physical scars—her stretch marks—and Finn's emotional ones, and wondered which cut deeper.

"But one thing hasn't changed. I still want you as badly as I did then. And I think you want me." He leaned into her, his hands still on the doorjamb, his chest brushing across her breasts. His mouth gently skimming her jaw.

She breathed in deeply and was lost. This room. This man. That godawful Brut. How could she ever think she'd be able to maintain a cold, clinical view to this sex experiment?

She couldn't. She must have known that somewhere in the back of that planning-within-an-inch-of-your-life mind of hers.

It was an unnerving realization, but it was not enough to pull her out of her haze of desire for Finn. A loud exhale full of her tumultuous emotions sent his head away from her neck so that he could see her face. "Tell me you want me, Liz."

Her nod was not enough for him. "Tell me," he prodded.

She could see how important this was to him. For him to know that she wanted him. So wrapped up in her own implications of this evening, she hadn't thought about how potentially momentous Finn could see this occasion.

Now or never. Three years, numerous pounds, and it all came down to this. She tried to ease up on herself. Life would still go on if she blew this. She would learn from this experience and get better where she needed to so she'd be ready when she entered into a meaningful relationship. As she'd said all along, it was only Finn. It didn't really matter what he thought of her, did it?

So why did she want this to go well more than she'd wanted anything in her life?

She laid her hands on his chest, felt his strong muscles tense underneath and met his gaze. "I want you." It was a near whisper. She started to lower her eyes, unaccustomed to such frankness when it came to passion, but stopped herself. *Find out now what you can and can't handle, Lizard. Test your limits. This is your chance.*

With a sense of boldness usually reserved for business negotiations, she lifted her chin, almost in defiance, and repeated with more conviction, "I want you."

His hands left the doorjamb and settled on her waist. "Good. I've waited eighteen years to hear that, Elizabeth."

She was shocked to feel tears begin to well up in her eyes. Oh, man. Just what she did not need now. Emotions. Not when she wanted to have sex!

He squeezed her waist and she was saved from messy emotions by thinking of the still slightly jiggly flesh he must be feeling. It worked. The moistness in her eyes quickly dissipated. It was part self-preservation that caused her to take his hands in hers and move them from her waist to her breasts. Mostly, it was because she thought she'd explode if he didn't touch her there. She was pretty sure she'd explode if he did, too, but *that* explosion would be a good thing.

His mouth crashed down on hers. She opened with no coaxing. Their tongues tangled and she thought that she might have just found something that tasted better than chocolate. It was sweet and soft and lasting. She caught his rhythm right away, matched his movements. His hands stroked her breasts with a soft touch that seemed out of place with his strength. She felt her nipples pebble under his hands, and the sensation thrilled her. He slid a hand around her back and gently pushed her to join him as he took a step backward, into the room. Toward the bed.

She gladly followed, but reached out and turned the light switch off as she took her first step. He stopped abruptly, causing her to crash into his chest. Through all this movement, their mouths remained completely fused together. He reached back behind her and turned the switch on. It was as if there were a power surge because just as suddenly she turned the light back off.

"No. I want to see you, Liz," he gasped, managing to take in some badly needed air and resume his penetrating kiss once more.

She tensed at his words, but let it pass, knowing she had thought this scenario through. She reluctantly broke from the kiss and moved to the dresser by the door and lit the candle she'd placed there earlier. Her foresight had once again saved her. Hah! Let Alison make fun of her lack of spontaneity all she wanted. Lizzie would never be caught unawares.

"There. That's better than that harsh light, isn't it?" she asked, and led him away from the wall, and light switch, before he could answer.

The room was cast in a warm glow that allowed them to see each other, but was faint and soft. "I don't know. I want to see you very clearly when you're beneath me and coming," he said, his voice low.

The comment put her back on her game. She could verbally volley with Finn like there was no tomorrow. Probably because up until now that was all she'd allowed. She gave him a wicked smile. "You're assuming you'll be on top."

His grin split his hard face. "Oh, I'll be on top all right. That's always how I pictured you, beneath me, squirming, calling my name, holding my face in your hands like you do…" He cut himself off and she could tell he had said more than he'd intended.

He lightened his tone. "Of course, after the first time, you can be on top…" He took her hand and led her, stopping at the side of the bed. "Or on the bottom…" He turned her around, her back to him and unzipped her dress in a swift motion. "Or on your side…" He brushed the shift from her shoulders, down her arms, easing it past her waist and hips and let it drop to the floor where she stepped out of it and he nudged it away. "Or on all fours…" He turned her around to face him and his eyes swept her from head to toe. "Or hanging from the canopy for all I care."

She felt her knees almost go out from under her, but caught herself. She musn't show how affected by Finn she was. She needed to keep her cool on the outside. Even if she was burning up—and soaking wet—on the inside. "You're assuming there'll be more than the first time," she said, but only met his impish grin with one of her own. They both knew once would not be enough.

She watched as his gaze traveled over her. It took great will power not to visibly suck anything in or stick anything else out. She wore a white lace and satin bra and panty set. It had intricate beading along the top edge of the cups and the vee inset of the panties. Normally she wouldn't wear white undergarments with a black dress, but she did tonight. She had chosen white knowing that Finn still harbored that good-girl innocence thing he'd always pinned on her. Rightfully so, at the time.

She saw him look at both bedside tables, presumably for a lamp to see her better, but she'd removed them earlier, spreading books and papers from work around so that there was no obvious place where they'd been. He seemed to accept there'd be no more light shed upon her, and he looked at her once more. "God, but you're a woman, Liz."

*Is that good? I guess it was better than being called a man, but…*She guessed it was a compliment, but years of shopping in the "woman sizes" sections of department stores made the term stick in her throat.

He seemed to sense her hesitation. "I mean, all those soft curves…you're so beautiful."

The word she picked up on—soft—resonated in her ears while "beautiful" slid past.

Screw it. He wanted her, curves and all. Looking down and seeing his growing erection outlined by his khakis drove that point home. It also made her realize she stood near naked to his fully clothed. She stepped forward and set about evening the playing field.

She rapidly undid the buttons from his shirt and pulled it from his pants, eliciting a hiss from Finn as the material dragged across his penis. She didn't care, she wanted to see his chest. She was a little more careful unzipping his pants and easing them down his lean hips. He stepped out of them and kicked the pants and his shoes off at the same time. He leaned down and stripped off his socks, and took Lizzie's sandals from her feet. She took the moment to measure the man he'd become.

She wasn't disappointed.

His was not a body created in a gym like the executives she knew. It wasn't a body sculpted for physical greatness like the athletes she represented. It was a body honed from hard work, from lifting and piling and carrying. His back and shoulders, hunched over to administer to the straps of her sandals, were strong and broad, the muscles snaked across his bones and corded together at the base of his neck.

When he stood again, wearing only his boxers and a shit-eating grin that made her nipples tighten, she garnered a view of his sumptuous chest. Dark brown hair whorled across it, then trickled into a line which led down past his boxers. Needing to see where the line ended, as if looking for the pot of gold at the end of the rainbow, she pushed off his boxers and was rewarded with the sight of a fully aroused, pulsing erection.

She brushed the back of her hand against it and delighted in the whoosh of breath that left him. She turned her palm in and gently took him in her hand and began a slow stroke, reaching the entire length of his generous shaft, lingering at the velvety soft head and back down again.

Finn's head was thrown back in enjoyment and Lizzie basked in his pleasure. She could feel him tensing and pulsing under her hand, hear his sharp breathing become more and more labored the faster she stroked. He suddenly seemed to realize there was a woman attached to the hand getting him off. His head sprung back, his eyes, heavy-lidded and a deeper blue than she remembered, gazed at her.

His hands went to her back, presumably to undo her bra and she sidestepped him, scooting onto the bed. She wanted to be lying down when she was naked for the first time. That way, if she kind of held her arms at her sides and arched her back a little, everything fell into place in the most flattering of ways.

The sudden loss of her hand from his dick made Finn very aware of her movements, but didn't seem to mind her move to the bed.

He lifted her legs, which dangled down the side of the bed, and followed them as he placed them in the center of the mattress, himself over her. He eased her legs apart to allow him room to kneel above her.

This was perfect. Exactly the position she wanted to be in. She reached around and undid the clasp of the bra herself. She slid the straps and cups from her slowly, holding them in front of her breasts, watching Finn's eyes devour her. It would seem to him as if she was doing a slow striptease, or was bashful. The truth was, this way she could arrange her heavy breasts at their best vantage. She lost her train of thought when her hands brushed across her nipples and she let out a gasp, unaware they'd become so sensitive.

Finn watched every movement. As if he was determined to make that gasp come from her himself, he tore the bra from her hands. He saw the aching buds that had caused her gasp, and placed his hands on both her breasts, cupping their fullness, lifting, brushing his thumbs against her nipples. She gasped again, and a self-satisfied smile played on his mouth.

He slid from the bed and headed toward his pants. Finding them, he reached into the back pocket and threw a handful of condoms onto the bedside table. "So I don't have to stop to find them later, when I'm not sure I'll be able to function." He got back on the bed, in the exact same position he had been before, right down to his hands fondling her breasts.

She smiled. "It's okay. I'm on the pill." She had started taking the pill four months ago, in expectation of becoming sexually active again this summer.

Always have a plan.

His hands stilled momentarily at her words, then began to caress her again. "Not good enough," he said.

She thought about what his ex-wife Dana had done to him, the trust and faith he must have lost along the way, and only nodded her understanding. Besides, there were still STDs to think about. She knew she was clean, but didn't want to tell Finn the way she knew that particular fact was that she hadn't had sex in fifteen years. If he wore a condom, they could avoid that conversation altogether.

His hands skimmed down her waist and she closed her eyes in dread. To her delight, his hands only briefly lingered on her waist, lowering further. His hands stilled and she opened her eyes. He was watching the play of his deeply tanned hand against her lighter-skinned hip and the shocking white of her panties. Three very distinct shades of color.

His other hand left her breast now as he slipped his fingers around the elastic waist and slid her panties over her hips, past her thighs, and over her feet. He held them in his hand for a moment and Lizzie saw his gaze move from her panties to her body. A swallow of fear passed her throat as she envisioned his face scrunching up in disgust and saying something like, "I'm sorry, there's someplace I need to be," and scurrying for the door. Or worse, losing that glorious erection.

She'd be back to square one on her plan, but knew she'd never be able to try again after suffering another such humiliation. A lot was riding on this. She scoured his face for any sign of disgust and watched as his eyes narrowed and his mouth hardened. What did that mean?

He laid his hand on her mound and pressed lightly. "God, Liz, I can't remember wanting a woman more in my entire life than I do right now."

She knew it was the claiming of something he had been denied before and not an overwhelming desire for her body that he was feeling, but she didn't care. *She passed inspection!* Granted, she was in the most conducive position and there was only the dim candlelight from across the room for him to see her by.

She'd take it.

She raised her arms along her sides, which, she knew pushed her boobs together in a rather pleasing way, and reached for him.

He fell on her, but caught his weight on his arms at the last moment. He settled in, rubbing his hard dick against her, making room for himself, her legs opened just wide enough to let him in, but close enough to keep contact with his hips and thighs.

She let out a soft sigh as the contact hit her. She looked up to see him staring down at her. Out of habit—out of necessity—she reached up and cupped his face in her hands, their eyes locking. They had been in this exact position many times before, but always with the barrier of several layers of clothes. To feel his rough hair against her breasts, along her belly, was exquisite.

To have such close physical contact with someone—anyone—again after so long nearly made Lizzie weep. She knew she'd missed being touched, but she hadn't realized how much she missed touching someone. It felt so good to have warm, pulsing skin beneath your palms. To feel crisp chest hair tangle in your fingertips.

He nuzzled her neck and collarbone, kissed below her ear, and brought his head back up again, her hands still gently cradling it. He looked at her eyes, pupils dilated with desire, and in a low voice, said, "Tell me what you want, Liz. Anything. I want to make you happy."

The words seemed to shock them both. Did he know how unhappy she'd been? Could he tell this was her first time in fifteen years? Would she die of embarrassment if he called her on it?

He rolled his hips, giving her a taste of how he'd help her find happiness and said again, "Tell me what you want."

It was an open invitation if she could find the guts to take it. What *did* she want from him? She wasn't entirely sure, but didn't think she could say something along the lines of "I want to know that I am sexually satisfying to a man, that I can come without the aid of a vibrator, that my body does not disgust you and that I can have fulfilling, mind-blowing sex. And oh yeah, then I'm going to go find someone else to have it with on a long-term basis."

Instead, she held his face close to hers and said, "Kiss me."

It was a gentle kiss. At first. Her hands went from his face around his neck and nestled in his soft hair, which was getting shaggier as the summer went on. She kind of liked it that way, a little wild, like Finn himself. She twirled her fingers in the soft nest. His mouth grew more insistent and she met his need with her own. The kiss deepened. He softly nipped at her lower lip, she playfully sucked on his tongue.

The kiss went on and on, lazy and slow. His chest tight against her breasts, his hands roaming her body. It was the realization of his hands that made Lizzie break the kiss, catching her breath. She felt his hands moving over her hips and thighs, belly, they seemed to be everywhere at once, leaving a trail of tingling skin in their wake.

The kiss broken, he lifted his head from hers, raising himself up on his forearms, his hands leaving her body and resting at her face, gathering strands of her hair.

"Tell me what you want." His voice was stronger now, gathering steam as their bodies were gathering tension, gathering desire.

She took her hands from his nape and held his face once more, but instead of bringing his mouth to hers, she guided his head down her neck to her breasts. She positioned him just where she wanted him and whispered, "Suck me."

Why not. He'd asked what she wanted. Good girl and whore rivaled inside her and she knew she'd let the whore win tonight. It'd be a lot more fun.

He groaned his approval of her request and latched on to a nipple and began to suck. She nearly jumped off the bed. God, she had no idea her breasts were so sensitive. Had she ever known that? Her back arched, wanting to be closer, seeking the sweet heat that came from Finn's mouth and shot directly to the core of her. So good. She'd merely meant this as a stop along the way, a bone to throw Finn, knowing he was such a breast man. She had no reason to suspect she would be the one writhing from pleasure.

But this was all part of it. Finding out what she liked, what her body wanted. And it wanted Finn to do these delicious things to her.

He seemed to pick up on her revelation and switched to her other breast as his hands massaged and pushed the two together. His tongue switched from nipple to nipple, wetting both, spending time at one, then the other, sucking one deep as he pinched its mate.

It was driving her to a frenzy and he knew it, seemed to anticipate her every whimper with the strong use of his tongue and mouth. After one particularly strong roll of her hips, begging him for something more, he raised his head and looked at her. "Tell me what you want."

Lizzie thought about what she wanted most to say, what she wanted most to feel. Could she bring herself to ask for it? She took his head in her hands once more and led it away from her breasts, wet and glistening from his mouth. Past her tummy and hips, allowing Finn to place soft kisses as he went, down to her nest of curls. She was wet with desire, could see it herself. She watched Finn's nostrils flare as he took in the scent of her. Waited for his reaction and silently sighed relief as he unselfconsciously licked his lips.

"Lick me."

His tongue was on her before she had the words out. His hands spread her outer lips and he nuzzled his nose into her, teasing her clitoris from its hiding place. It didn't need much coaxing, as if it knew what it was missing, and decided to join in the fun. She became engorged and throbbed, a perfect target for his seeking mouth.

Oh my, my battery-operated friend never did that! As his thumbs held her open wide, and his mouth coaxed and teased her nub, he slipped a finger inside her. She knew she was very slick. She also knew she was very tight, a fact that Finn learned on his own a few seconds later as he added another finger and nearly filled her up. As if he realized she would have to be very soft and relaxed to take him, he set about in all earnestness trying to make her come.

Not a hard task.

She was already on the brink from the deep kisses and the attention paid to her breasts. The stroking of his tongue on her tingling clit quickly brought her to fever pitch. His fingers inside her picked up a rhythm that his tongue matched. Lizzie held his head in her hands, her fingers interwoven through his hair, simultaneously pushing him away and pulling him closer as the physical sensations awakened her long-dormant body.

This was not like those few times her senior year of college. There was no numbness now, no feeling of "is this all there is?". Her body was finely tuned and nerve endings she never knew she had were singing at the top of their lungs.

She felt the tightening that comes just before the explosion, but it was nothing like she experienced alone, through her own ministrations, dreaming of a faceless, nameless man. This was real. And intense. And it was Finn's mouth taking her there.

The tightening changed to a dead calm and she knew the she was headed over. Finn sensed it too, and clamped his lips down on her clit and sucked her deep into his mouth as his fingers swirled inside her, reaching up, trying to push her over.

Her body convulsed its sweet release. What normally lasted a few seconds when Lizzie was alone, what had never happened when she'd done it with a partner in college, went on and on with Finn.

He made sure of it.

His mouth played over her sensitive skin, lapping, sucking, as he added a third finger just as she was coming down, sending her spiraling up yet again. He held her hips in place with his other hand, her writhing and rolling taking her away from him more than he would allow. Finally...*finally*, he eased his fingers from her and gently kissed her clit goodbye and allowed her to gently fall back to earth, cradling her hips and buttocks, chin resting in her curls.

Slowly, her breathing returned to normal, and she felt him make his way back up her body, stopping at the same places he had on the way down. Her hips. Her belly. Her breasts. Her neck. Kissing each place with a tenderness he reacquired since his strong handling of her moments earlier. Leaving a trail of her own moistness on her skin with his mouth.

"Tell me what you want," he whispered once more into her neck.

Her arms skimmed down his back, squeezed his tight butt, reveling in its hardness, and swept to the front of him. She took his penis, throbbing now, pulsing with need. A need she understood, even thoughs hers had just been met. She reached over to the table, tore open a condom and rolled it onto him like the pro she in no way was. She guided his shaft to her opening and said, "Fuck me."

He grabbed her hips and plunged himself inside her. She gasped, stilled. When he realized it wasn't from pain, that, yes, she was very tight, but her long orgasm had made her wet and open to him, he began to pump into her.

His strokes were long and hard. Lizzie wrapped her arms around him, and instinctively drew her legs up and around his waist, drawing him deeper inside.

She felt so full, so...so...she didn't want to think something schmaltzy like "complete" or "like a woman", but that was what it felt like to have Finn Robbins deep inside her. Clutching her hips and burying his face in the crook of her shoulder as he gasped her name. She clenched her internal muscles causing him to groan and pump harder. She was thinking about what else she could do to please him during his turn when she felt the tension beginning to build in her again.

Surely not. She wasn't going to have another orgasm? So

soon? And with Finn inside her, not from having her clitoris rubbed or licked? The idea was so new to her she dismissed it, but it soon was back as the unmistakable feelings of spiraling were upon her. It hit her so unaware she bit into Finn's shoulder. He didn't even notice, so close to his own release.

Her shudders and spasms carried him over and he pumped quickly into her three more times then buried himself deep and spilled. Her orgasm milked him and the rolling of his hips was met with her own.

He lay on top of her for a long time, the weight of him welcomed by her arms wrapped around him, her calves slung over the back of his. After a while he got up and went out the door, kissing her on the nose as he left her. She heard the water in the bathroom run, figured he was disposing of the condom, and waited for him to return. When he did, he rolled her over to pull the covers free from under her, climbed in beside her and covered them both.

He spooned her from behind, his hand at first resting on her hip, then sliding down to her tummy in a movement similar to the one she did to herself every morning. She knew she should care, a little voice inside her was saying "his hand's on your tummy, roll over, move the hand, put it on your boobs, something, anything, to distract him!" but she couldn't find the energy to obey the voice. It faded away, its volume turned down.

Finn nuzzled her neck and they lay quietly, each deep in their own thoughts, each nearing sleep.

"You were definitely worth the wait, Elizabeth," he whispered as they both drifted off.

Sixteen

—⚬—

Call Sybil

LIZZIE BRUSHED THE SIDE of her bed Finn had slept on and felt nothing but the cool sheets. She checked the alarm clock. Early, but not that early. Had he left to sneak back into the farmhouse before his kids woke up? Certainly understandable, but she was disappointed. She'd hoped for an encore performance this morning.

She heard movement from downstairs, water running in the kitchen sink. God bless old houses where you could hear every movement. Thank goodness no one else had been in the house last night, for they sure would have heard an earful.

She found her beat-up terrycloth robe—one of the few pieces of clothing she'd kept from her former size—and slipped it on, loving the way it wrapped around her body nearly twice. She was gone from her bedroom before she even realized that she hadn't put her hand on her tummy this morning. She padded downstairs in bare feet, but when she rounded the corner to the living room she stopped, frozen in her tracks.

Finn stood with his back to her dressed only in his jeans, slung low on his hips, his broad, tan back slightly bent as he looked at the knick knacks and photos in the curio cabinet in front of him. The reflection of his face in the glass cabinet doors shone at Lizzie like a mirror. In the morning light, she easily saw every nuance that passed over his face as he looked at the family photos.

The image was familiar to her, seeing Finn like that. A suffocating pain shot through her chest as she was hurled back in time, her memory betraying her with its startling clarity.

She'd gone to see him at the theater one night after the second showing had started and she knew he wouldn't be very busy. She'd walked to Houghton by herself, not daring to tell even Alison and Katie that she was going. She'd been out of high school three weeks, summer was in full swing, she already had loads of tips from waitressing to take to State, and her tan was coming along nicely.

And she couldn't stop crying herself to sleep at night.

Finn had called a week before and said he wanted to see other girls. When she asked if that meant in addition to her or instead of her he didn't give her a straight answer, but hemmed and hawed his way off of the phone.

He hadn't called since.

She knew it was over, but she couldn't stop herself from taking that fateful walk to Houghton to see him one more time. Maybe she'd act cool and sophisticated, calling his bluff, and say he was right, they should see other people too, but still continue to see each other—how about tomorrow? Maybe she'd throw pop in his face and call him every blue word she knew—and Alison had taught her a lot of them, much to Katie's chagrin. Maybe... maybe she'd tell him she'd sleep with him—right now, in the projection room if that's what he wanted—if only he'd take her back.

Fantasizing about the pop throwing, her gait became slower as she realized she was more apt to play out the latter scenario.

He didn't seem all that surprised to see her. Leery, watchful, but not surprised. Maybe he envisioned her throwing pop at him as well. Perhaps it was an incident that often happened to him.

They made excruciating small talk for a few minutes, Lizzie still deciding which road to take. Finn said he had to go back upstairs to the projection room. She just nodded. He reached out and squeezed her arm.

"It was good to see you, Liz. Take care of yourself," he said. They had been near the door to go into the theater, next to the stairwell. He led her directly across the lobby to the exit doors, then turned back and headed up the stairs.

It was a definite dismissal and she put her hands out to the glass doors to leave. She paused at the door, looking out into the evening twilight. Being so far west that it should really be in the Central time zone, but remaining on Eastern time, the Copper Country remained light until ten or eleven o'clock in the summer. It was a kid's paradise, playing baseball so late into the evening. The walk home wouldn't even be really dark until she was just about to her house.

The cool glass on Lizzie's hand shocked her. She took a step back, then another. Her dignity already in shreds, she decided to go for broke and wait for Finn to come back downstairs.

She'd definitely sleep with him. Enough of this good-girl crap, he was a man and he wanted a woman. And she was going to be one for him. Would it matter just this once if she altered her life plan? Moved up the virginity timetable a few years?

Her stomach churned with dread as she waited, then some movement coming from the doors in front of her made her lift her head. The door reflected the lobby behind her and she saw Finn making his way down the stairs. She stood still for a moment, trying to get her courage up, to turn around and face him, but she needn't have bothered. As soon as he saw she was still there, had waited for him, he came to a quiet halt on the fourth step from the bottom. Not realizing she could see him in the reflecting window, he silently turned around and made his way back up the stairs, creeping like a thief in the night, intent on waiting until she left before returning downstairs.

The thoughts that ran through Lizzie's mind right then would unwittingly affect the rest of her life. As she hustled through the doors and made her way back to her side of the bridge she could have been thinking, "What a snake! What a jerk! Who does he think he is!?" But those weren't the thoughts that ran through her humiliated brain.

Instead, her eighteen-year-old, broken-hearted mind raced with, "What did I do wrong? What could I have done differently? Did his other girlfriends kiss better than me?" and the piece de résistance, "Does he like someone prettier/thinner/better than me?"

The memory played like a movie in Lizzie's mind as she sat on the stairs in her parents' home—the place she still thought of as *her* home—and watched Finn.

With the hindsight of a woman who had faced life's challenges and won, she realized now how pivotal that night had been for her. She hadn't faced it before, had never really thought about that night, about how shattered her pride had been. How disgusted with herself she was for even going to the Mine Shaft. How she'd never told anyone about it to this day, not even Al and Kat. She thought her problems with intimacy and trust had begun with her sexual debacle three years later, but she now knew it had been birthed that night.

She wrapped her arms around her knees and rested her cheek against the soft robe. She allowed a tear to trickle down her cheek, making no attempt to wipe it away. That girl in the theater lobby deserved a tear or two. She hadn't cried that night—had not cried any more over Finn Robbins.

She did start making frequent trips to the Dairy Queen.

A soft sigh escaped her lips, but Finn was still oblivious to her presence behind him. She wondered what in her mother's curio cabinet could have him so engrossed, then gasped as she realized he was staring at the family photos of her at twice her size.

There were at least a dozen photos in front of him. One with her and Zeke when he got his wings, him looking devastatingly handsome in his Navy whites, straining to reach an arm around her girth for an embrace. One of Lizzie looking happy in a chic, designer suit, albeit seven sizes larger than the ones she wore now, in front of the office doors with the Hampton Public Relations sign on her first day of business. One with her parents at a Red

Wings game, she in a XXXL Pete Ryan jersey.

One of her on her high school graduation looking crisp and young and full of dreams. Later that night she'd whimpered Finn's name as he'd held her on a blanket at the beach, frightened of what her body was feeling, of emotions that seemed just out of reach.

Lizzie's gasp was what made Finn finally aware of her and he turned to face her. There was a questioning look in his eyes and compassion in his voice—not pity, she would have died to hear pity—when he said, "Tell me what happened to you, Elizabeth."

—⟋⟍—

It seemed fitting that she told him of the last fifteen years at the beach. He had bared his soul to her here only a month ago, and it was here that they had shared so many heated moments years earlier.

She threw on shorts and a tee-shirt, Finn gathered his shirt and shoes, they put the coffee he'd been making before the pictures distracted him in a thermos, grabbed two mugs, and drove the short distance. It was too early for anyone to be there. They had to park on the highway and walk in because the gates to the parking area wouldn't open for several more hours. It was a lovely, clear morning, destined to be another glorious day. The water, still and mirror-like, held Lizzie's attention as always. Once settled on the blanket and each with a mug of coffee in their hands, Finn needed to only voice a soft "Liz?" to get her started.

It all spilled. Probably too quickly, it seemed hard for Finn to keep up. Things she'd never put into words seemed so clear to her now.

She didn't tell him about remembering the night at the theater after their break-up, she didn't want him to know that she'd seen him, didn't want him to know how much that had shattered her.

And she didn't mention the failed attempts at a healthy intimate relationship. It wouldn't do her any good for him to know that last night was only about pushing her sexual envelope.

But she did tell him everything else that had happened to her. She explained to him about cravings and hungers that never seemed to end. How sometimes, after leaving an office full of close co-workers and a social gathering that included dinner with friends she cared deeply about, she'd return home and feel so alone that she'd get back in her car and drive to the nearest McDonald's. How she'd order two large pops because she didn't want the counter person to think the large amount of food she'd ordered was going to be eaten by only one person.

She croaked out a laugh as she told him that part. "Like a kid at McDonald's gives a shit how much I eat. Like they're going to call the Big Mac Police on me." Finn only gave her a small smile and waited for her to continue.

She put into words how exhausting being "the nice one" had always been to her. She never felt that she could hurl a bitchy comeback, or put someone in their place the way Alison could. She could never attract men with the ease that Katie did. She worked hard at being so friendly, so accessible to everyone. Having a few candy bars on the drive to work was a self-granted reward, of sorts, for all she did. She didn't have anyone at her condo to say, "fantastic job, Lizzie" when she got home, so she let Papa John say it for her.

She told him how she felt like a double agent at times, so capable and competent in her professional life, and such a total fuck-up when it came to anything else.

How humiliating even taking a shower was every day when you needed to lift up your stomach to wash under it. Mirrors and especially clothes —something she'd loved all her life—and any sort of athletic activity, became things she dreaded. Her disregard for her body was like a black hole that she hadn't seen herself falling into. When she was so deeply ensconced, she could see no way out.

She stopped talking for a while, just stared at the lake. She'd never get tired of looking at that lake. Finn just lay beside where she sat, waiting patiently. He probably needed to get to the farm, but made no sign of moving, showed no signal for her to hurry up and get on with it. For that she was grateful. It was painful to talk about this, but he was easing the way for her by being silent.

Her voice was lighter and her whole body seemed to ease as she told him of her turnaround.

It hadn't been easy. The first time she had sent a plate of her beloved fettucini alfredo away half finished because she was full— something that had never stopped her from cleaning off the plate before—she'd almost burst into tears.

The foreign object her face became when washing it and would come into contact with cheekbone instead of fleshy cheek. The Samson-esque importance she gave to her hair, not cutting it other than trimming the ends, since she'd started to lose weight. The length in some indefinable way proportionate to her weight loss.

She explained about journaling, how that morphed into the tablets and lists she always carried around.

"What was it that made you start to lose weight?" he asked.

She had no intention of telling him about meeting Davis. Thinking his name now, she struggled to picture him in her mind. She was surprised to find it took her several moments before she saw him, dressed in an Armani suit, dashing into a meeting. She'd started to think that maybe her epiphany moment would have come regardless of meeting Davis. She sensed she'd been at a point in her life—a now-or-never moment—when she'd have the strength and courage to begin a new chapter in the saga of Lizzie Hampton.

"I was ready. It was as simple as that," was all she said.

He sat up and crossed his ankles, his long legs resting along-side hers. The khakis he'd worn to the dance looked nearly white next to her legs, now deeply tan from days in the strawberry fields. A slight pink from the parade graced the surface of her knees. He placed his hand on her thigh, a gentle touch of a friend, not the sexual one of a lover. "Liz, not a thing about you is simple, it never was."

A small smile played on her lips, she leaned her body into his, then away, giving him a small sway of understanding. He laughed and mimicked her motion, leaning a little harder than she did, nearly throwing her off balance. She came back at him, putting her whole body behind it and they tumbled over, Finn pulling her to him as they rolled off the blanket and onto the grass, still wet with the morning's dew.

Their smiles were wide with amusement as Finn rolled them back to the blanket, anchoring Lizzie beneath him. He peppered her face with wet kisses, making exaggerated smacking sounds with each one, until she was laughing the laugh he professed to love so much.

He rose up on his elbows, his face over hers. She was reminded of a similar position last night, though with fewer clothes. She traced his face with her fingers, letting them come to rest on his full bottom lip. She watched her fingers move with his mouth as he whispered, "Thank you for telling me all that, Liz. Thanks for trusting me enough to share it with me."

The words made Lizzie reel. It *was* about trust, wasn't it? She'd had to have a huge amount of trust in Finn—in anyone, really—to be able to say all the things she just did. The thought cheered her.

Just this morning she had remembered being devastated by this man, and now she was able to trust enough to lay herself bare. She felt more naked with him here, now, than she had laying with him in bed last night.

She gauged her internal barometer and felt something she was sure was…could be…may be…peace.

—⁓—

Finn dropped Liz off at her parents' house. Their embrace when she scooted out of the Jeep seemed different. Full of an understanding that hadn't been there before.

He felt honored, and just a little humbled that she'd chosen to tell him her story. There was an ease between them now. The pent-up anxiety about desperately wanting to be together was gone. He wondered if the desire would be gone as well, now that he'd finally slept with her. It seemed just the opposite. He wanted her again and again, now more than ever.

Yes, fucking Liz Hampton was now checked off his mental bucket list, but he wasn't entirely sure that a whole slew of new items hadn't taken its place. And every one of them included Liz.

So much about last night made sense to him now. The woman who had seemed shocked to see Liz was indeed shocked... at her appearance. It also made sense to him why someone like Pete Ryan, or any other man she'd come in contact with, had not pursued her with a single-minded determination to make Liz his wife.

Finn knew that overweight men and women had fulfilling relationships, but he also knew that Liz would not have pursued a relationship when she felt that uncomfortable with her own body. Hell, it wasn't even that she felt uncomfortable with her body, it was like she had cut off all connection with her body whatsoever. Why would she try to have a relationship with a man who would be accepting of her obesity—and Finn knew there were good men like that out there—when the whole point of the obesity was to abstain from having a personal, intimate relationship with a man?

But why? What had made her shun all intimacy? From what she'd said it had begun around her senior year of college. Had something traumatic happened? Had she been abused, or raped? He didn't think so. He thought Liz would have told him that.

In the end, it didn't matter what had triggered it, he only wished to hell he could have been there to help her through it.

She was so honest. After the game playing and hidden agendas of Dana, it renewed his faith that there were indeed people who told it like it was.

He thought back to their lovemaking. He had noticed her inhibitions, of course. Saw her hesitation when she told him what she wanted. It had been one hell of a turn-on for him. His good girl gone bad. He couldn't remember ever coming so hard as he had inside of her.

He'd thought that her inhibitions were directed at her choice of partner. His wrong-side-of-the-tracks mentality could not lie still. He'd thrilled in the way he'd made her come undone, the way she'd moved beneath him, the sounds she'd made.

Now it made more sense. Her needing the lights off, seemingly orchestrating her movements. And her hesitancy in bed. It had been about her body, not about him as he had thought. The realization was unsettling.

He passed Bob's Mobil on his way back to Houghton. Today's Bible verse read, *"God loves a cheerful giver."*

He smiled to himself. Liz was in good with the man upstairs, then, because he didn't know anyone who qualified more than she as a cheerful giver. Giver of her time, her resources, even of her body, which may have been the hardest thing for her to give.

He thought about that for a minute, placing it amongst the information he'd just learned about her.

Sure, she was a cheerful giver, but at what price? If she'd been more of a bitch like Dana, would she have turned to food for solace? Was obesity her cost for always being "there" for everyone? Who had been there to cheer her up, who had been her sounding board? He knew she was tight with her family and Katie and Alison, but they weren't with her on a daily basis.

If he had it in his power—and he knew that he didn't, not really—he would see that Elizabeth Hampton never felt the need to order two pops from McDonald's again.

Seventeen

—◆—

√ Get more condoms
√ Get lemons for Clea
√ Call Sybil

"**LIZZIE, HONEY**, we're concerned for you. We think it's great that your confidence has returned, that you're having great sex, but having great sex for this long without emotions entering into it just isn't possible. Not for someone like you, anyway," Katie said with warmth and concern.

Before Lizzie could ask for clarification on the "someone like you" comment, Alison piped in with her two cents. "You're in over your head, Lizard."

Lizzie put on a smile and laughed her friends' concern off, a habit she had honed to perfection over the years, "That's it from the psychologist? No deep analysis? No 'this stems from your childhood' crap?"

"Nope. Just....you're pretty much fucked, Lizard. And I think you know it."

She gave a half-hearted chuckle. "Wasn't that the whole point? Getting fucked?"

Katie jumped back in, taking Lizzie's hand in her own, "Oh, Lizzie, don't. Don't joke this away, not this time. This is too important."

Lizzie's eyes darted around the picnic table looking for…
what? She didn't know. Maybe a big vat of chocolate to duck her
head into? Finding no such vat or any other treat, and knowing
she'd find no solace there anymore anyway, she braced herself to
face the music.

"Okay, I admit, I'm feeling more with Finn than I thought
I would. But maybe that's good, maybe its just an indication that
I'm ready to handle a romantic relationship."

"Or maybe that's just a huge rationalization," Alison said.

"What am I trying to rationalize? I knew that I was going to
have sex with Finn before I came here, why do I need to rationalize it now?"

"Not the having sex part. The *only* having sex part." At
Lizzie's questioning look, Alison continued. "You are not the type
of person to have casual sex, so you've created a relationship with
Finn to warrant the sex. It's okay. You just need to realize what
you're doing so you can put a stop to it before you get hurt."

"Put a stop to the sex?" It was almost a whimper, the thought
of ending those blissful nights in Finn's arms unbearable.

"No, put a stop to forcing a relationship that isn't meant to
be, that could never happen, just to rationalize having sex with
someone you're going to leave in a few weeks."

"Why could it never happen?" she asked.

Katie and Alison exchanged glances. Katie gently said,
"Lizzie, you don't really think you and Finn have any kind of
future together, do you? You see, this is what I was afraid of." She
looked over at Alison with an accusing glance. "This is what I told
you would happen that first night we went to the theater to hunt
down Finn."

Alison raised her hands in surrender. "Hey, I'm not the one
with the asinine find, fuck, and forget plan."

Lizzie ignored them both, saying more to herself than to
her friends, "There could never be any future with Finn." It was
a statement, but there was just the slightest lilting of her voice at
the end, creating a question.

"No, of course not, he's got those kids," Katie said.

"And you don't even like kids, not to mention how snotty Annie is to you," Alison added.

Lizzie thought of the progress she and Annie had made since the day of the exercise bike, but kept the information to herself, only numbly nodding with her friends as they continued their tag team.

"Obviously he can't leave the area, not with the farm," Katie said.

"And your business is in Detroit, you can't leave there," Alison added.

Just yesterday Lizzie had reread the proposal her account executives had given her about taking on partners. If that happened, she'd be able to work from any location. Flying to meet potential clients, which would be what she'd concentrate on, could be done from anywhere. With the internet, email, texts, and faxes, she could set up shop in her old bedroom and not miss a beat. Not that she would, but still…she was not nearly as tied to Detroit as her friends seemed to think.

And, God, how she loved this place. It wasn't fair to be here in the summer, when the Copper Country was at its best. Of course, it was pretty spectacular in the fall, too. If only she was visiting in January, she'd be chomping at the bit to get back to Detroit.

Wouldn't she?

"And, I know this sounds snobby, but could you really see yourself with a man who never even went to college?" Katie asked.

"It does sound snobby, but unfortunately, it's accurate," Alison added.

Lizzie thought about the life lessons that Finn had learned at the hands of his mother, from Dana, even Annie's illness. She wondered if you could ever buy that much education? Sure, she'd read more books this past year than Finn probably had in his whole life, but he was hardly stupid. He had made the farm work, had become a businessman with no training.

Lizzie had looked through his books and financial statements when setting up the foundation for Annie. Something she felt kind of uncomfortable doing, but Finn didn't seem to mind. He had a long-term business plan to improve the farm with new equipment. He also had a very well thought-out and researched business plan for a horse boarding and training operation. The plans had been put on hold when Annie was diagnosed, but still seemed doable. If not for Dana's extortion, the farm would be turning a good profit and Finn's horse boarding/training business might be flourishing. They'd never know.

"Plus, of course, all you ever were to Finn was a conquest," Katie said.

"And you could never settle for anything less than full commitment," Alison added.

Ah, they had her on that one. Or did they? She couldn't be sure, but she thought that Finn was experiencing the same draw that she was. She'd purposely tried to stay away from the farm, to give him time away from her, time with his kids, time for the farmwork, and he would always call by late afternoon, wondering where she was, when she would be coming by?

After they had sex, he would pull her close and hold her, just breathing her in, content to lie together until he needed to leave.

Since that first night, they hadn't been able to spend the entire night together, and he had been the one to lament that fact on more than one occasion. Not her, him. He was feeling it too. They were both careful to still refer to what they were doing as a fling, but they hadn't mentioned her leaving in quite some time. Of course it was understood, but still, it wasn't something either of them brought up.

But a summer fling, good as it may be, was all it could ever be, right?

Why?

Because of all the reasons Katie and Alison just brought up!
Oh yeah, those reasons.

Still, she had valid responses to each of their points, even if she voiced them only to herself.

"Well, now that we've got that settled," Katie said and started to pack up her things.

"Yes. We feel better about the whole situation now, Lizzie," Alison added.

Lizzie was dazed. Had they really settled anything? She seemed more muddled than when she'd arrived. She knew a dismissal when she saw one, so she gathered up her things and hurried off, thinking she still had time to get to the farm to help Clea with dinner.

—⁓—

As Lizzie drove off, Katie purposely lingered.

"Honestly, Al, as a psychologist, I would have thought you'd come up with something better than plain, old-fashioned reverse psychology."

"It worked, didn't it? She was definitely thinking of objections to each of our points, even if she wasn't saying anything."

"I know, but we were so obvious, I expected her to see right through us."

"She can't see anything through that haze of love she's in," Alison chuckled.

Katie smiled. "It is pretty obvious, isn't it?"

"To us, anyway. Okay, now that we've got her thinking about it, let's pray to God Finn doesn't break her heart again and we've got a replay of eighteen years ago on our hands." Alison's pragmatic streak shone.

"You don't think he would, would he? She's obviously the best thing that ever happened to him."

"He did it once, who's to say anything's different?" Alison said.

"You're right, maybe we should have just kept our mouths shut."

"No. She needs to realize she's in love with Finn. But she needs to realize it by herself. And if he does break her heart, she needs to know that she can survive," she thought on that for a minute, then added, "without the help of Ronald."

"Ronald?" Katie asked.

"Ronald McDonald."

—⁓—

A strand of hay dropped from Lizzie's hair. She snatched it from the dinner table and placed it under her napkin before anyone could notice. She looked around the table to see if her embarrassment had been witnessed. Stevie shoveled mashed potatoes into his mouth with a continuing rhythm, taking no time to swallow before the next forkful hit, his eyes intent upon his plate. Annie was rattling on about some show she had seen on the Disney Channel that afternoon. Clea's eyes darted to her plate as Lizzie's met them, an all-knowing smile playing on her mouth at seeing the hay, but pretending not to notice for which Lizzie silently thanked the older woman.

Then she looked at Finn. His eyes were on her hand that was still holding the napkin in place over the damning piece of hay. His gaze moved up her arm, pausing at her breasts, over her mouth, still swollen from his kisses, and rested on her dazed eyes.

His look said volumes. It said he knew what she was hiding under her napkin. It said he knew how that hay had gotten in her hair in the first place. And it said he wouldn't mind repeating the act again—their literal roll in the hay—as soon as possible.

She gave him a scathing look, but he only laughed and returned to his meal.

It had been three weeks since the first night they'd had sex. Three weeks from the night they had both thought to quench their thirst for each other, then put some distance between them.

They'd made love every day.

It hadn't been easy. Sometimes Finn would come over to her parents' house after Stevie and Annie were asleep, asking Clea to turn her monitor on, or even to sleep in the farmhouse for the night. A few times Clea took the kids somewhere for the evening and Finn and Lizzie would hurriedly come together in his bed. He was down to only one night a week at the Mine Shaft because of the berries being in prime season, but hey'd made use of that one night, doing it in the projection room after closing.

Just tonight, he'd cornered her in the barn while everyone else was inside getting dinner ready. While stretched out on a bed of hay, the sweet scent of strawberries lingering in the air, he'd given her the most satisfying orgasm she'd ever had.

That was the funny thing. It got better every time. Lizzie hadn't seen that one coming. She knew she was becoming more comfortable with her body around Finn, though she still never allowed him to see her in the daylight or to have the lights on while they had sex. He understood her hesitancy and never pushed her. She knew that with her comfort level with her body rising, it would only make sense that her comfort level with sex would rise as well. But it was rising at a much faster rate.

She was good in bed! Well, maybe not good, but better than she ever thought she'd be. It was a shocking revelation for her.

But that was what she'd set out to do, so she really shouldn't be surprised. Her plan had worked like a charm. She now felt able to begin an intimate relationship with a man suitable to her future.

Problem was, she didn't really want to anymore.

Clea's voice drew Lizzie from her thoughts. "I'm sorry, Clea, what did you say?" They were just finishing up the dishes, the kids had gone into the living room to watch TV and Finn was at the desk going over the newest figures Lizzie had put together on the fundraiser.

"Would you come out to the trailer with me for a minute? I'd like to show you something," Clea repeated.

"Of course." Lizzie followed Finn's grandmother from the farmhouse and across the lawn to the trailer.

"Make yourself comfortable, dear, I'll just go get what I wanted to show you," she said and disappeared into what Lizzie assumed was Clea's bedroom. Lizzie followed the woman's directions and made herself at home on the couch.

Clea returned after only a short while holding a shoebox,

joining Lizzie on the couch. She held the box on her lap, finger-ing the lid. "I've thought about showing you this for some time now, and I've gone back and forth on whether or not to do it." She paused, saw she had Lizzie's attention, and continued. "Mind you, I'm not giving these to you—they're not mine to give—and I ask that you don't open them." Again she waited, still running her hands, aged and withered from life and hard work, along the corners of the box. "But, I do think you should know that these exist, and you can do with that information as you please." She handed the box to Lizzie.

"I found them in the back of the closet when Finn moved out of here and back into the farmhouse after he and Dana were married. I think he completely forgot about them. He's certainly never mentioned them to me." She nodded for Lizzie to open the box, sensing her trepidation.

As Lizzie lifted the lid off the box she was assaulted with the scent of cedar, probably from the closet where the box had resided all these years. Inside were sealed letters. More than twenty of them. None had postage marks or even stamps on them. They had never been sent.

Every single one of them was addressed to her at Michigan State.

She flipped through them, crushed that they were sealed and knowing she couldn't break Clea's request not to open them. But oh, how she wanted to know what they said. She noticed that ten of the letters were addressed to her dorm room her freshman year, seven to the dorm she lived in her sophomore year, and five to the apartment she lived in her junior year. None were addressed to her senior-year apartment.

"I don't understand? How…how did he know where I lived?" Her voice was soft, and she cleared her throat to repeat herself, but it wasn't necessary.

"I'm not sure about the other addresses, but I do know that he called your mother shortly after you left to go to college for your freshman year to get your address," Clea said.

Lizzie pawed through the envelopes again, as if not believing what she saw the first time. "My mom? She never told me he called."

"I happened to overhear that call, that's how I know. He asked your mother not to tell you he called. He said he wasn't sure if he'd write, wasn't sure you'd be happy to hear from him, so it would be better all around if your mother didn't mention it."

Lizzie silently sat on the couch, stunned. He *had* written to her. He just didn't send the letters.

"How he got the other addresses, I'm not sure. Probably the same way."

"I…I don't know what to say. I don't really know what this means," Lizzie said. Her hands were still funneling through the envelopes, the feel of the paper cool against her skin.

Finn had written to her at college. Lizzie couldn't wrap her mind around it. Had she meant more to him than she'd realized? It certainly appeared that way. "Why didn't he send them?" She didn't even realize she'd voiced the question out loud until Clea answered.

"Pride, I expect," she quietly said.

Lizzie's head shot up from the box, startled. "Pride? What do you mean, pride? He was the one who broke things off with me."

"Something I believe he regretted soon after if the way he moped around here that summer is any indication. Steven, Finn's father, my son, died when Finn was only ten. Linda tried to make a go of it, but she'd just had Phoebe, and…" Her voice trailed off.

Lizzie knew that Finn's mother was an alcoholic and that Finn's father was dead. She didn't know, until now, how young Finn had been when his father had died.

"That's when they moved in here with you?" she asked.

"Yes. I sometimes wonder if Linda might have been better off on her own. If maybe having me close by to help didn't allow her to…indulge more than she would have if she'd had sole responsibility of those kids." It was obvious to Lizzie that Clea had replayed the scenario in her memory many times, looking for a different outcome.

"Or maybe something tragic may have happened if you hadn't been around, Clea. You were a godsend for Finn and Phoebe. I know Finn thinks so."

Clea smiled faintly. "Maybe, dear, maybe. We'll never know, will we? We play the cards we're dealt.

"Anyway, by the time Finn was fifteen, Linda was out of control and Finn took over with Phoebe. I know it was awful for him. There were times he'd come home after being out with friends and they would have seen Linda in town, falling down drunk, going off with some man or another. It gave Finn a very jaded perception of women, I'm afraid. One that didn't die when Linda did several years ago, and one that was certainly reinforced by that ex-wife of his."

Lizzie only nodded, having had a similar reaction to the woman the one time she'd met Finn's mother.

"When he met you, I thought he'd finally be able to let that all go. But, for whatever reason, he let you go instead. I always thought he didn't want to bring you down to what he thought his level was."

Finn had said something similar to her and she hadn't believed him, thought it was just a line to get her to forgive him for past sins and join him in a summer fling.

Clea took Lizzie's hand in her own. "You do know Finn always thought he wasn't good enough for you, don't you?"

Did she? Yes, she guessed she did. She knew he'd always harbored a wrong-side-of-the-tracks mentality when it came to her, and that his prideful streak was a mile long. But she never expected it was of this magnitude. Enough that he wouldn't ask her back after he'd let her go?

The memory of his blow-up after she bought him that shirt confirmed to her that yes, Finn Robbins would have a hard time swallowing his pride and asking her to come back to him. Throw in that he never really thought he deserved her. It all added up to a box full of letters sitting in a closet for eighteen years.

What a waste. She could almost cry for the kids they were. Finding the love of your life so young, and not being mature enough to see it through. Letting things like pride and lack of esteem rule your heart. She was as much at fault as he was, adhering to some crazy life plan that ended up getting shot to hell anyway.

Lizzie froze, realizing what she'd just said to herself. *Finding the love of your life.* The epiphany was as strong and clear as the one she had the day she met Davis Cummings. She had loved Finn. She had found the love of her life at eighteen.

She took a deep breath, feeling her chest tightening with the knowledge. Why had she denied it back then? That was simple. As intense as her feelings for Finn were, she was practical enough, even at that young age, to think that it was only lust, that she could not possibly fall in love so young.

After all, she'd had a plan.

Besides, if she was in love with Finn, wouldn't she want to show him off? Trot him out in front of the entire senior class of Hancock High? But she hadn't. She didn't like the way he dressed, was embarrassed that he worked at the Mine Shaft three years out of high school. And she lived in fear of being somewhere with other people and coming upon Finn's drunken mother.

But Lizzie wouldn't deny it to herself any longer. She had loved Finn. Deeply, and with a conviction that had not faded after eighteen years. And if she were really honest with herself, she'd admit that she loved him still.

Damn. Damn. Damn. This was not part of her plan.

Eighteen

—◊—

√ Buy more condoms
√ Do something nice for Clea
Call Sybil

FINN HEARD LIZ call out to him and he directed her to the back of the barn where he was working. "What did Gran want?" he asked when she reached him.

He sensed, more than saw, her shrug. "Oh nothing. Just wanted to show me some pictures of you as a kid."

Knowing there were no childhood pictures of him in the trailer—they were all in the family albums kept in the main house—but not wanting to push Liz, he let it slide. He wasn't stupid enough to bang his head against the wall of a woman that didn't want him to know something. "Mmm," was all he said.

"What are you doing?" she asked. She was standing directly behind him. He could feel her knees graze against his back as he sat on his haunches patching a hole in one of the stalls. Damn, but even her knees could make him hard. And he'd just had her in this same barn a couple of hours ago. Get a grip.

That was the problem, he'd lost his grip entirely where Liz was concerned. The promise he'd made to himself at the dance— to finally sleep with her then cool things down—had flown out the window that very night. And the idea of keeping his distance from her now was laughable.

When he held her in his arms, when he was buried deep inside her, his hands clutching her full hips, her hands cradling his face, he knew he was dealing with much more than a summer fling.

Thank God he was involved with Liz and not some traitorous bitch like Dana. Liz had been very upfront about not needing any commitments from him. But this was Liz, and Liz was not the type to jump into flings. Though they had not yet spoken about anything beyond the summer, Finn knew Liz shared the same deep feelings as he did. He felt it when they made love. And that's exactly how he'd come to think of his time with Liz, making love. He had another week at least—because no way would she leave before the fundraiser was over—to broach the subject with her.

The subject of a future together.

It would take some doing. He couldn't leave the farm right now, so she would have to relocate. He felt shitty asking her to do that, but he knew she loved this area. He could see it whenever they were near the lake. She couldn't take her eyes away from the calming water. Besides, that was probably the least of the sacrifices he'd be asking her to make to have a future together. There was Annie and Stevie. Liz and Stevie were tight, but it was still touch and go with Annie. Finn knew that most of that was Annie's fear about the upcoming surgery, so that would soon come to an end. Gran already loved Liz, and that feeling seemed mutual, so he didn't really see a problem there.

Finn only knew he couldn't let her get away again. It had been the biggest mistake he'd made in his life, but in a way he couldn't regret it. If he hadn't broken things off with her, he would never have hooked up with Dana, and there'd be no Stevie and Annie. Yeah, things had been pretty shitty with Dana and with Annie's illness, but Finn became paralyzed with fear at the thought of life without his two children.

Just like he'd come to feel about life without Liz.

She'd done the one thing that Finn thought impossible—restored his sense of trust.

God, she was such a genuinely good person. To come into his life and give so much, without asking for anything in return. Well, technically she did ask for something…a summer fling. But to his way of thinking, that wasn't asking anything of him, it was his pleasure. He knew he didn't deserve her, but this time he wouldn't let that stop him. He'd live his life trying to earn her love.

He was sure Liz loved him, just as he knew he'd always loved her. She was probably just a little gun shy. That was likely for a couple of reasons. First, he'd burned her before. Sure it was a long time ago, and she said she had forgiven him, but he knew he'd hurt her. Second, she'd been through a lot the last few years losing weight. Finn didn't know much about that kind of stuff, but figured something that dramatic would probably screw with your mind a little. Though Liz didn't seem to harbor too many hang-ups about that. Or if she did, she hid them well.

Still, he wished he could get her to see her body the way he saw it. Full. Delectable. Delicious. Sexy. Desired beyond belief. He'd been thinking about how to go about that when she found him in the barn.

"Just patching a hole," he said. He tilted his head up to look at her but she was looking away, around the barn. Finn followed her gaze and saw her noticing the different patches not only in this stall, but all around this far end of the barn. The holes were mostly patched, but the patching was all new, and in various degrees of drying. Some had been patched as recently as yesterday or the day before, and a few were drier, indicating they had been done longer ago. All were relatively newly patched.

He finished the patch and rose to his feet, putting his tools away, even though another hole was only a few feet away from where he worked.

"Why aren't you going to do that one?" she asked, pointing to another hole with her tan leg, her sexy toes poking from her sandals.

"Another time," he said, pushing past her and taking the tools to the makeshift workbench along the far side of the barn.

"Don't rush on my account, I'm in no hurry, in fact, I'll help if you want." She moved to his side, reaching for his hammer.

Finn chuckled. "No, it's okay. I just wanted to do the one tonight. The others will wait till another time." He intercepted her arm that reached for the hammer and placed it on his chest instead. "I can give you another job, though, if you're so interested in working with my tools," he said with a grin.

"Ha. What are you, in eighth grade? That sounds like something Stevie and his buds would say," she said, but she wasn't angry. Her hand smoothed up and down his chest, seeming to like what she felt.

Finn damn sure liked what *he* felt. He couldn't believe he was getting aroused again so soon. It was only a few hours ago that he'd tumbled Liz in the hay like the proverbial farmer's daughter. He was thirty-eight years old but his body responded to Liz like he was a randy teenager. "Let's get out of here. I don't think you want to pick all that hay out of your hair again."

She stepped into him, curling her arms around his neck, placing her face on his chest. "I asked Clea to sleep in the house tonight. I want you to spend the night with me, is that okay?"

Okay? Hell yes it was okay. He hadn't been able to sleep with Liz in his arms since that first night. He hated slinking away from her bed in the middle of night. Like she was some hook-up he couldn't wait to get away from. Nothing was further from the truth.

"Hell yes, it's okay. Let me go check on the kids, then let's go." He started to move, but she held him fast.

"Finn? Why are all these holes patched so weirdly, like they were done at different times, but all recently?" Her eyes scanned his handiwork.

Damn. How much to tell her? "That's exactly why. They were patched at different times. I finally got around to starting the repairs a few weeks ago." Again, he tried to walk away. This time she let him go, standing firm. He took a couple of steps before he realized he'd lost her. Turning, he saw she wasn't satisfied with his answer.

"Why not just patch them all at once? Like now, we could have them all done in no time."

"No, that's not how I'm doing it," he said firmly. She seemed to bristle at his tone and he figured he'd have to explain it all. Damn, how to do this and not sound like a total sap?

He took a deep breath and stepped back, half sitting, half leaning against a sawhorse. "Do you remember asking me that night at the beach when I told you about Dana and Annie why I wasn't more furious?"

She nodded, her glossy black hair bobbing with her. "Yes. You said I should have seen you then, that you were furious. And you had the holes…" Her voice slowed as the situation was dawning on her. "…In the barn to prove it." She waved her hands around the back area. "So this is the outcome of your frustration?" At his nod, she asked, "Okay. But why start patching them now? And why one at a time?"

His shoulders sagged, just a little. *Shit. Just tell her, maybe it won't sound as pussy-whipped out loud.*

"I came in here the morning I got back from your place. That first night we were together. It was still pretty early, so instead of going into the house, I came out here first. I walked back here to get something and saw that hole." He pointed to the largest hole, now patched and painted. "I'm not sure why, probably having just been with you. How good you are, Liz. How sweet. I don't know, but I felt like I needed to get rid of that hole, so I patched it. I was just about to do the next one when I heard Stevie up and in the yard, so I went to the house."

She stood staring at him. He knew she was probably embarrassed at his words, Liz just couldn't handle a compliment. He went on, determined to see this thing through.

"Anyway, I only patched the one. Then after we made love the next time I came out and patched another one. Again, I planned on patching them all, but I stopped after the one."

She started looking around, seemingly counting the patched holes and the ones still to patch, realizing the amount of fury that had gone through him all those years ago by the sheer volume of damage. And also the amount of time they had spent in bed by the number of patches.

"It kind of became a thing. Each time we got together I'd come out and patch another hole." He had her attention again. "This is going to sound corny as hell, Liz, but it was like each time we made love it wiped out one more bad thing that had happened in my life. The patching seemed to be a way to acknowledge that."

Had he still owned his horses, he was certain he'd be able to hear their hearts beating, the barn had gotten so quiet.

His eyes never left hers. God, he was so in love with her. She was staring straight at him, his beautiful Liz, scared to death of the things he was saying, but so desperately wanting to hear them. He could do that for her, at least. It was hard, and not in his nature, but he could let her know how special she was, how beautiful. That she wasn't just loved because she had always been "the nice one", but because of the wonderful, generous, loving person she had become.

Damn. He could see she didn't know what to say. He shouldn't have told her about the holes. He hadn't intended to, but Liz brought out an honesty and integrity in him he'd been sure he'd left behind in the divorce lawyer's office. The day he'd sold his daughter's future for his and his children's freedom.

He rose from the sawhorse, started to say something, but her tender look stilled him. She moved to him, took his hand and led him to the front of the barn to the door. "Come home with me," she whispered. He followed, saying nothing.

—∿—

Finn led her into her bedroom at her parents' place, shut the door and turned on the light switch. Liz automatically moved to turn it off and he gently grasped her hand. "Not this time. Tonight, we do things my way." He could sense her trepidation, but he pushed it aside. He knew his intentions, he wasn't going to hurt her. Not if she trusted in him like he trusted her.

She started to move toward the bed, but he held her firm where they were. They stood in front of the closed bedroom door, which held a full-length mirror. He turned her to face the mirror, standing behind her, his hands firmly on her shoulders.

"Tell me what you see," he whispered into her ear, brushing her hair aside to bare her neck. His breath sent a chill through her and Finn thrilled to know he could make her body respond to him so easily.

She seemed to sense what he was trying to do, what he was *going* to do, and her body tensed. Then she relaxed and shot back with a jaunty, "I see Clea's fabulous cooking right here," she placed a hand on her right hip, "and here," her left hand on her behind. Her tone was light, teasing, but Finn saw no amusement in her hazel eyes.

This was going to be harder than he thought. Damn. He didn't let her joking distract him. "I'll tell you what I see, Liz. I see a very beautiful woman."

A nervous smile graced her beautiful mouth. "Finn, you don't need to do this. To sweet talk me. I'm a sure thing." She nudged her elbow lightly into his gut, to emphasize her joke. She started to move away from him, but he clamped a hand around her waist to keep her still.

"Don't, Liz. Don't joke this away. I know it's hard for you to take a compliment, babe, so just be quiet and listen. Okay?" He wasn't really asking her permission, but he stared at her reflection until she met his eyes and slowly nodded.

His fingers reached around her, through her arms which hung limply at her sides, to begin unbuttoning her blouse. It was a cotton short-sleeve blouse and was easily disposed of, thrown across a nearby chair. The tan of her chest and arms seemed even deeper compared to the pale cream of her tummy and the tops of her breasts that peeked above her bra.

He slid his hands down her sides, feeling a soft quake from

her. He undid the button and zipper to her shorts. He felt her squirm, but he held her hips in place as he pushed the shorts down to the floor. He directed her to step out of them, and when she did, he kicked them to the side.

Her panties and bra were of a soft, robin's egg blue. Satiny innocence that demanded his attention. "So pretty," he whispered, letting his tongue glide against her neck. He was rewarded by a soft sigh as she leaned back against his chest.

Needing to feel her hot skin against his, he eased her away from him only long enough to peel off his tee-shirt and jeans. He then pulled her back to him, he only in boxers and she in bra and panties. Her panties were high on her waist, covering way too much in Finn's opinion, but they were cut high on her leg, giving him a welcome view of her thighs. They had both discarded their footwear at the front door.

He ran his hands up her arms, not knowing if the tingling began with him and he passed it on to her, or the other way around. It didn't matter. What mattered was the effect they had on each other. Had always had on each other. Would have on each other forever. He'd waited for it to ease, to lighten. But the fire for Liz only grew more intense.

He reached to her back, to undo the clasp of her bra. Her hands came up, covering herself just as he undid the hooks and began to brush the straps from her shoulders.

"Finn," she began, hesitation in her voice.

"Ssshh. Let me." He took her hands in his, feeling the round globes beneath and tried to gently pry her fingers loose.

"Let's lie down," she said.

"No. I want you here, in front of the mirror." He gave her hands another tug and she allowed him to take the bra away from her.

No longer having the support of the sturdy bra, her heavy breasts hung low and full. He heard her groan, but ignored it, his stare not leaving the heaving flesh, the puckered areolas, the blushed, hardening nipples.

"God, you have unbelievable tits, Liz," he murmured into her neck as his hands reached for them.

She beat him there, cupping them herself. "Yeah, unbelievable that they're down here, when they should be up here," she said, lifting them to the higher position they'd occupied in her youth.

He couldn't help but chuckle, but then brushed her hands away and took the mounds into his own hands, letting them lower to their natural position. He began to caress the flesh, feeling it tighten and firm under his gentle touch. His thumbs brushed across her nipples, watching in the mirror as they visibly tightened. "No, they're right where they're supposed to be. In my hands." It was corny as hell, but he meant it. "They're big and full and real…"

"And thirty-some years old," she added.

"Right. They're the breasts of a woman, Liz. And they're incredible." He pushed her breasts together. "God, how I want to bury myself in them. Bury my mouth. Bury my face. Bury my cock." He allowed his eyes to leave the image of his hands on her and found her eyes in the mirror. She lowered her warm eyes, not able to watch him, or not able to hear his blunt words, he wasn't sure which. It didn't matter, he'd give her more of both.

He kissed her neck, tracing his tongue back and forth across her pulse point. Sucking on her tender flesh until he'd marked her. Childish, he knew, but he liked the idea of Liz wearing his brand.

He didn't want to ever leave her breasts. Could play with them for hours, which he had on one occasion in the barn. This was better. It had been dark then, and seeing Liz's flesh blush, watching the arousal on her face, not only feeling but watching the tight puckering, was intoxicating. He raised a hand to her lips directing her to take his fingers in her warm, wet mouth, fully saturating them. She did, and he returned to her nipples, his slick fingers now playing a tantalizing push, pull, and pinch game.

She rubbed her ass against his erection, reminding him she still wore her satin panties. Not for long. Amidst a low growl that grinding her sweet ass against him brought, he left her breasts and moved his hands down her sides to the waistband of her panties.

Apparently she had forgotten about her panties as well, because her back stiffened against his chest as he moved to take them from her. "Finn, let's move to the bed," she whispered, her voice quavering.

"Not yet, babe, I need to see all of you." Before her hands could reach his, he slid her panties down her hips and thighs, right to the floor. She reluctantly stepped out of them and nudged them aside.

He realized she must have been using different swimsuits when she was at Alison's because there was no definite tan line, just a fading of deep tan into pale, creamy skin. The tan of her legs and arms was much deeper due to the days she spent in his strawberry fields. There was a strip of tan at her belly where Finn figured she had lifted the top of that thing she called a tankini. Just a sweet little strip of tan right at her belly button. It wasn't even as wide as his hand. He placed his fingers along the strip, unable to take his eyes from the delicious contrast of skin tones. God, he'd missed out on so much these last few weeks not being able to see her clearly while they had sex. It had always been with that one damn candle burning all the way across her room. Or in the barn after twilight with only the dimming daylight coming through the slats of the walls. They'd kept the door of the barn closed and locked because Liz turned out to be a bit of a shrieker, much to Finn's delight.

He turned his gaze to her face and watched as her eyes took a quick inventory of her fully naked body, then dropped to the floor, not willing to look at herself any longer.

Had he lost her? It wasn't his intention to humiliate her. Hell no, he just wanted her to see herself as he saw her. A gorgeous, mature, curvy woman that made him feel like no woman ever had.

"What do you see?" His hands smoothed down her hips, tempted to dip into her raven curls, sure he would find her wet with desire. He fought down the temptation, wanting to take it slow, even though her bikini wax shaped her glistening curls into a kind of landing strip. *So he could find his way home.* He'd felt it before, but finally seeing the neatly trimmed hair just about sent him out of his mind.

She shook her head, unable, or unwilling, to answer his question. He wrapped one hand around her waist, guided to the little strip of tan, and his other hand went to her chin, lifting it. Daring her to meet his gaze in the mirror.

Not one to back down from a challenge—not his Liz—she met his stare, and lifted her chin out of his hold.

"You want to know what I see?" she said, defiance in her voice. She didn't wait for his nod to go on. "I'll tell you what I see. I see a woman who abused her body for years and now must pay the price. I see droopy boobs, a flabby belly, inner thighs that jiggle when I walk. And stretch marks. Lots and lots of stretch marks." The breath whooshed out of her and Finn wondered if she'd collapse in his arms. She didn't. In fact, she stood even straighter, moved away from the warmth of his chest, leaving him bereft of their shared heat.

"Some people call stretch marks badges of honor," he offered up. His hands grazed the silver marks at the tops of her breasts. The same marks he'd noticed the first night she'd been at the farm and he'd gotten her blouse off. His touch moved lower, feeling the slight rise of the marks along her abdomen and hips. It was funny that they seemed like such a big deal to her when they didn't diminish his desire one bit. He would never have thought twice about them if she hadn't pointed them out.

She snorted. "Yeah, badge of honor if you have a baby to show for your troubles." She started to go on, but he could see he needed to get her out of this frame of mind.

"Okay. That's what you see. Now let me tell you what I see." He took her shoulders and pulled her back against him, pushing his firm erection into her ass and lower back, driving home the point he was about to make; that no matter how she saw herself, she made him unbelievably hard.

His hands began to touch her everywhere. Feather-light touches all over her body. His fingers continued their sweeping as he kept his eyes pinned to hers in the mirror and began speaking.

"I see a woman whose full breasts were not only made to nurse babies, but were made for a man's pleasure." His fingers trailed across her nipples. "I see a woman with wide hips, for easy birthing, or for a man to grab onto as you ride him." His fingers bit into the flesh at her hips and he pulled her tighter against his cock, rubbing himself against her. She let out a soft moan, but her eyes never left his, even as her head fell back against his shoulder.

"I see a woman whose tummy is a soft pillow to rest my head on after I've gone down on her." Her hands finally moved for the first time since he'd pulled her bra out of her grasp. They went to his arms, but instead of stilling him, or pushing him away, they rested on top of his. Her hands on top of his hands, wanting to follow him as he adored her body. Wanting to believe him. Needing to believe him.

He would make her believe, because it was the truth. He loved her body.

"I see a woman whose pussy gets drenched every time I touch her. Who comes hard when I rub her clit and whisper in her ear how bad I want to fuck her." His hand, with hers atop, skimmed through her curls and proved his point when his fingers easily slid through her soaking cleft. Her clit was already peeking from its hood, hard and throbbing. He began to slowly stroke her and a low moan of delight escaped her lips.

"I see all those things, Liz, all those parts. But you know what I see when I look at the whole? Do you know what I see?" His voice was rough with arousal. His stroking picked up speed now, and his other hand, still entwined with hers, returned to her breasts. His kneading was no longer gentle, and he could feel her responding to his rougher touch. She liked it a little rough, his good girl. She also liked when he talked dirty to her, he could see that in the way her body trembled.

"No," she answered, barely able to get the word out. His eyes wouldn't allow her to look away. He instinctively knew she wanted to see his eyes when he said what he intended to say. "What do you see?" she asked.

"I see the woman I'm in love with." At her deep intake of breath he released his hold on her and spun her around to face him. He crushed his mouth down on hers, devouring her warm, sensuous lips, gliding past with his tongue, intent on finding hers. He did, and they tangled their wetness against each other as their bodies pressed tight, her tits crushed to his chest, his hard dick shoved into her mound.

He couldn't believe he'd just said that. He knew it was true, but to say it. Jesus. But as the words tumbled out of him, Finn felt a lightening from his chest. He trusted Liz completely. Even if she didn't feel the same way—and he had a strong suspicion that she did—telling her that he loved her would be okay. Liz would never hurt him. Would never flaunt his love for her, or use it like a weapon as Dana had his love for the kids. No, Liz was the one person he could trust with his heart.

He started moving backward to the bed, not letting go of her body or her mouth. When the back of his legs came in contact with the edge of the bed, he turned and gently eased them both down to the mattress, pushing the comforter out of the way, wanting to feel the cool of the sheets against the heat of their skin.

The embrace and kiss broke as they situated themselves on the bed, Liz reaching for him as soon as she was lying down. She held his face in her hands. Finn could see the shine of unshed tears in her eyes. Oh hell, he hadn't wanted to make her cry. But he had to let her know what he saw when he looked at her. What he felt every time he looked at her.

Now, away from the mirror, looking directly into each other's eyes, he needed to make sure she knew his words weren't just a pep talk for her failing self image. He kissed her tenderly once on her lips and again told her how he felt.

"I love you, Elizabeth Hampton."

—🙞—

It wasn't like before, Lizzie thought, and not only because this time the lights were on. No, tonight was different. She wasn't thinking about how her body felt to Finn, she was thinking about what Finn made her body feel. Actually, she wasn't thinking at all, just feeling. And it was wonderful.

He'd seen her at her worst. In bright, harsh light, standing naked. Not lying down, where she could position herself to a better advantage. No, there she stood, letting everything hang out, or down, as the case may be.

Seeing herself, *really seeing herself*, in the mirror in front of Finn was one of the hardest things she'd ever done. And the most liberating. She'd disclosed to him her harshest opinions of herself, totally believing them, and yet hoping beyond hope, he could see past them.

Obviously he had, because he still wanted her. His hunger, his lust, his desire were plain in his eyes. It wasn't pity or understanding, or compassion that shone from those gorgeous blue peepers. No, it was pure want. Pure need.

But best of all, he loved her. Finn Robbins was in love with her.

"Prove it," she whispered to him. "Make love to me, Finn."

He ducked his head to kiss her. To be able to fully concentrate on the sweet sensations that his mouth brought hers instead of where his hands may be roaming—and what they may be finding—gave new depth to Finn's kisses. Had she known how soft his lips were? How the rough texture of his tongue was tantalizing against her own? How, when she sucked on his tongue, he shivered?

They'd been together nearly every night for the last three weeks and yet Lizzie's body hummed like it'd never been touched.

She turned off her mind, not willing to lose this wondrous awakening that was tempting her to self analyze. Why think when Finn's mouth was doing a torturous dance down her neck, skimming across her chest, teasing her tightening nipples.

Again, his words in front of the mirror came back to her, filling her with a boldness that excited her. She lifted his mouth from her tingling breasts and held his face in her hands, making him look up at her. She slowly shook her head from side to side. "Unh, uh," she said. "You had your way, now it's my turn."

She found she wanted to be in charge of this session. Her learning curve over, her confidence restored, she wanted to hold the reins. The image of his horses brought her next idea.

At his questioning look she gently pushed on his chest, entangling her fingers in his crisp chest hair as she did, until he was on his back. She leveled up to her elbow, leaning over him. God, she loved his chest, so broad, so strong. She bowed her head in reverence to it, licking his nipple as she did, receiving a shaky exhale of approval. She took in the scent of him, the familiarity of it now a comfort to her. He smelled of hay and Clea's kitchen and, of course, Brut.

She sat up and slid one leg over his waist, sitting low on his belly, straddling him. Instinctively, she hunched her shoulders, trying to seem smaller, trying to minimize. Catching herself, she sat up straight, even arching her back slightly.

No hiding beneath Finn's strong body this time. She started to rub herself against the rough hair that made a vee down Finn's belly, loving how it felt. Looking down, she saw how her wetness moistened his hair, making it glisten in the bright light. The sheer eroticism of the sight made her moan.

His hands slid up and down her thighs, the friction causing a delicious heat. She inched her way backward, rising as she did, so that she could grasp his erection in her hand. She stroked him with one hand as her other raked across his chest leaving white indentations in her wake.

"Jesus, Liz, put me inside you," he hissed, but she wasn't rushing. She took her hand from his chest and raised it to her own mouth, licking her palm several times while her eyes locked on his. She then continued to stroke him, able to slide along his length more easily, picking up speed.

His hands slid from her thighs to her breasts, teasing and taunting her as she was him. When a particularly playful tweak caused a gasp from her, he said again, "Put me inside you." It was as close to begging as she'd ever heard from the proud man, and she decided to put him out of his misery. Or at least give him a different kind of misery.

When she pressed him against her core they both lost their breath. She eased him to her entrance, sliding him along her cleft, totally saturating him. She slowly lowered herself onto him, resting her hands behind him on his muscled thighs. She sat, back arched, head thrown back, more exposed than she'd ever been.

Woman on top, no big deal, right? But would he ever know what it took for her to reveal herself to him like this? To invite his perusal of her body? When she glanced down, the look in his eyes made her realize that he did know what she'd offered him.

"You're beautiful when you ride me," he said. He reached his hands out to smooth her hips then slid to her butt. "You have such a great ass, Liz, perfect for this. Perfect for me to hold on to." His hands began to knead her cheeks, rocking her into a forward motion that she quickly found and took over herself.

She leaned forward, letting her breasts hang down to find his waiting mouth. The suckling sounds he made spurred her own desire and her movements picked up speed.

The force of her orgasm caused her to pull her breast from Finn's mouth and arch back, small shrieks of delight escaping her. Shudders racked her body, her fingers bit into Finn's waist and chest as she rode out the wave, only to be caught by another as he reached out and stroked her where their bodies joined together. He teased her with his touch until she could take no more, than allowed her to come down.

As her breathing began to reach normal, he grabbed her hips and bucked his still throbbing erection into her. "Ride me hard, Liz. Make me come," he groaned.

She did.

And he did.

When she had thoroughly milked his body, she collapsed on top of him and he rolled them to their sides, facing each other. They gazed at each other, wearing dopey grins, waiting for sanity to return.

"Oh. We didn't use a condom," she said. She hadn't noticed at the time. Surely Finn must have realized?

He held her close, tangling his fingers in her hair. "You're on the pill, right?" he asked.

"Yes…" she said. But that wouldn't be enough for him, not after what Dana had done. God, he wouldn't think she was trying to trap him or playing some kind of game with him, would he?

"We're fine then," he said, kissing her forehead.

She realized that just as she had just put all her trust, all her faith, in Finn by baring her body to him, so had he to her.

Pulling away from him slightly, she took his face in her hands. She knew he loved it when she held him like that. She'd done it when they were dating years ago. She had held his face above hers that first night on his grandmother's couch and had known, even then, that she would need to memorize every feature of his strong face. Felt sure that it was the face she would want to conjure up for the rest of her life.

She held that same face, now aged and weathered, and played with the idea that maybe this time she wouldn't have to memorize it. Maybe this time she wouldn't have to rely on memories.

"I love you, Finn Robbins," she said. It was the first time in her entire thirty-six years that Lizzie said the words to a man, other than her father and brother, and yet they rolled off her tongue with ease.

He kissed her softly, so gently she wasn't even sure his lips met hers. He rolled her over to spoon, as had become their routine.

His hand rested low on her tummy. She didn't even notice.

Nineteen

√ Go over EVERY Annie Aid detail – AGAIN!
√ Call lawyer about partnership proposal questions
√ Get to-do list for Annie Aid to K&A
√ Get bottle of wine for each K&A
√ Send flowers to Sybil – and DON'T call her anymore

THE WEEK BEFORE the fundraiser was full of last minute details and duties. Finn and Lizzie found it harder to be alone, but find time they did. Their lovemaking took on a new sweetness, with no more sense of urgency.

Lizzie once again went over the partnership proposal her senior staff had written, making notations and suggestions in the margins. With the partnership, she envisioned being able to work from home around three weeks out of each month, and travel to Detroit and various spots around the country to meet clients the remainder.

She decided to do it. To give up complete control and take on partners. Now she just needed to figure out where that home office would be. Without a doubt she would be moving back to the Copper Country. But would she be moving in to Finn's house right away, or would they wait until Annie had her operation and had gone through physical therapy? She knew she was welcome to stay at her parents' house for as long as she wanted. Or maybe she'd sell her condo and buy a place on the lake up here. Something small, where she could live and work for now, then be a place where she and Finn could take the kids later.

Later? What precisely would be happening later? No exact words of the future were spoken between Finn and her, but there was a definite understanding that they'd be together. Wasn't there? He'd said he loved her and she'd told him the same. Didn't that mean he wanted to be with her beyond next week? Her inexperience in the relationship department left her wondering. She didn't want to ask Katie and Alison. She hadn't even told her two friends about this new, deeper understanding. It still seemed so personal, so pure, she wanted to keep it to herself a while longer. After the fundraiser, when her parents returned, she'd sit them all down and tell them of her decision to move home and make Finn and his family a permanent part of her life.

She was thrilled with the success of the fundraiser, though not surprised. Advance ticket sales had ensured that not only would all the expenses be covered—and there were a lot, with chartering a plane to get all the athletes to the remote area—but would pay for Annie's operation and future medical and physical therapy bills. Lizzie estimated that tickets bought the day of the event would help put a dent in the mortgage on the farm so that the Robbins family would be on solid ground.

That she hoped to one day be a part of that family, she kept to herself.

The Friday golf outing and picnic had a huge turnout. Stevie's pals manned the holes and caddied for the celebrity golfers. Stevie and Lizzie drove around the course in a cart during the tournament checking on things. Stevie was in heaven. He'd given the girl from the Strawberry Festival—again dressed in purple, Lizzie noticed—the coveted last hole to work, where the golfers tended to hang out and wait around after they finished playing. Stevie introduced the purple-clad girl, named Heather, to Lizzie.

Lizzie had Finn bring Annie to the course just as the tournament was ending so she could meet the athletes that had come to her benefit, and so that they could meet her. Petey, of course, acted like they were old buddies in front of the other jocks, flirting and teasing with Annie, much to the little girl's delight.

Finn seemed slightly dazed at all the events and attention given to the cause, basically trying to stay out of Lizzie's way.

The Stanley Cup arrived on Saturday morning and was taken to the rec center, where a line of people that swept around the entire building gathered to have their picture taken with the hallowed trophy and the hockey players of their choice.

Though he posed with the trophy when asked, Petey was careful not to touch it, bowing to the superstition that all pro players had. Never touch the Stanley Cup unless you've won it. He hoped to lift the trophy over his head in victory himself some day, so he wasn't about to tempt the hockey gods.

Petey rubbed the Colorado Avalanche players' noses in the fact that most people requested the hometown hero pose with him and the cup even though he'd never won the trophy. The Avs retaliated by flashing their championship rings in Petey's face.

Lizzie soothed egos and gave Petey a warning, and the afternoon progressed smoothly. Just another day of dealing with petulant men that made a living playing boys' games.

Later that night, Finn, Lizzie, and Alison all pulled into the parking lot of the rec center at the same time in their respective vehicles. Clea would bring Annie and Stevie later in the minivan. Lizzie and Finn had driven separately, figuring she may need to stay later than everyone else to see that her clients all had a good evening. The three each rounded their vehicles and smiled at each other.

"Lizard, you look great," Alison told her friend.

Lizzie loved the dress she'd chosen for this special night. A periwinkle blue sundress with wide straps that crisscrossed her tan back. She'd worn her hair up to show off the back of the dress.

"She's right, babe, you look terrific. Great dress," was all Finn said, but his eyes told her more. She could see the hunger in his blue gaze. It made her shiver in the warm August night.

She waved the compliments away and turned to Alison. "No Brandt tonight?"

"He's coming later. I came early to see if you needed any help."

Lizzie squeezed her friend's arm. "Thanks, Al. And yes, I need help. There's a pile of boxes in the back of the truck that need to be brought in."

Finn reached the back of her vehicle before she could. "I'll get them, you two look too pretty to be hauling boxes."

Alison smiled at the compliment. "Thanks, but you look pretty spiffy yourself, so don't you get all dirty, either."

"Thanks. New shirt," he said, sharing a look with Lizzie. They both knew that it had been a major turning point for them when she'd bought him the shirt for the dance. "The color will bring out the blue in your eyes," was all she'd said when she'd handed it to him, preparing herself for the inevitable blow-up. None came. Only a soft "Thanks, Liz." She'd raised her brows in disbelief and he'd only laughed and walked away, murmuring something about old dogs and new tricks.

The trio's attention was diverted from the boxes in Lizzie's Navigator when a school-bus-yellow Hummer turned the corner and began heading through the parking lot toward them.

"You've got to be kidding me," Alison said.

"I can't believe someone up here actually bought one of those things," Lizzie added. "I didn't think they were even still making them."

"They're not. But this one looks pretty new."

Finn shrugged. "What? I think they're kind of cool."

Lizzie and Alison rolled their eyes at each other. "Please. Those things are so obnoxious. Why not come just come out and say 'I have a small penis, therefore I'll drive a huge vehicle to make up for it'," Alison said.

Amidst laughter from all three, Lizzie added, "Besides, those things are really expensive. Most of the houses around here cost less than what you pay for those. Who up here has that kind of money to throw away on transportation?"

After only a second, Alison and Lizzie simultaneously barked, "Petey." They both giggled. "I am going to give him such shit over this," Alison laughed, and Lizzie nodded her head in agreement, already thinking of taunting things to say to her friend about his new choice in vehicles.

But it wasn't Petey who got out of the vehicle when it came to a stop, it was Ron and Katie. Alison and Lizzie only stood staring as the couple approached them. Ron and Finn shook hands, sharing the requisite "Hey, man" greetings. Finn led Ron to Lizzie's vehicle and each took a heavy box and headed inside.

After the men had gone, Katie turned to her friends. "Don't. Don't say a word."

Alison and Lizzie looked at each other, helplessly, then both broke out laughing which caused Katie to groan. "I know, I know. I can't believe he bought it, either. I can't believe he'd even want one of those things. Or how he even found one. Do you know how much that thing's going to stick out around here? I'm so embarrassed."

"Why'd you let him buy it, then?" Alison asked, and Lizzie looked at Katie questioningly as well.

Katie let out a sigh of exasperation. "I didn't *let* him buy it. He just bought it."

"You didn't know he was going to buy it?" Lizzie asked.

"No."

Lizzie and Alison looked at each other, thinking that maybe such things happened in marriages. What did they know?

Katie continued, "The worst part is, he used the money we'd set aside to use for in-vitro."

Lizzie's gasp of disbelief covered up Alison's "fucking asshole" that was whispered only for Lizzie's ears, not wanting Katie to overhear neither the sentiment nor the language.

Katie's beautiful blue eyes teared up and Lizzie noticed that her friend looked older than she'd ever seen her. Tired. Listless. It was startling a change.

"Oh, KitKat," Lizzie said. She and Alison automatically moved to comfort Katie, but were interrupted by Ron and Finn, who took the rest of the boxes from Lizzie's vehicle. Both Lizzie and Alison noticed the warning look that Ron shot his wife as the men walked by.

Lizzie and Alison moved to their friend. As they patted her back and gave sounds of encouragement, Katie whispered, "Fucking asshole." Alison and Lizzie both jumped back from the embrace as if bitten by a snake. They stared, amazed at Katie, not able to comprehend that the foul epithet had come from their friend.

Katie shrugged her shoulders, and seemed to emotionally gather herself. "Okay. Enough. So I have a huge yellow monstrosity instead of a baby, big deal." The three women stood awkwardly, such an unusual feeling for them, until Alison broke the silence.

"At least you won't have two o'clock feedings with that thing," she quipped. The lame joke was enough to get them moving, and they headed toward the building.

"Where's Brandt, Al?" Katie asked.

"Coming later."

"You guys sleep together yet?" Katie asked, knowing no subject was off limits between the women. Especially after what she'd just disclosed to them.

"No. I don't know if he's not interested or what. I've given him plenty of opportunities, but so far he hasn't taken the bait," she said.

"And yet he's the one who's calling you, right?" Lizzie asked, trying to get a handle on the situation.

"Yeah, he's all over me, except he's, you know, not...*all over me*," she said.

The three laughed. "Maybe he's just a gentleman," Katie offered.

Alison sighed. "I suppose. And I suppose I should be glad, but I'm going out of my friggin' mind. My sexual frustration level is at defcon four."

Again the women all laughed. "I see you're not suffering from the same condition, though, Lizard," Alison said.

Lizzie almost played dumb, but realized that tactic was useless with these two. "That obvious, eh?" she said with a smile on her face.

"Oh please. Here I am not getting laid and Katie has to be seen in that…that…" Having lost all words for the vehicle, she merely pointed at it. "And you're positively glowing. At least have the decency to be embarrassed."

They entered the building while Lizzie made a conscious effort to turn down the wattage on her happiness for an effort of solidarity with her friends. As they came into the lobby, Finn turned, met her eyes and flashed a huge, dirty-minded grin. Lizzie lost all previous thoughts and returned the smile as her friends only chuckled and rolled their eyes.

—⁓—

The dance that ended Annie Aid was well attended and, by all accounts, a huge success. Finn knew that his kids were having the time of their lives. Annie was never off the dance floor, and most of her dance card was filled with hockey and football players who moved around her chair with the agility that comes from evading defenders on the field or ice.

He hadn't seen much of Liz tonight. She'd warned him that she'd have to spend most of the evening schmoozing with the athletes. Making sure the ones that were her clients were being well taken care of, and dazzling the ones that currently weren't her clients with the hope of changing that status.

He also sensed something flaky was going on with Katie and Ron, so he steered clear of them. Brandt had shown up and was very attentive to Alison, but Finn didn't spend much time with them, either. He mostly held down the fort at a table with Gran, keeping an eye on Annie on the dance floor and watching Stevie make a play for some girl dressed in purple. After the fourth celebrity athlete came up to Stevie and greeted him, the girl in purple sidled up to him, figuring that's where the action was.

Careful, boy, watch out for her motives. Finn shook the cynical thought from his head. Not all women were like that. Not all women had hidden agendas. His eyes swung to Liz on the other side of the hall, talking with a group of women who looked to be about her age.

Case in point.

Was there ever a more open, more honest woman alive than Liz Hampton? The idea that this incredible woman belonged to him made the blood rush to his head and he found he needed to get some air. He told his grandmother he was going to step outside. She nodded and added that she'd be taking the kids home soon.

Pete Ryan intercepted him as he made his was out a side door. "Hey man, I was hoping I could catch you alone. Can I talk to you for a sec?"

Curious, Finn nodded and moved outside, the hulking hockey player following. When he turned around, Pete handed him a business-size envelope. "What's this?" Finn asked, not moving to open the envelope.

"It's my contribution to the Hannah Robbins Foundation," he said.

Finn handed the envelope back. "No, man. Thanks, but your contribution was your time and effort at this event. Liz told me about the calls you made to get a lot of these guys up here. And you alone were the draw that got so many people to come. No, that's more than enough. But thanks."

Petey pushed the envelope back to Finn. "Take it. It's done."

Puzzled by the man's words, Finn opened the envelope to find legal papers from the bank. After quickly perusing the documents he realized that it was the mortgage for the farm, paid in full. He stared up at Pete, an incredulous look on his face.

"Margo, from the bank?" At the light of recognition on Finn's dazed face, Petey went on, "She and I were in the same class in high school. I've known her forever. And I do mean 'known' her…as in the Biblical sense." He raised his eyebrows in a roguish way. "Anyway, I asked her what would be the best way to help, to ensure Annie's future. She said that it looked like the fundraiser would cover the operation and upcoming medical expenses. She said that what would really help out was to get the farm out of debt. She mentioned some business plans you'd taken her a while back about how to modernize the farm and a possible business with horses?" He waited for Finn to catch up.

Finn nodded, saying, "A boarding and training set-up. Possibly breeding down the road." It was said more to himself than to Pete, but he nodded.

"Right. That's what she said. That it would be doable if the farm were out of debt. So, there you go," he said, matter of fact, like he paid off people's mortgages every day.

"I can't accept this." Finn handed the note back to Petey.

"Sure you can," Petey nudged the paper back at Finn.

"No, I really can't. I can't accept your charity." The pride in his voice was evident.

Pete studied his feet for a while. "Listen," he finally said, looking at Finn. "*You* aren't accepting charity. This is a donation to the Hannah Robbins foundation, a charitable organization. I know, because I'm on the fucking board of directors. I could just give money, but I thought this would give everyone involved a little more peace of mind."

"Why are you doing this?" Finn asked.

Pete seemed uncomfortable, looking away, but finally said, "Listen, I adore Lizzie. She'll tell you that I did her the favor by being her first client and getting some of my buddies to join on, but the truth is, I'd have hung up my skates a long time ago if she hadn't been there, pushing me, egging me on, being my sounding board. Being my best friend."

Finn should have felt a pang of jealousy, but he didn't. He knew exactly what Pete meant. And that was the reason he loved Liz, that she was so giving, so able to take on the problems of the people she loved. He only nodded his understanding to the hockey player. "So why this? This helps me and my kids, not Liz."

Pete looked at Finn. "She's in love with you, you know," he said quietly.

"I know," Finn responded, just as quietly. He looked down at the paid bank note in his hand, knowing that it was Liz, as much as Pete, he owed for it. "I don't deserve her."

Pete laughed. "Of course you don't." He only held a hand up as Finn's head shot up at the rebuke. "But then, nobody deserves her. Nobody's fucking good enough for Lizzie."

He waited until Finn digested that, seemed to agree, and nodded his head.

"Besides, it's a good write-off," Pete said, obviously wanting to lighten the moment.

Not any better with this giving and receiving stuff, Finn smiled and thanked Pete again then started to turn.

"Just don't hurt her," Pete called after him. "She's…she's fragile. I know she acts all business and totally in charge of everything, but she's not used to mushy love stuff. Just…just don't break her heart."

Finn turned to face Pete. "I did once and it was the stupidest thing I've ever done. I won't let her get away again."

Happy with that, Pete shook Finn's hand and both men went in opposite directions. Pete toward the lobby where two of his teammates were having a chew, and Finn to find Liz to tell her what'd just happened. He was uncomfortable with the whole thing and he knew Liz would be able to put it all in perspective for him. She had that effect on him.

Before he could track down Liz, Gran and the kids found him.

"I'm going to take the kids home now. It's been a long day for everyone."

Annie could barely keep her eyes open, but her angelic face was flushed with the excitement of the weekend. Finn walked them out to the minivan, waiting discreetly as Stevie said good-bye to the purple girl. Heather, he thought Liz had said the girl's name was. When he swung his exhausted daughter into his arms she whispered in his ear, "Wasn't it just the best day ever, Daddy?"

He settled her into her seat, buckling her in and ruffling her hair. "It sure was, sweetheart. The best day ever."

Annie seemed to remember something and looked around the parking lot. "Where's Lizzie?"

"She's still inside, honey. She has to stick around until the end. Why?"

His daughter relaxed once again. "Oh. I just wanted to say thank you. But I'll tell her tomorrow."

A lump grew in Finn's throat as he watched the minivan drive away. Tomorrow. They would now have a lifetime of tomorrows to say thank you. And please. And I love you. And pass the bread and every other mundane thing that members of a family said to each other.

Passing his Jeep on his way back, he decided to put the bank note Pete Ryan have given him into the glove box. It stuck in his craw to accept the gift. It reminded him once again of all that Liz had brought to his life, all she had done for him and his children. All the things he had not been able to do himself.

The prickling feeling he now knew was his stubborn pride began to burn at the back of his neck. Seeing Liz would ease it. He went inside through a side door that the minivan had parked near for easier access to look for her. Not seeing her in the main room, he headed toward the lobby, but saw the back of Katie's and Alison's heads in a side foyer. Figuring Liz was probably with them, he headed in that direction. Liz wasn't with them, but before he could ask the women where she was, the words coming from Katie stopped him and he stood quietly to listen, the women unaware of him at their backs.

"I mean the woman is beaming, just beaming," Katie was saying.

"Yeah, I guess this plan of hers was a good thing after all," Alison said.

Finn knew he should let the women know he was behind them, but he didn't. Something stopped him from making his presence known.

"I guess so. Maybe she knew what she was doing. I have to tell you though, I was pretty concerned when she first told us about this master plan of hers," Katie said, taking a sip of her wine.

"With good reason," Alison said. "I mean, when your best friend says she wants to fuck an old boyfriend so she can test out her new body, I think concern is in order."

The women sipped at their drinks as Finn thought about their words. He hadn't realized that Liz hadn't slept with anyone but him since she'd lost weight. It made sense, though, as shy as she had been about her body in the beginning. He found he liked the idea.

But something wasn't right with what they'd said. Yes, Liz was getting used to her new body with him, but she hadn't even know he was still in town until she'd run into him that night at the Mine Shaft, right? What did they mean "her master plan"?

A vision of one of her tablets, one she always quickly shoved back in her purse when he was around, came to mind. It was labeled "the plan" across the font in red marker.

The cool fingers of doubt swept across the back of his neck and he was just about to question the women when they began to speak again.

"Well sure, but what really bothered me was the whole sleeping with Finn only so she could be prepared for her relationship with this Davis Cummings."

"Yeah, that was really unlike Lizard, I admit, but…"

Still stinging from the hit his pride had taken from Pete Ryan's generosity, the words cut Finn to the quick. He whirled and started back to the main room, not hearing Alison finish her sentence.

The door slamming behind him alerted the women that he'd been standing behind them. They just didn't know how much he'd heard.

"Oh shit," Alison said.

"Ditto," Katie said, and the women rushed after Finn.

Twenty

—⁂—

√ Make Yooper baskets for athletes
√ Buy new dress
√ Make sure photographers are attending

HE HAD TO FIND LIZ. Had to hear from her mouth that what her friends had said wasn't what he thought. A niggling voice in the back of his mind kept telling him it was true. That it all made perfect sense.

There was no way someone like Liz Hampton would want someone like Finn Robbins for anything more than a good fuck. That's what she'd come here for, and that's exactly what he'd given her.

No, he tried to tell himself. She had told him she loved him. His Liz wouldn't lie. She was good, and clean and honest. They were going to have a future together. He and Liz and Stevie and Annie would be a family.

But the voice that had continually reminded him who he was—who he would always be—plagued him. *You're nothing but the son of a drunk who can't even provide for his own children.* He swallowed hard and tried to shake the thought. No, Liz saw him for more than that. She saw him for what he had tried to be, for what he *could* be. She'd told him so.

Women lie. Women have always lied to you. Your mother. Dana.

Now Liz. The only time she told the truth was in the beginning, when she said she just wanted a summer fling. Was everything else a lie? Especially the loving him part?

He found her in the lobby of the rec center, hugging some man he'd never seen before. Someone who had obviously just arrived. The guy was decked out in a fancy suit. Who the hell wore suits to a community dance in the Copper Country? A sliver of ice-cold dread shot through him.

This was him. This was the guy. This was who Finn had primed Liz for. The guy that was going to reap the fruits of Finn's labors. The one who would have a life with Liz.

She saw him then, but didn't seem to notice his fury as he stalked toward her. Probably too busy pressing herself against that asshole.

Pete Ryan was also in the lobby talking with a couple of guys in the corner. Finn recognized them as clients of Liz, had met them yesterday, but, not following sports, didn't remember their names.

When he reached her, Liz calmly turned to Finn and said, "Finn, I'd like you to meet Davis Cummings, a friend and colleague of mine. Davis, this is Finn Robbins. Finn is Annie's father."

Annie's father? That's how she introduced him to this Davis guy? Not even a token "friend" label?

Pride and fury waged a war within him. They both won out when he lifted his hand to Davis and said, "Davis Cummings? Oh yeah, you're the guy Liz has been practicing for."

Finn felt a twinge of gratification when he saw the shock on Liz's face. She looked past Finn to see Alison and Katie entering the room with looks of horror on their faces. She was always sharp, so he wasn't surprised when she quickly put together what must have happened. "Finn," she started to say but was cut off by this Davis character.

Shaking Finn's hand, he said, "I'm afraid I don't understand. Lizzie's been practicing what for me?" Davis's glance left Finn and searched Liz's face with something that bordered on delight that she was doing something with him in mind.

The look sickened Finn and he lashed out. "She's been practicing fucking, Davis. And she's been practicing with me. It's been quite a chore, let me tell you, but she's finally getting pretty good at it."

Complete silence filled the lobby. Pete stepped away from the two men he was talking with and moved toward Liz, seemingly coming to her defense. Jesus Christ, the woman had so many men willing to come to her, to help her, what the hell was he thinking that he could offer her any kind of life? He saw Liz wave Pete away, but the hulking man stood close by, ready and waiting.

"Finn, you don't understand. That was before. My plan... things have changed, now."

Her plan. The words were shrill to Finn's ears. He grabbed for her purse and searched through it for the tablet he knew would be inside. There were several. He pulled the out one titled "the plan" and let her purse drop to the ground. He sifted through the pages until they came to rest naturally on the page that had seen the most use.

Several items were on the list, all but one checked off. Finn's eyes zeroed in on the last line.

Find, fuck, and forget Finn Robbins.

Images screamed at Finn. Dana's young, pretty face underneath him murmuring it was okay, she was on the pill. Dana's weathered face screaming she'd rage a holy terror if he didn't hand over the money. His mother telling him she'd stop drinking and start being a better mother to Phoebe. And Liz. Cradling his face and telling him she loved him.

It was the last image that hurt the most, cut the deepest. For it was Liz who he trusted more than anyone. She was the nice one. The good one. The one who did for others. The cheerful giver, for Christ's sake. She'd come up with some diabolical plan to use him to satisfy her curiosity about her body, then go home to some designer suit-wearing douche.

And it would have been almost bearable if that's all she'd done…slept with him once or twice, then went back to this asshole that stood beside her.

But she hadn't done that. No, she'd slept with him for a month, pulling him deeper and deeper under her spell. She'd spent every day at the farm with his family. With his kids. God, she'd been so great with his kids. And it had all been just part of some plan.

The pain slashed deeper at Finn and he felt the overwhelming need to slash back.

He waved the tablet in her face. "And I thought you were too good for me! I actually thought I had to aspire to be the kind of person you were. So kind, so generous. So *honest*." He practically spit out the last word, intending it to burn Liz.

It hit its mark. Liz stumbled back as if his words had been a physical blow.

She grabbed the tablet from his hands, saw what he'd been looking at him, and said, "It's not checked off. IT'S NOT CHECKED OFF!" Her voice shook, pleading.

"Why not? You certainly found me, and we know how much often you fucked me, Elizabeth." He dug in his back pocket and came up with a pen. He took the tablet back from Liz and slashed a mark through his name. "It's checked off NOW!"

He threw the tablet down at Liz's feet. He had to get out of here. Thank God Gran had already taken the kids home. He couldn't bear to go back into the festivities and hunt around for them. There was no telling how many people knew about Liz's little folly. Was he now the laughing stock of the Copper Country? Would he become known for his stud services for out-of-town visitors? He started to leave, then thought of something, and turned to Liz once more.

"Just one last thing. You are on the pill, aren't you?"

Dumbfounded, Liz nodded.

"Good. At least that's one thing I don't have to worry about."
She tried to reach out to him, but he pulled away from her. "Han-

dle all the fundraiser and foundation stuff through Margo. I don't want to see you again."

Seeing the crushed look on Liz's face just about brought him to his knees. That he hurt so badly for her even after knowing what she'd done to him made him want to hurt her even more, and he knew just the target. He turned to Davis and said, "Good luck, man. Hope you like it with the lights off." He heard the strangled sound come from Liz, but he couldn't face her.

He walked past her and out the door of the rec center.

—∿—

Lizzie didn't turn around to watch him go, nor did she need to see his reflection this time to know that he wanted to get as far away from her as possible.

She stood silent, not believing what'd just happened.

After a moment, a lifetime habit of putting other people at ease caused her to look around at the stunned faces in the lobby. Putting a smile on her face she said, "Don't worry, everyone. Just a simple misunderstanding. Nothing to worry about. Why don't we all go back into the dance?"

She started to move forward but Alison and Katie each took an arm and swung her around, heading outside. Out of the corner of her eye, she saw Petey step forward and take Davis's arm, leading him into the rec center, the other men following.

Outside, Katie placed her arm around Lizzie's shoulder and Alison stepped in front of her, tilting Lizzie's chin up to look her in the eye. "Not this time, Lizard. No laughing this off, or pretending it didn't happen. You were just barbecued in there. Feel it, Lizzie."

Lizzie started to say something. To make light of it. To make a joke of some sort. To brush her friends aside and tell them they were making something out of nothing. She started to say all of that.

What came out instead was a sob of pain so deep it rocked her entire body. It was the type of soundless cry that babies made before they could get out a substantial wail. Her shoulders shook and she struggled for breath. When her lungs finally filled, she was able to get sound out. The cries took her friends by surprise. But only for a second, then they recovered and began comforting Lizzie, leading her to Alison's car.

Lizzie wasn't sure how they got her home. She was vaguely aware of Alison driving and Katie following in Lizzie's SUV. Good. She sure as hell didn't want to return to the rec center the next day to get her car.

They were in her bedroom now. She stripped off her dress. The dress she was so proud of. The one that had lit Finn's face up so brightly only hours earlier. *Was that tonight?* Time seemed out of proportion to her.

She crumpled the dress up and threw it in the corner, causing Katie and Alison to look at each other. Lizzie stepped into some drawstring gym shorts and the largest tee-shirt she could find, then hunted for her bathrobe. Finding it, she wrapped its generous material around her twice, and pulled the belt tight. She moved to the bed where her two best friends sat and laid down between them.

"Let's call Domino's," she said in a quiet voice.

Katie and Alison shared a look of panic. What to do now? If this was any normal breakup scene, they would of course call Domino's and Little Caesars, and take a run to the nearest convenience store for six or seven pints of ice cream.

But they couldn't do that for this break-up. That would send all the wrong signals to her. That hurt could be healed with food. There was no way Alison and Katie would start any sort of downward spiral for her.

She knew the spot she'd put her friends into. "I'm just kidding," she said. She could feel the sigh of relief that emanated from them. But Lizzie knew she wasn't kidding. She knew that more than anything she longed to forget about this horrid night with a little help from her friends. And she didn't mean Katie and Alison. She meant her pals like Ben and Jerry. Her buddy Papa John. And, of course, the woman who knew all her secrets, Sara

Lee.

She cried on their laps for an hour. They stroked her hair and cooed words of comfort to her.

"Isn't anyone going to say 'I told you so'?" she asked.

"About what, honey?" Katie asked, rubbing Lizzie's back.

"That my plan was stupid to begin with, and how you both saw it blowing up in my face from the start."

Alison and Katie looked chagrined. "Well, since we're partly responsible for it blowing up in your face, we don't have much of a right to say 'I told you so', do we?" Katie gently said.

Lizzie waved her hand, a blanket forgiveness. She knew that she should have been honest with Finn the minute their relationship turned serious. Should have told him why she'd come to town. That she had intended on getting together with Finn from the start. That showing up at the Mine Shaft had been no coincidence. That it was originally to be nothing more than a summer fling, but now she was in love with him and desperately wanted a future together.

It was her honesty, her integrity, that Finn valued most, and she'd betrayed that. She couldn't blame her friends for her omission.

"I told you so," Alison said. Katie punched Alison in the arm, but Lizzie only laughed. God, how she loved these women.

Finally, she told her friends to go home, that she was okay, and she just wanted to get some sleep.

Her friends looked skeptical, but she convinced them to leave.

The second they were out the door, Lizzie threw off her robe and grabbed her sneakers and car keys. She intended to drive straight for the convenience store at the other end of Hancock. The only place that would be open this late. Instead, she felt the Navigator head for Houghton. It was if she had no control over the vehicle as it headed toward the Robbins' farm.

No. No. No. She wouldn't beg and grovel at this man's feet. Memories of that long walk back from Houghton years ago when she'd gone to see Finn at the theater after he dumped her came raging back. Did she really want to humiliate herself that way again?

She wouldn't have to make that decision because Finn's Jeep was not in the driveway at the farm.

Where was he?

She headed back to Hancock, going through town, past the turn up to her parents' place. Back toward her original destination of the convenience store. When she got to the store she drove past, not even looking into the window. Not sure she could take the temptation of seeing the shiny glass freezer doors knowing what treasures lay behind them.

Lizzie drove on to the beach. She hoped to see Finn's Jeep there, but the gates were chained shut and there were no vehicles along the road. She parked the truck, grabbed two blankets from the back, and slowly walked to the spot where she and Finn had always gone. Laying one blanket on the ground, she wrapped herself in the other and sat down, hugging her bent knees to her chest, staring at the lake, letting its softly swirling waves lull her. It did its magic, as the water, and the Copper Country, always did.

She achieved such a sense of calm she almost half expected to turn to her left and see Finn lying beside her, one arm under his head for a pillow, the other thrown over his face.

The sadness struck her again. She lay back on the blanket, rolled up into a fetal ball, and tried to hear the water lapping over her sniffling.

She awoke some time later shivering from the cool air, amazed that she'd been able to sleep. Gathering the blankets, she made her way back to the Navigator, all hopes gone that Finn might show up at their special place.

The clock on her dash read four fifteen. It was pitch dark as she drove through Hancock, not seeing another single car on the road. She reached Bob's Mobil and put her blinker on to turn up the hill, when she saw something that made her screech into the gas station's lot and slam on her brakes.

Up on a ladder resting against the marquee, dressed in pajamas, was Bob, in the midst of changing the Bible verse.

His pickup truck—or what Lizzie assumed was his truck—was parked right next to the sign. Lizzie saw how it all must play out. Bob would wait nearby in his truck until no one was out, pull up, quickly change the sign, and drive off, obviously going home and back to bed.

Lizzie was dumbfounded. She'd seen the "Changing of the Verse"! She couldn't wait to tell Alison and Katie. She rolled down her window as she pulled the Navigator alongside Bob's truck.

He looked down at her from his ladder. What a pair they made. Bob in his pajamas perched high on a ladder and her still wrapped in her blanket, red eyes puffy from crying.

"Lizzie," Bob said, with a nod.

"Bob," was all she could say, returning his nod.

She started to say more, but stopped when she looked at the verse Bob was in the midst of assembling. It was the Corinthians verse that was often read at weddings. So far Bob had posted "Love is Patient. Love is…" He hadn't finished yet, and she found she didn't want to see him complete his task. She knew how the verse went of course, but she kind of liked the way it stood now. Love is…fill in your own blank.

She powered up the window and drove home, knowing she would never mention to anyone what she'd just witnessed.

—∞—

Finn spent the night driving aimlessly for a while, then found himself at Eino Ruotala's farm twenty miles outside of town. Eino was whom he had sold his horses to. The barn where the horses were stabled was unlocked and Finn quietly made his way down to the stalls that held his beloved animals. He had only done this once before, a few weeks after they'd been taken away. He hadn't allowed himself to come back since even though Eino, understanding his loss, told him to stop by any time.

The beautiful animals still knew his scent and nickered their welcome.

"Hey guys," he whispered. It was all he trusted himself to say, afraid his voice would crack. He went to all seven of his former pride and joy, pleased to see they had obviously been well cared for. Petting and nuzzling, but not daring to go into the stalls themselves for fear he'd never want to come out.

He sat on a bale of hay directly across from the stalls and thought about the day he'd watched them being taken away. He loved the animals, had raised every one of them himself from birth. Hell, he'd even birthed two of them all by himself. He ranked the day he sold the horses second—only behind the day he found out about Annie's condition—as the worst of his life.

Not so much for the loss of the horses themselves, though that had stung like a son of a bitch. But it had been more than his horses that had been taken from him that day. He'd lost all sense of hope, of goodness, in mankind. It'd been Dana's treachery that made selling the horses necessary. It'd been fate, or God, or karma, or whomever he'd pissed off, that had not let the tiny vertebrae on his precious baby girl develop properly. All the other shit that had happened to him in his life he could take, hell, he probably deserved, but not his baby girl. She was so innocent and pure.

He felt as helpless the day they'd taken his horses away as he had the day he'd sat down with the doctors when they explained his daughter's condition. Helpless, bitter, betrayed, and seething mad. Absolutely sure he'd never have any hope or calm in his life again.

But Liz had restored that, not even realizing what a precious gift she'd given him. All to have it snatched away again.

This betrayal hurt even more because he just couldn't believe that Liz Hampton was capable of such a cold-blooded seduction. Had life really changed her that much?

He snorted at that, causing the horses to shuffle uncomfortably. Of course it did. Look at how life had changed him. Goddamn, he wasn't even sure if he felt worse for himself or for Liz, he loved her that much. It tore him apart to think that life had made her yet another calculating bitch like Dana.

He dreaded telling the kids that Liz was gone from their lives. Annie would pretend to be glad, but Finn knew his daughter had come to care for Liz, had come to depend on her as the mother she'd never had. Oh, Gran had been great with Annie, but Annie needed a mother and Liz had filled that role, however briefly. Stevie would be the most hurt. He'd pretend not to care or notice, but Stevie was Finn's son and he knew the wound would cut deep. He vowed to be there for his son, try to help him through this. Hell, maybe they could help each other.

Some hours later, Finn rose and left the barn to drive home. At least Annie would get her operation, have money for recuperation and the farm would be in the black. He had tried to pay for it once with his horses—his heart—but that hadn't worked, thanks to Dana. He guessed it only made sense that now he pay for it with his heart after all.

And that was okay with him, he'd gladly live with heartbreak if it would mean Annie had a shot at a normal childhood. But God, it hurt to know he wouldn't have Liz in his life anymore.

Twenty-One

√ Get athletes to airport
√ Meet Davis for breakfast
√ Go back to bed

DAVIS SHOWING UP at the dance had been a complete surprise. He texted her, and Lizzie met him for breakfast Sunday morning, getting only a measly three hours sleep after her foray to the beach. She apologized for leaving him the way she had.

He brushed her apology away with a wave of his hand. "It was fine. Pete and the other players took care of me. I ended up staying at Pete's, as a matter of fact. Seems your Annie Aid drew enough people to fill up all the hotel rooms."

Lizzie nodded. "Yes. It was quite a success. If I'd known you were coming, I'd have made arrangements. We kept a couple of rooms open for just such a reason." As she spoke the words, she felt the Yooper casualness fade from her voice and her business tone take its place.

"Pete's place was fine, though I didn't get much sleep," he smiled. A devastatingly handsome smile, she noticed, but not with much interest.

"No, I suppose not. Petey's place was probably party central after the dance."

He leaned across the table and laid his hand gently on top of hers. "It doesn't look like you got too much sleep last night either, Lizzie."

She knew what her eyes looked like, she had splashed cold water over them several times before meeting Davis at the restaurant. "No. No, I didn't."

His hand squeezed hers. "Do you want to talk about it?"

She looked at him hesitantly. "I don't think I can talk about this, Davis. Not with you, anyway."

He seemed to understand and sat back in his chair, nodding slowly. "That's fine. I just want you to know one thing,. We've been dancing around each other for a couple of months now and I came up here, not only to congratulate you on a wonderful event, an event that several of our players were involved with, but to put an end to the dancing."

Oh great, dumped twice in two days. Not that she'd even been Davis's to be dumped. She wondered if it was too late to change her breakfast order of fruit salad to stacks and stacks of pancakes. "I understand," she said to him.

He looked closely at her. "I don't think you do. I don't know what you had going with the man I met last night, it's really none of my business. But I came here to tell you I want to start seeing you, Lizzie, exclusively and frequently."

Oh. She wasn't being dumped after all. Quite the opposite in fact. Oddly, the thought that Davis wanted to begin a relationship with her was not the least bit appealing. "I don't know Davis…I don't think…"

"Look." He cut her off. "You don't have to say anything. Obviously you're in a pretty weird place right now. But once you get back to Detroit, back to your real life, and things get back to normal, let's discuss it again, okay?"

Her real life? Back to normal? Would things ever be back to normal for her? Was her old life to be considered normal? Funny, she couldn't think of anything more normal than standing in Walmart picking out a new tank top for Annie, or helping Clea clear away the dinner dishes.

When they parted, he gave her a soft peck on the cheek, nothing more, but his eyes held a promise of things to come.

Driving back to her parents' place, she realized the date. Exactly eight weeks since she'd first come to town. In eight weeks she'd managed to find Finn, get him to sleep with her, get comfortable with her new physique, and was now in place to begin a relationship with Davis Cummings. She didn't miss the irony of how her original plan had come to full fruition.

She'd never been more miserable to have successfully completed a plan in her life.

She got the athletes off on their chartered plane, presenting them all with thank-you baskets full of traditional Yooper things, right down to a flannel shirt and orange touque. The guys loved them, donning the bright knit hats, made for deer-hunting season but worn year-round by the locals, right in the airport. She even managed to snag a new client in one of the Russian Avs and had been promised a follow-up meeting with the Lions' hot new running back. The fundraiser had been very good for her firm. She would've let Finn know so he wouldn't feel so indebted to her, if she thought he'd speak to her.

In a daze, she moved through the next few days. She met with Margo at the bank to go over the final numbers from Annie Aid. She resigned from the Hannah Robbins Foundation board of directors, even though Margo begged her not to.

"This was your brainchild, Lizzie, you should stick with it," the banker said.

"No, it'll be fine now. The funds can be administered through you and the bank. Promise me, though, that if, say years down the road, Annie needs another operation or something, you'll contact me."

"Of course, but surely you'll be aware if something like that happens."

Lizzie only gave a small smile, but she knew that Finn would not keep in touch, would want her nowhere near his family. There'd be no shoebox of unsent letters this time, not if his parting shots at her were any indication of how much she'd hurt him.

Her parents called from somewhere in Tennessee. They were on their way home after spending a week with Zeke. Her mother sensed something was wrong with Lizzie when she asked her daughter about the fundraiser, but Lizzie brushed her mother's concern away. They asked if Lizzie would like them to stop in Detroit on their way home. Knowing that it was out of their way, that going through Chicago and Wisconsin would be faster, and not really wanting them to see how Finn Robbins had once again devastated her, she said no.

Zeke called, making idle talk until she realized that Petey had probably called him.

"Petey tell you I got dumped?" she said, always able to cut to the chase with her twin.

"Yeah. Sorry." He didn't seem to know what else to say. She knew guys in general were bad at this sort of thing, but Zeke was woefully out of practice at being there for her after a break-up.

"It's okay. I'll get over it," she told her brother.

If only she believed it herself.

The ten-hour drive back to Detroit seemed like twenty. What she wouldn't give to have Annie and Stevie fighting in the back. The silence was deafening.

She didn't keep her staff on pins and needles, approving the partnership plan her first day back in the office. The next two months were spent hashing out the details, signing legal documents and occasionally being talked off the ledge whenever she'd start freaking out about letting go of her baby.

—❧—

Lizzie answered her doorbell late one evening in mid-October to find Finn standing on her doorstep.

"Today was Annie's operation," he said.

No hello, no greeting of any sort, just right to the point. He hadn't changed a bit. Then she looked more closely at him and realized she was wrong. His face looked drawn and worried, much paler now that the summer sun had left the Copper Country and his tan had faded. His hair had just been cut and he was wearing a crisp dress shirt under a sports coat and slacks that were severely wrinkled. Probably from sitting in a hospital waiting room all day.

It was all she could do not to nuzzle her nose into his chest and breathe deeply.

"I know. I called the hospital, but they wouldn't tell me anything because I wasn't family. How is she?" she asked

"Good. Out for at least ten hours. They want to keep her perfectly still, so they have her totally juiced up. They wouldn't let me anywhere near her for the night. But the operation went great. The doctors are pretty optimistic." He looked past her, into the living room. "Are you busy? Can we talk?"

"Oh, I'm sorry. Come in, come in," she stammered, not believing her own brief lapse in manners. She waved him to a chair in the living room, then sat on the couch to his side.

"Finn, I think you should know that…" she began, but he cut her off.

"No Liz, let me. I can't tell you how sorry I am about the things I said that night at the rec center. It was childish and hurtful and you have to know I didn't mean a word I said."

She bowed her head, looking at her hands folded in her lap. "I know you didn't," she said, and heard his sigh of relief.

"Thank God. I wouldn't have blamed you one bit if you'd slammed the door in my face." He leaned forward, his knee brushing hers. "But I'm so glad you didn't. Liz, about us…"

"Finn, I really need to tell you…"

But neither of them got to finish as the door to the kitchen swept open and an apron-clad Davis Cummings entered the living room. "Lizzie, your palate is in for the night of its life. Oh, sorry, I didn't know we had company."

Lizzie could see the muscles of Finn's jaw tighten, saw the blue of his eyes turn steely as his gaze went from Davis to Lizzie, then took in the two half-empty wine glasses on the coffee table.

"Finn, you remember Davis Cummings, don't you? Davis, Finn stopped by to give me a progress report on Annie. Her surgery was today." She looked at Finn, silently wishing that he'd come for more than that, but knowing he hadn't. Just seeing the way he reacted to Davis' presence convinced her that he was still mad at her.

"Right. And now that I've done that, I'd better get going and let you two enjoy your dinner." He started to rise and Lizzie fought the panic she felt at the thought of him walking out the door. Walking out on her. Again.

"You're welcome to stay, Finn, I'm sure Davis made plenty." She tried to hide the pleading in her voice.

Finn looked at Davis, then at her. "No. Thanks anyway, I want to get back to the hospital. I just wanted to let you know how she was doing."

"Thank you for that," she said, following him to the door.

He turned at the entrance and said low, for her ears only, "And to apologize."

"There was no need, but apology accepted," she said. She reached a hand up, to touch his cheek, but saw him recoil, and quickly dropped her hand. "Goodbye, Finn."

"Goodbye, Elizabeth," he said, then turned and left.

—⚊—

Damn. Damn. Damn. Of all the nights to finally cave in to Davis" offer to let him cook for her. He'd been after her for weeks to let him loose in her kitchen but she'd put him off. The bad mood she'd been in all day, knowing today was Annie's surgery, finally made her relent. She figured if there were a man in her kitchen, she'd be less likely to drop everything and high tail it to Ann Arbor to see Finn.

She loved seeing him again, but took his visit for what it obviously was, a mere courtesy call. After all, if it hadn't been for the fundraiser she'd helped pull together, Annie probably wouldn't even be having her operation today.

But she didn't want his thanks, or even his apology. She wanted him to tell her that he still loved her, that he couldn't live without her, that the two months apart had been hell for him.

They sure had been for her.

"Lizzie? Dinner's ready," Davis said behind her. She started toward the kitchen, but only made it as far as the couch before her legs gave out and she crumpled into the soft cushions, sobs racking her body.

Oh God, not more crying! It seemed like that's all she'd done for the last two months. She would have sworn there wasn't enough water left in her to shed, but the tears kept tumbling. It was so odd to feel bad instead of shoving the pain down with food. Odd, but good.

She knew she'd get through this night, just as she had all the others since she'd come back to Detroit. It actually got easier every day. It was just seeing Finn again that set her off.

She could hear Davis moving to her, felt his weight on the couch as he sat next to her, sensed his hesitation. No wonder, he'd never dealt with anything other than the fun Lizzie, the nice Lizzie, the always up Lizzie. He'd be appalled at this pile of sobbing woman. Lizzie found that the thought didn't really bother her. She cried. So what.

Davis waited patiently until she got her crying under control, even found her some tissues. When she felt able to talk she turned to him, but he held his hand up for her to stop.

"Me first, Lizzie. I know you've been putting me off since you've been back, that I've been the one calling and you were the one with all the excuses. I guess I just figured that you really were too busy catching up to go out with me like you said, but obviously it was more than that." She waited for him to go on, there really wasn't much she could say, what he said was true. "I don't know what you had with that guy this summer, but you're not over him, are you?"

"No," she whispered. "I'll never be over him, Davis."

"Who is he, anyway?" he asked.

He hadn't asked her about Finn during their phone conversations since she'd been back, and for that she was grateful. She didn't know how she would explain Finn to Davis. Or to anyone for that matter. How did she explain emotions that she herself were only now coming to terms with?

"He's the man I fell in love with eighteen years ago. The man I'm still in love with," was all she said.

She watched as he absorbed the information, and like the classy guy he was, gave her a squeeze on the hand. "I understand, Lizzie, and it's okay. Now, how about some of my famous chicken kiev?"

"Do you mind if I take a raincheck, Davis?" Then she spoke words that had not passed her lips before. "I'm not hungry anymore."

—⁓—

It wasn't rage or fury that Finn felt this time as he walked away from Liz. It was defeat.

So that was it. She'd made her choice. He would just have to live with it. He had come to her place for more than a progress report on Annie and to offer the much-deserved apology. He had come to make amends and to hopefully make a clean start.

When the doctors informed him that his daughter was resting comfortably and that the operation had been a success, his first thought had been of Liz. He followed his instincts and, after being told he wouldn't be able to see Annie for at least twelve to fourteen hours, he made his way to Novi to see Liz.

On the drive over, his mind raced with all he wanted to say, starting with "I'm sorry" and ending with "will you marry me".

He'd only gotten the first part out before her new man had interrupted them.

The thought of anyone else's hands on Liz's body nearly made him drive off the road. Would he know how to touch her? Would he make her feel good about her body? Would he love her like Finn did? Was it possible for anyone else to love Liz Hampton the way he did? He didn't think so.

Needing a distraction lest the vision of Liz straddling Davis Cummings drive him insane, he turned on the radio, hitting seek to find the first station he could and cranking up the volume. As a commercial ended, a lone guitar sang out and Finn realized it was a Springsteen song.

He turned the radio off and drove the rest of the way in silence.

Twenty-Two

—⚡—

√ Call Margo
√ Get new boots, jacket, mittens
~~Call Sybil~~

THE BLUSTERY JANUARY wind whipped at Finn as he wheeled Annie up the ramp and into the farmhouse. Stevie had already shoveled and sanded so the push wasn't as strenuous as it might have been. He made a mental note to thank Stevie for doing the shoveling while he and Annie had been at her physical therapy session.

It seemed like he was doing much more of that lately—thanking and praising Stevie—than he ever had before. He and his son had definitely turned a corner. No more breaking curfew or any other bullshit. He'd like to think it was all that quality time he'd spent with Stevie since the end of the summer, and that was surely part of it, but Finn knew that the threat of being grounded, and therefore not seeing Heather, was the real reason behind Stevie's turnaround.

"How'd it go?" Finn's grandmother asked as they entered the kitchen.

Finn wheeled Annie to the large throw rug just inside the door where the snow from the wheels of her chair could melt. He began the task of ridding his daughter of her many layers of winter clothing. "Pretty good. Tell her, Annie."

Annie's eyes lit up, matching the pink glow of her cold cheeks. "Five minutes today, Gran."

"Five minutes? Oh, honey, that's wonderful. That calls for some hot chocolate," she said, and turned to the refrigerator to get out the milk.

Annie's progress was now being measured in the amount of minutes she could stand up with her full weight on her legs. She hadn't taken any steps yet—the therapist wanted to wait until she got to ten minutes before they attempted that—but she was adding nearly a minute each session so it wouldn't be long before they tried.

Five minutes felt like five hours when Finn had to watch his baby girl standing there, grimace on her face, gritting her teeth, determined not to grab on to the support bars at her side. A couple of times the therapist had asked him to leave the room during the exercise because he seemed to be in so much pain watching his daughter that Annie had gotten upset. He soon got a hold of himself and now passively sat watching Annie and her therapist while inside his heart pounded and his palms itched to jump to her aid. Sitting on his hands seemed to help.

"Stevie home?" Finn asked.

"Yes, he's up in his room. Don't forget you've got that man with the horse coming in an hour."

How could he forget? He'd been totally taken by surprise when Margo had called him out of the blue last week and said she knew someone who had recently bought a horse and was looking for a place to board it. She asked if she could give them Finn's name and number. He'd started to say no, that he wasn't prepared to board a horse, but stopped himself. The barn was fit enough. He had plenty of hay. All he needed to do was clean out some of the stalls and get some feed. He'd told Margo to go ahead and give the guy his number.

A man called a few days later and discussed arrangements and fees with Finn. He was dropping the horse off this evening.

It wasn't the same as having his own horses, but it was a start.

He'd plowed the snow out of the corrals so he'd have a place to exercise the horse. He and Stevie had put snowshoes on last Sunday and made a trail past the strawberry fields and a ways into the woods. The kids seemed as excited about the prospect of having a horse in their barn as Finn was.

With cautious optimism, he'd dusted off the business plan he'd written years ago for his horse boarding and training operation. Yeah, it was a start.

Finn was in Stevie's room an hour later, going over his son's homework with him, when he heard a vehicle pull into the driveway. He quickly made his way downstairs to get his winter gear on.

The doorbell rang as he was sitting in a kitchen chair pulling his boots on. When he called for his visitor to come in, the door opened and a cold burst of air brushed through the room and right to Finn's face, which was already frozen…with disbelief.

"Liz?" his voice cracked and he tried again. "Liz? What are you doing here?"

"I came to see a man about a horse," she said with a small shrug. At Finn's look of incomprehension, she continued, "I'm EH Beach."

"You're…you're…?"

"Yes, I'm the person whose horse you're going to board."

"But I talked to a man." Finn sputtered.

Lizzie nodded. "A co-worker, making a call on my behalf."

"Why the code name?"

"Would you have agreed to board my horse if you'd known it was me?" she asked.

Realizing he wouldn't have, and why he wouldn't have—mainly that he was pissed as hell at her—reminded Finn that he shouldn't be so damn happy to see Elizabeth Hampton standing in his doorway. Scowling, he said, "EH Beach, eh? EH, Elizabeth Hampton."

She smiled. "I threw in Beach for old time's sake."

He snorted as he rose from the chair, his boots tied tight. He swung his jacket on and grabbed his gloves. "No, I don't suppose I would have agreed to this if I'd known it was you." He was standing in front of her, both of them at the doorway. Damn, if she wasn't adorable in her little white parka with a fuzzy fleece collar, and white Nanook boots with her jeans tucked in. Her knit mittens were striped with white and light blue and matched the hat she had on, pulled low over her ears.

"Okay then, let's see this fine piece of horseflesh an experienced buyer like you picked out." He opened the door for her, but she was looking past him, toward the living room.

"Are the kids here, can I say a quick hello?" She made to move around him, but he grabbed her elbow, spun her and started her out the door.

"No, you can't. I don't want you seeing the kids, Liz. This is business deal. Let's get your horse unloaded and into the barn, then you can take off."

What the hell was she up to? Why was she even in town?

He didn't believe for a second that she'd suddenly become interested in owning a horse. He was thinking that there might not even be a horse at all, that the whole thing was just a way to see him, but then he saw the horse trailer attached to her Navigator. *Why would she want to see him, anyway?* She was all set back in Detroit with her douchebag new boyfriend. One that cooked for her, no less. Hah, there was a kind of sweet irony that Liz would end up with a guy that loved to cook. Maybe she'd get fat again.

But Finn found that he couldn't wish for anything bad for her. He wanted her to be happy, he really did. It just stabbed him like a knife that her idea of happiness did not include him and the kids.

So, why was she here? Could it really be as simple as buying a horse and needing some place to board it? Why him? Didn't she realize how badly it would hurt him to have to deal with her on any kind of regular basis? That he ached without her? That since seeing that Davis character at her place, only the ongoing care of his children could keep him from pulling one of Gran's quilts over his head and staying in bed until spring.

He ignored the hurt look on her face from his refusal to let her see the kids, and made his way to the back of the trailer. He unbolted the door, took out the ramp and led the horse out of the trailer. He felt the blood rush from his head as he got a clear look at the animal.

"Pegasus!" He turned to Liz. "How?"

"Eino said she was your favorite one," she said, as if that alone was explanation enough for why one of his horses, indeed his most treasured horse, was back on Robbins property.

"She is, but how did you even know about Eino?" he asked. He ran his hands along the beautiful animal. *God, how he loved her.* It took Finn a second to clarify to himself which female he was currently with merited the sentiment. "Peg," he said, as if declaring a winner.

"When I decided I wanted to buy a horse, I asked Margo if she knew anyone who wanted to sell. She gave me Eino's number."

He narrowed his eyes at her. "Asked her if she knew anyone who was selling? Or did you ask her who I sold my horses to?"

She shrugged. "I'm not really sure how I phrased the question."

"What are you up to, Liz?"

"What? Can't I buy a horse if I want to? Where else am I going to keep him?"

He turned away from her and started leading Peg to the barn. "You forget, Liz, I happen to know how much you like hidden agendas."

—⁂—

This was not going well at all, Lizzie thought as she followed Finn into the barn. She hadn't expected him to fall into her arms begging her to take him back when he answered the door, but she'd hoped it'd go a little better than this.

Here she stood, no lists, no tablets. For the first time in her life, she didn't have a plan. Oh, buying Finn's favorite horse was kind of a plan, but, beyond getting Finn to board the beast, she didn't have a clue. She'd just have to wing it.

Finn was already at the far end of the barn, putting Pegasus into a stall, when she joined him. She sat on a bale of hay across from him and watched as he began brushing her new horse. Neither of them said anything for a while, Lizzie settled in, taking off her mittens and hat.

"You cut your hair," Finn said.

"Mmmm, about a month ago," she answered as she brushed her hand through her new short cut.

"Why?" he asked.

She didn't know if she could explain her decision, one of many she'd made in the last two and a half months, so she only said, "I didn't need it anymore."

He looked at her, as if finally seeing her for the first time since she walked into his kitchen door, and nodded his understanding. "It's cute short. It suits you."

"Thank you," she said.

He brushed a few more strokes, then stopped. "You know, I think that's the first time you've ever taken a compliment from me."

"What do you mean?"

He put the brush down and picked up some other grooming tool, one that Lizzie didn't know the name of or even what it did. *Oh yeah, she was going to make a great horse owner.*

"I've never heard you just say 'thank you' to a compliment. You always crack a joke, or do a 'get out of here' kind of thing."

A silence fell over them as she thought on that. She watched as he worked, his love for the animal obvious. His hands swept across the quivering horse, along its flanks. He ran his hands down its leg, lifting its calf to check the condition of her shoes. She was reminded of the night at the beach when he had done the same to her and she told him the movement always made her think of him with a horse. Apparently Finn had the same thought because as he dropped the horse's leg he looked at Lizzie with a hunger in his eyes that made her think that maybe, just maybe, all was not lost.

"I never lied to you, you know," she said quietly.

He dropped his gaze from hers and turned his attention back to Peg. "You didn't tell me the whole truth though, either."

"No," she whispered, "I didn't."

When he didn't respond, but kept on with Peg, Lizzie turned her attention elsewhere. He had done a lot of work in here, she mused to herself. She held her breath as she looked at the wall where the patched holes were, not knowing what she hoped she'd find. The entire wall was now repaired and good as new. She didn't know what to make of that.

—⚜—

Finn followed her gaze and knew what she was thinking about. He placed a blanket over Peg and put a bucket of feed within her reach, made sure she had plenty of water, then stepped out of the stall, closing the door behind him.

He came to the bale of hay and stood in front of Lizzie. "How are things in Detroit?" he asked. He couldn't bear to ask her about Cummings. Were they still together? He stole a look at her hand and saw no engagement ring, then chastised himself for looking. The guy would have to work pretty fast to have a ring on Liz's finger in only a few months. Of course, Finn had wanted to put one on her last October. He didn't let himself think about that. That was different, he told himself, though couldn't expound on why that may be true.

"Last time I was there, everything was fine," she said.

Puzzled, he asked, "What do you mean?"

"I haven't been in Detroit since before Christmas."

Visions of Liz and Davis cavorting on white sand beaches almost stopped Finn from asking, but he was curious. "Where have you been?"

"Here. Well, to be exact, at three-twelve Lighthouse Drive."

Finn knew that Lighthouse Drive was a street on the water in Hancock. He waited for Liz to go on.

"My new home," she said.

"What about your business?" he asked.

Her hazel eyes looked up at him. "Hampton and Associates is doing fine. I work from an office at my new place, and so far have only needed to leave the Copper Country once, to meet a prospective new client. I took on partners to free myself up more. And so I could move back here."

Finn caught his breath. God, she wouldn't tease him like this, would she? Would she purposely seek him out and tell him she'd moved back to town when she had no intention of ever being a part of his life? The woman who could devise a plan to sleep with a man a few times to gear up for a real romance could do something like this. In fact, it would be right up her alley.

Suddenly Finn knew that Liz was not that woman. Had never been that woman. Not the Elizabeth Hampton he knew. And loved. Whatever her original intention had been last summer—and he'd be the first to admit it was pretty fucked up—she'd fallen in love with him and wanted to be with him.

Finn. Not Davis Cummings.

With a new sense of assurance, he raised his leg, resting it on the hay bale next to her hip.

"Tell me about Davis," he said, leaning toward her. He rested his arm on his knee and placed his face level to hers, daring her to meet his gaze.

Meeting him head on, as he knew she would, she said, "Nothing to tell. The first time I saw Davis since the night at the rec center was the night of Annie's operation."

He knew it. No way could good girl Liz Hampton sleep with a man she wasn't in love with. He could kick himself for not sticking around that night at her place and finding out the truth of the situation. His damned pride. He vowed to never let it get in his way with her again.

"I won't lie to you, Finn, and I won't omit anything this time. He called quite a bit once I was back in Detroit. I kept putting him off. What you walked in on that night was him making me dinner and me planning on telling him there could never be anything between us. I've always liked Davis, and thought at one time that he'd be the perfect guy for me. But we are—always were, really—just friends."

"Why? Why be just friends if he's the perfect guy for you?" He knew he was skating on thin ice. He couldn't be sure she wanted him back, and he was opening himself up to potential heartbreak by taking this route, but he had to know. Had to hear her say it.

"Because he's not the perfect guy *for me*, not really. You're the perfect guy for me, Finn, you always were."

He realized just how much Liz was opening herself up by being here, by coming to him after he'd walked out on her. Twice. Three times if you count what happened eighteen years ago. Her courage and strength humbled him.

"Finn," she said, "about that tablet…that list…"

He put his hand up, cutting her off. He turned around and walked out of the barn.

—⁓—

Lizzie watched as Finn left the barn. What now? Did she chase after him? Did she wait? Was he coming back? Should she sit here until spring if that's what it took?

The hay was cold under her butt and she was just about to give up when he returned.

He held a tablet, not a steno like the ones she used to carry, but a legal-sized pad. He thrust it in her face.

"You're not the only one with plans, Liz. Here's my list."

"Finn, wait, I said…" He pushed the tablet under her nose, stopping her.

Her hand trembled as she took the tablet. The light in the barn was dim, but she was able to read Finn's list.

Annie starts walking. It was checked off. Lizzie looked up at Finn, tears stinging her eyes. "Oh Finn, is she…"

"She's close," he said, "any day now." He motioned her back to the paper. "Keep reading."

The next item was also completed. *Get Stevie something for making the honor roll.*

She smiled. "I'm not surprised. He's one sharp kid." Finn nodded, she returned to the next item. *Start horse boarding business.* Check.

"I'm your first client," she said, looking up at him.

"That you are," he answered. He nodded toward the tablet. "There's one more item on my list."

She looked back down at the yellow paper. *Marry Elizabeth Hampton.* Her head tilted back to see him. His blue eyes—eyes she saw every night when she'd lie awake in bed—stared down at her.

"It's not checked off," he said. The words she'd spoken at the rec center echoed in her ear.

She smiled, and pulled the pen from his hand. She slashed it across the paper. "It is now."

—✲—

"Elizabeth," he whispered. She was in his arms the next instant. His mouth sought hers and was ecstatic to feel it open beneath his. She tasted wonderful, like winter and mint, fresh, clean. She tasted like the woman he loved.

"You feel so good," she sighed, catching the breath that he had robbed from her in his desire to taste her. She was clinging to him, tearing at his jacket, trying to find the zipper.

He did the same, unzipping her jacket, putting his hands on her sweater, needing to feel her body, the only body he'd ever desire. His hands brushed under her sweater, going right to her breasts. She let out a squeal as his freezing cold hands touched her warm skin. He instantly released her, but she pressed herself against him, not wanting to lose contact.

"I forgot how hard it was to makeout in the wintertime. Cold hands, too many layers. Just one of the many things about the U.P. I'll have to get used to again." She laughed the boisterous laugh that he loved so much, the laugh he'd been aching to hear these past months.

"God, Liz, I missed you so much." He looked into her eyes, letting her see the warmth and love that came from his own.

She cradled his face in her hands as she whispered, "I love you, Finn. I want a future with you."

"Me too, babe, me too. But, I'm a package deal, Liz. Love me, love my kids." He knew he was safe saying the words.

"Done and done," she said. She was nuzzling into his neck, trying to get past the layers of warmth to breathe in his scent.

"Come on, let's go in and tell Gran and the kids." He started zipping her up, putting her mittens over her hands, pleased to see they were trembling as much as his were.

"I can't wait to see them, I've missed them so much," she said. She waited for him to put her hat on her, allowing herself to be garbed for the Copper Country winter as she'd been by her mother when she was a child.

He pulled the hat down tight, covering her ears, kissing the tip of her nose as he did so. "It's not going to be easy, Liz. We've got a long road ahead with Annie's recovery. Your business, the farm, the horse boarding business. I'm not sure how it's all going to shake out, but I do know that we're going to spend the rest of our lives together, figuring it out."

She held his hand as they walked toward the farmhouse, lights burned from its windows making it seem alive with warmth.

"Don't worry," she said, "I'll come up with a plan."

—◠◡◠—

The Worth Series continues with

WORTH THE DRIVE
THE WORTH SERIES BOOK 2:
THE PRETTY ONE

—◊◊—

WORTH THE FALL
THE WORTH SERIES BOOK 3:
THE SMART ONE

Try Mara Jacobs's romantic mystery series

BROKEN WINGS
BLACKBIRD & CONFESSOR, BOOK 1

—⁓—

AGAINST THE ODDS
ANNA DAWSON'S VEGAS, BOOK 1

AGAINST THE SPREAD
ANNA DAWSON'S VEGAS, BOOK 2

Find out more at
www.MaraJacobs.com

After graduating from Michigan State University with a degree in advertising, Mara spent several years working at daily newspapers in Advertising sales and production. This certainly prepared her for the world of deadlines!

Most authors say they've been writing forever. Not so with Mara. She always had the stories, but they played like movies in her head. A few years ago she began transferring the movies to pages. She writes mysteries with romance, thrillers with romance, and romances with…well, you get it.

Forever a Yooper (someone who hails from Michigan's glorious Upper Peninsula), Mara now resides in the East Lansing, Michigan, area where she is better able to root on her beloved Spartans.

Mara first published in October of 2012 with 2 romantic mystery series and the contemporary romance Worth series. You can find out more about her books at **www.marajacobs.com**